THE
LAST DRAGON
CHARMER
BOOK 1

VILLAIN KEEPER

THE
LAST DRAGON CHARMER
BOOK 1

VILLAIN KEEPER

LAURIE McKAY

HARPER
An Imprint of HarperCollinsPublishers

The Last Dragon Charmer Book 1: Villain Keeper
www.harpercollinschildrens.com

Library of Congress Cataloging-in-Publication Data

McKay, Laurie.
  The villain keeper / Laurie McKay. — First edition.
    pages cm. — (The last dragon charmer ; book 1)
  Summary: Nothing is more important to Prince Caden of Razzon than slaying
a dragon, but his quest proves more difficult than he thought when he and
his nemesis, the sorceress Brynne, are unexpectedly trapped in magicless
Asheville, North Carolina.
  ISBN 978-0-06-230843-6 (hardcover)
  [1. Princes—Fiction. 2. Heroes—Fiction. 3. Dragons—Fiction. 4. Magic—
Fiction. 5. Asheville (N.C.)—Fiction.] I. Title.
PZ7.1.M437Vi 2015   2014038650
[Fic]—dc23   CIP
                                                                             AC

Typography by Robert Steimle
14 15 16 17 18   CG/RRDH   10 9 8 7 6 5 4 3 2 1
❖
First Edition

For my mom, who read this fifty-one times, and my sister, who read it fifty, and my brother, who read it twice. For my family and friends, who've supported me. And especially for my dad, who we all loved and who we all wish could've read it, too.

Contents

THE
LAST DRAGON
CHARMER
BOOK 1

VILLAIN KEEPER

1

THE RED HAZE

For the second time in Caden's life, King Axel hugged him. Caden's bed was unmade from when his father had roused him. The embers in the fireplace crackled. In the flickering light, his sword and staff collections cast odd shadows on the stone walls.

When his father let him go, he stood in shadow and spoke in whispers. "Gather your things quietly and leave. Slay your dragon. When you return, I'll name you an Elite Paladin like your brothers."

Suddenly, Caden was fully awake. "You're sending me on my quest?"

"Yes. Now, hurry."

Caden didn't hurry. He yearned for the honor that came with the title Elite Paladin more than all else, but such quests didn't start at night and in secret. When his seven older brothers had left for their quests, it had been under the bright winter sun and to the cheering of crowds. They'd all been at least fifteen turns, not twelve. Now the kingdom was asleep. Until a moment ago, Caden had been asleep.

For such a large man, King Axel moved on silent feet. He kept glancing to Caden's door like he expected a crypt devil to snatch Caden and drag him to the catacombs. "By the final chime of the night bell, you are to be atop your horse and beyond the castle wall."

Outside, the night was black and cold. Caden was supposed to leave like his brothers, under the blinding sun. His father's face was supposed to be bright with pride, not hidden in shadow.

"Why not wait until morning?" Caden said.

"Yours isn't the place to question your king."

It was Caden's sworn obligation to serve his father, the king, and protect the people of Razzon. That didn't include following orders blindly. His father knew that. He was the one who had told Caden that. Caden did the proper thing, and reminded him.

King Axel kept his voice low, but Caden felt the iron in it. Like all royals, the king had been gifted at birth with an ability to help him through the challenging life ahead. His was resolution. His will was absolute. He never changed his mind once he'd made a decision. "Tonight, it's your duty to do as I say," his father said as he strode toward the hall. "I'll free your horse. Leave through the Southern

Tower." At the doorway, he turned. "Make me proud."

Caden felt his words catch in his throat. Before he could say he would, the king was gone. For a moment, Caden stared at the doorway. Then he dressed and packed.

His coat was the color of the dimming sky, the color of Razzon's royal family. The imperial Winterbird was embroidered in silver and gold threads on the back. Strapped across his back, he felt the comfortable weight of his best sword. The blade was sharp enough to split gilded armor.

In the distance, he heard the low, soulful bellow of the night bell. He squared his shoulders and hurried to the far side of the castle and the upper entrance to the Southern Tower.

The Southern Tower held the quarters of the first queen, the mother of Caden's brothers. Fifteen years after her death, only the king ever entered. The door creaked as it opened, and Caden felt unease as he stepped through and onto the staircase.

The stairs were cut into the stone walls and carpeted with silk-trimmed blue wool. The banister was carved with reliefs of dragons and knights. He peered over it. On the ground floor, set in glittering gold and silver tiles, was a giant mosaic of the imperial Winterbird—the same symbol adorning Caden's coat.

The second chime of the night bell rang out, and Caden dashed down the steps. He paused at the bottom, his feet on the Winterbird's wing. A portrait hung on the expanse of the wall. The first queen stood beside young versions of his brothers, lined up from first-born to seventh-born: Valon first, then Maden, Lucian, Martin, Landon, Chadwin, and, finally, Jasan. She looked kind and was smiling at them.

He felt out of place beside the painting. There were no portraits of Caden's mother, the second queen. No closed-off towers were dedicated to her memory. She'd been sent away soon after his birth and no one would speak of her, not the servants or guards, not his father or brothers. The portrait made him wonder if she ever smiled at Caden like the first queen smiled at them.

The third chime of the night bell bellowed. Caden left the portrait and ran.

Outside, the snow fell in soft chunks. Razzon was the land of winter. Always, it snowed. Caden whistled and his horse, Sir Horace, charged from the night. His coat was the color of dim-lit frost, but his mane was blinding and white. Breath fogged from his nostrils like smoke. He was the eighth finest horse in the realm, a Galvanian snow stallion trained by the Elite Guard, a horse befitting a prince.

The king might not share his burdens with Caden, but Caden could change that. He could make his father proud and show he could be trusted. He could slay a dragon. Then his seven older brothers would finally accept him as one of them. Caden reached up to pat Sir Horace's mane.

"We will prove ourselves," he said.

In obvious agreement, Sir Horace raised his magnificent head and whinnied.

Caden glanced back at the castle. It was a tall shadow against a black sky. He swore that when he saw it next, a dragon would be slain by his hand, and he would be named an Elite Paladin like his father and brothers.

He rode through the night then for the next two days. He traveled up and down the great slopes of the Winterlands, through ice-covered forests that tinkled like green glass, stopping only for sleep and meals with Sir Horace. It was on the third day that he found hope. In a fishing village near Dark-Eye Lake, he saw a collapsed house and burned-out field. He heard rumors of a dragon.

Dragons were the side effects of bad magic. The villagers claimed one had formed from the anger and hate as a spellcaster and his rival fought. Unleashed, the dragon was ravenous. It devoured the spellcaster and his rival, destroyed the house, and then disappeared into the mountains.

Caden rode to a high slope to survey the area. In the distance, he saw the beginnings of the Springlands, home of the meadow gnomes and tree elves. Home, too, of his childhood playmate, and occasional tormentor, the thief and sorceress Brynne.

She was the daughter of the powerful spellcasters

Madrol and Lyn, and heir to the mind magic of the night mages. Often, Caden's father contracted her parents for jobs unfit for the honorable Elite Paladins, jobs requiring magic and questionable scruples. Always, she caused Caden trouble. He rubbed his back, remembering the time she'd spelled him to grow a snow fox's tail. Such was the dangers of spellcasters. When they weren't losing control and spawning dragons, they were causing mischief and fluffy white tails.

He shook off the memories. With luck, the dragon hadn't traveled beyond the snows yet. Better to fight a beast born of magic in the Winterlands, the lands of the Elite Paladins, than in the magic-infested Springlands. Caden scanned the border. Just before the soft snowgrass gave way to lush meadows of yellow and purple violets, he spotted a scorched trail in the snow.

"A fire dragon," he told Sir Horace. "I was right."

Sir Horace seemed unsurprised. Unlike Caden's brothers, Sir Horace knew Caden's judgment was sound. He trusted Caden.

They followed the singed trail along the border. It was night when Caden caught sight of the dragon. Its scales were smoldering embers, its teeth molten iron. Its eyes were cinder black and it smelled of smoke. Dragons were known to take on the qualities of the emotions from which they were born. Those born of anger often had the character of fire.

Caden felt his heart tingle and his breath hitch. His quest would be done in moments. Above, the moon shone brightly and illuminated a band of thick clouds and falling snow. He dismounted and drew his sword—the sound of metal scratching metal sliced into the night.

The dragon turned. Its breath burned the green and white grasses. Nearby frosted tulips caught fire. The leaves of the blizzard oaks melted.

Before Caden and the dragon could battle, though, the frozen ground under Caden's boots cracked. The snow glowed the sickly red of bad magic. Beside him, Sir Horace reared up. Ten strides beyond, the fire dragon cocked its smoldering head and watched. Dragons were mere memories of beasts much greater than themselves. They might be the side effects of magic, but they couldn't *do* magic. The fire dragon looked as confused as Caden felt.

The sickly glow curled around Caden's legs and waist. He dropped his sword and grabbed for Sir Horace's reins, but it was too late. The ground broke as if there was no mountain beneath it, and the red magic tugged him down.

Head over feet, Caden fell. Beside him, Sir Horace went around and around, tail over muzzle, his frightened whinny piercing and loud in the red haze.

Within moments, a figure plummeted down beside them. Her hair trailed behind her like a train of dark fabric. She seemed as caught as them, and they became three:

Caden, his horse, and the girl, falling into red.

Like a braid of blood and fire, the bad magic seemed roped around her waist. She thrashed and tugged at it, and her hands glowed gold.

With one hand, Caden caught Sir Horace's reins; with the other he reached for the girl. No one should die alone. Not Sir Horace, not this girl. "Grab my hand!" he yelled.

She looked up and clutched for him. Their fingers locked. Their tumbles evened to a fast fall.

Caden felt air roar by his ears. Wind rushed against his back. They sped toward something. Their end, he feared. When his sixth-born brother, Chadwin, had been killed six months ago, his father had cried. Caden tried not to think of the pain and disappointment he'd cause by dying.

The girl squeezed his hand and shouted, "We're stopping!"

They weren't stopping. Never had Caden moved at such a speed, and the pull from the magic seemed to be only growing stronger. "What?"

He'd but a moment to wonder when the golden glow from her hands flared. It burned through the red haze like a small sun. Like rocks thrown from tower walls, they slammed into hard ground.

Caden hit back first. He gasped for breath. Above him, the sky was dark and star filled. No snow fell. Sir Horace landed at his side. His flank rose and fell with hard breaths. The girl crashed on her stomach with her cheek pressed to the ground.

She stumbled to standing. Caden rolled over and did the same. They were on a road, but a strange one. It was smooth like pressed dirt, yet hard like stone. To his right, he saw a bookshop. To his left, a wide window with a display of chocolates. He recognized the wares but not the language on the signs. On the walkway beside the road, the streetlights weren't lit with magic or fire. They seemed to have captured lightning.

He turned to the girl and, now free of the haze, knew her at once. It was Brynne. He'd known her since he was four and she'd irritated him for just as long. Last he'd seen her, her people had been traveling toward work in the Summerlands. He frowned. That was also the last he'd seen of his prized gnomish dagger.

She was dressed in the silvers and golds of spellcasters. The practiced magic of their order always shone in those colors. Her sleeves and high collar were embroidered with red and blue threads, reminders of the sister colors of the dark magics. Red for magic born of hot emotions like anger and jealousy. Blue for destruction and indifference. It was always these magics and dark motives that loosed dragons. From what Caden had seen of sorcerers and dragons, it was a warning too rarely heeded.

With a blink, the dazed look in Brynne's eyes

disappeared. It seemed she also recognized him. "You!" she said and peered at him. "This has to be your fault, prince."

Caden had been moments from slaying a dragon, from returning home to his family. He was the one who should be angry. "What have you done, sorceress?"

"Me?" she said. "I was napping"—she motioned to the ground and to the sky—"and then I was ensnared. With you." She pointed at Sir Horace. "And it."

"Sir Horace is not an it," Caden said and crossed his arms. "And neither he nor I cast this trapping spell."

She put her hands on her hips. Her cheek was scraped. "Well, I didn't do it," she said.

"You're the only spellcaster I see," he said.

Around them, the city sparkled. There were square buildings of metal, stone, and glass. Many had red or brown canopies above the walkway. Come morning, the area would likely be busy.

Where the road forked, there was what looked like a small park nestled between the buildings and roads. The gentle sound of running water came from within it. Sir Horace rolled to his feet and trotted toward it, his tongue hanging from his muzzle.

Brynne narrowed her eyes. "That magic wasn't mine," she said, but her words came out weak. Her face paled. "My magic saved us."

Caden rushed to catch her as she fell. Truth be told, red glowing magic traps didn't seem like the work of her or her people. But if Brynne hadn't ensnared them, who had—and why?

Like an afterthought, his sword clattered down beside them. He lowered Brynne to the ground and glanced around once more. Around them, the air was strange and cold. This was most certainly not their world.

A LAND WITHOUT DRAGONS

Nothing was more important to Caden than slaying a dragon, and he needed to get out of the strange city and back to doing just that. He'd been so close to his goal. He bit back his frustration. All quests were ripe with obstacles. He would overcome this one.

In the morning light, the city around him seemed more foreign. It was surrounded by mountains, but they were small and worn and looked shades of blue and gray. They weren't the sharp, snow- and rock-covered slopes of the Winterlands. The buildings were also small—most a mere three to five stories—and many had simple geometric ornamentation. Even the tallest, a glass and metal structure, failed to touch the clouds. They were nothing like the soaring towers and ornate castles of the Greater Realm.

On the road between the park and the walkway, a

smelly metal transport puttered by him. The streetlights turned off by themselves, seemingly aware morning had broken. People began to trickle into the area.

Caden was stiff from sitting on the bench and keeping guard. At least his enchanted coat kept him warm. He stood, loosened his muscles, and straightened his posture. His brown hair, which he kept regulation short like the Elite Paladins, was mussed, and he flattened it in hopes of a more dignified appearance.

In the night Brynne had snuggled close to a kneeling Sir Horace. She'd rested long enough, though. Caden nudged her with his foot. "Wake up, sorceress."

She snapped open her eyes and frowned like it took a moment for her to place where she was. Sir Horace was also rousing. He pushed to standing and his shadow fell over Caden and Brynne.

Brynne stood and was silhouetted by the winter sun. She was as tall as Caden, and at twelve years, ten months, and two weeks, she was one day older, a fact she never let him forget. Her dark hair hung to her waist. Her gray eyes glinted silver like she was born under the moon. With a glare, she sniffed her sleeve. "I smell of horse," she said.

She'd no reason to complain. Horse was a good smell. "The sooner we get home, the better for us all," Caden said. "Magic us back." He could still track and slay the dragon. He knew where it was, knew of its fire character. If they hurried, the dragon could still be his.

Brynne bit at her bottom lip and glanced around. "Let me think on things." Then she closed her eyes as if trying to sense the unseen. Her brow broke with sweat. After a moment, her cheek twitched, she opened her eyes, and rocked on her feet. Caden reached out to steady her, but she shoved him off. "The spell that brought us here was strong, but it's fading. I'm not sure I can track it and find a path back." She twisted her hands together. "And I'm not sure how such a return spell would even work."

Caden frowned. "I thought you were skilled."

Brynne put her hands on her hips. "Magic isn't that simple, Caden," she said. "And the magic that brought us here was powerful and *dark*." She motioned to the road and shops around them. "I can't just wave my hands and bring us from here to home. I don't even know where *here* is."

Perhaps she could be more useful with more information. "I can find that out," he said. He was tired of sitting and waiting. It was time to speak with the locals. "Wait."

Brynne looked annoyed with the order, but plopped down on the bench and waited. Across the road, there was a shop with paintings of cats in the windows. A woman was unlocking the door. She wore a green coat and balanced on shoes with sharp-looking heels. While Brynne and Sir Horace watched from the small park, Caden approached her. Best he stay on guard. Obviously, the shoes were weapons.

He cleared his throat to get the woman's attention.

The woman turned to him, key partially twisted in the lock, and stared at his sword. Then her gaze flickered to his right and widened. No doubt she was impressed at the majestic sight of Sir Horace on the square across the road.

Caden leaned back into the woman's line of sight. "What is this place?" he said.

He'd spoken in the Greater Realm's common tongue, but the weapon-heeled woman scrunched up her face like she didn't understand. Caden felt his stomach turn. All peoples of the Greater Realm knew the common tongue. He'd hoped this world wasn't as foreign as he suspected, but it seemed more and more that it was.

For her part, the woman frowned. "Sweetie," she said, "I don't understand you." Her tone was smooth, there was a pleasant drawl to her vowels, and she sounded kind. He felt more confident she wouldn't attack him with her shoes.

Also, while she may not have understood him, Caden understood her. Any language he heard, he could master. It was his gift of speech, bestowed on him when he was an infant. Like his father and brothers, and all princes or princesses born in Razzon, he'd been given a gift—a talent to aid him through the turmoil that was the royal life. His brothers were each given a gift to aid in battle. Valon was gifted with leadership, Maden with strength, Lucian with stealth, Martin with accuracy, Landon with fortitude, Chadwin with agility, and Jasan with speed.

By the time Caden was born, eighth prince of Razzon,

all the best ones were taken. In a moment of desperation, the Royal Bestower gifted Caden with speech—a talent that in no way helped with his swordplay, gave no advantage in battle, and was rumored to have last been gifted to a rogue princess of the merchant people.

It was, however, useful in speaking with strange women in strange lands. He adjusted his words to match the rhythm she'd used. He felt the long vowels form on his tongue and the smooth cadence dance on his lips. "Where am I—" and because a prince was always polite, and it floated in Caden's mind as the polite thing to say, he smiled and amended his words to "Where am I, ma'am?"

She seemed to soften at that. People often softened when Caden concentrated on his words. "College Street and Broadway," she said, and twisted the key until the lock clicked. "Are you lost?"

Caden wasn't lost. He was stranded by dark magic with his horse and an untrusted sorceress. "I'm not where I need to be." He crossed his arms and looked at the hard, gray road beside them. A shiny, red transport zoomed by. Her reply didn't sound like the name of a realm. He tried again. "I need the name of the world."

The woman looked confused. "What do you mean?"

In Caden's royal opinion, it wasn't a difficult question. He kept his questions to the sharp-heeled woman simple and direct after that, and returned to Brynne and Sir Horace with new knowledge. He switched back to their common language. "This is the 'downtown' of the land of Asheville. It's part of Carolina of the North, which is in the south." None of it made sense. Sir Horace and Brynne wore twin expressions of confusion. Caden sighed. "Also, she says her shoes aren't used for combat."

"That doesn't help me much. I've never heard of such places." Brynne seemed to consider. "We should find a local magic worker. Magic brought us, magic will get us home."

Sir Horace nuzzled Caden's shoulder. Caden reached and brought him closer. "No, we should find the local Paladins." He considered. This was a strange place. "Or this realm's equivalents. Paladins always render aid."

Brynne rolled her eyes and stretched. "Paladins always render trouble, prince. Everyone knows that."

While she couldn't devise a spell to return home, she did know one that would let her understand the local language. She cast it, and they split up. While Caden and Sir Horace went in search of more answers, she went to find magic.

None of the twenty-two people Caden approached knew of Paladins or sorcerers—not the woman with three kids, nor the man walking two dogs, nor the girls with packs on their backs—none of them. None knew of any dragons prowling the small mountains visible around the city either.

As the sun started to set, Caden tied Sir Horace to one of the self-lighting streetlights and went into a bakery.

Inside, it was warm and smelled like baking breads and the sweet pulp of venombark berries. The baker had brown skin and a rainbow-colored shirt. The counter was filled with rustic-looking breads. Caden forced his gaze from the delicious-looking food and addressed the baker. "I need to find a Paladin," he said in the Ashevillian tongue. Though he didn't really want to, he added, "or a sorcerer." At this point, he'd be happy to find a gnome.

"Just breads and muffins here," the baker told Caden. With a smile he handed out a tray of samples. "They're all vegan, all natural. Take some."

Caden didn't know what "vegan" meant, so it likely had no equivalent in his language, but he took three pieces— one for himself, one for Sir Horace, and one for Brynne. Outside, he ate the bread and untied Sir Horace. Caden's piece was chewy and healthy tasting, and he approved. Sir Horace, however, spit his out onto the street before Caden mounted and they returned to the park.

Brynne was fidgeting on the bench. "No one knows of magic," she said while Caden climbed down. "And two people tried to take me away when I said I slept in the park."

Caden handed her the bread and looked to the walk-ways—"sidewalks," in the local tongue. Many stared at Sir Horace, and one had yelled at Caden when Sir Horace had relieved himself. None looked like Paladins or sorcerers, for that matter.

They needed to be practical. It was possible they'd be stranded for longer than a day or two. The square was nice enough, but it was open and unprotected. "We need to find a better place to stay."

Brynne narrowed her eyes. "Yes, prince, that was my point."

As twilight fell, they searched together for a campsite, Caden atop Sir Horace, Brynne beside them. There were larger roadways beyond the downtown, divided into three and four lanes. The metal transports—cars—moved fast on them. They crossed under one busy roadway to get to a wooded area with houses, and finally made camp in the cedars between the downtown and a large inn with stone stacked walls and a large rolling red roof.

Caden surveyed his supplies—one small pan, a satchel, and a worn compass invented by the desertsmiths of Summerlands. The compass was an essential tool for any soldier, especially an Elite Paladin. The lid was engraved with a gentle snake, a tribute to the Sunsnake that turned the deserts. Inside it had a small lever with three settings. With the lever in the center location, it would navigate direction. Move the lever up, and it could test if a plant was edible. Move it down, and it directed the user toward freshwater.

For the next two days, they investigated. Each morning, Brynne cast her spell of understanding. It wasn't natural like Caden's gift of speech. It was fleeting magic that drained her energy and had to be renewed daily. She searched for information on moon phases and sun patterns, for spellwork, and for any way to strengthen her magic or help her discover the way home.

Caden was relegated to more practical tasks. He strengthened their shelters with twisted branches and cold mud, then hunted for food. He used his compass and satchel to find and collect edible tubers, berries, and drinking water. Afterward, he joined Brynne to explore the city. By the time they regrouped at the campsite on the third night, she was grumpy and Sir Horace was restless.

"The beast and I are hungry," Brynne said, and frowned at the roasting tubers on the fire. "I can steal us real food. We'll need some soon." Although not her friend, Sir Horace whinnied in obvious agreement.

The setting sun cast shadows through the cedar branches. Through gaps in the trees, Caden saw the first lights turning on in the city below. The noise from the roads was growing loud with cars.

He turned to Brynne and glared. "Future Elite Paladins don't steal," he said. "These will sustain us for now. They can for several days." Brynne looked as if she intended to steal food anyway. Caden sighed and tossed Sir Horace one of the tubers. "Eat it, Sir Horace. It will quell your hunger."

Sir Horace neighed and stomped at the frozen earth. The ground cracked under his hooves. Hot breath billowed from his nostrils like chimney smoke.

Brynne sat on a log that Caden had arranged as a bench and stretched her legs. "You understand that foul beast can't talk back, don't you?"

Her beauty aside, he grew tired of her insults. True, they were stuck here together and had formed an alliance. But he'd found food; he'd built shelters. It was time for her to do her part. "You need to complain less and be useful. Find us a way home already."

She arched a delicate brow. "My magic's the only thing that kept the forces that pulled us here from delivering us straight to them. You'd likely be dead if not for me."

She'd said that before. "So you think," he said.

Her face scrunched up like he was the one annoying her. "So I know, prince."

She seemed quite certain for someone who couldn't identify said forces, couldn't give a reason they'd been pulled from their different kingdoms to this strange world, and couldn't find a way back to the Greater Realm.

This he didn't say, but Brynne frowned like she knew his thoughts. She twisted her hands together and stared down at them. When she spoke, her voice was small. "It's not a simple spell. The more I learn . . ." She took a deep breath and continued. "The moon is different here. The phases change swiftly. I estimate a mere fourteen days from full moon to new one. And the sun casts different light. No one seems to know of magic." She looked away. "I think it will take years for me to master a spell to get home.

At least four, maybe more. Even then, I might not have the power to get all three of us home."

He heard her words but couldn't process them. "What?"

She reached as if to pet Sir Horace, but Sir Horace snorted and jerked away like the proud stallion he was. Backed by the setting sun, she seemed to glow. "We're stuck here. Based on my skill and the best alignment for a travel spell, it'll take years to return us. I'm certain. You, me, and"—she paused to level a sneer at Sir Horace—"the beast are trapped."

For a moment, he stared at her, caught by her dark beauty, but he was no fool. He knew who she was—a sorceress of questionable motives, a girl from a people of magic and thievery.

"You're wrong," he said.

Her confident expression seemed about to crack. "I'm not," she said.

Caden had a dragon to slay. His father was waiting. "I won't stay here."

She laughed, and, for the briefest moment, looked like she might cry. "Caden," she said, "we don't have a choice."

From the hillside, Caden watched night fall. The city glowed with white and yellow lights. Without clouds, the sky above was filled with stars, though none grouped in patterns he recognized. The moon rose. Already it was under three-quarters full.

He turned back and prepared some tubers he had collected for dinner. Brynne stood over him. She opened her mouth to likely throw out a comment about his cooking, but was interrupted by voices from the road below.

"Got some strange reports about the hillside. And someone said they saw a girl 'round here," a man said.

Caden turned. Sir Horace stood at attention. Brynne went wide-eyed and chewed on her bottom lip.

The man spoke again. "This way, boss," he said. He sounded closer. "You know, it's been over seventy-two hours. Odds are we aren't gonna find her."

"I know, Jenkins," a second, deeper voice said, "but I promised I'd keep looking."

"Yeah," Jenkins said. "No stone unturned. Right?"

"Something like that."

Caden hoped Brynne understood the men. She spoke the Ashevillian tongue with the aid of her spells, but the magic was fleeting and it was late in the day. "Get out of sight," he whispered.

"I've had enough of your orders, Caden," she said, but she became serious and battle ready. She stepped into the eastern shadows, becoming one with the night.

Caden patted Sir Horace's neck. "Quiet, friend," he said, and led the horse to the cover of the thick cedars that framed their camp's uphill side.

Brynne had questionable ethics, but she was his ally until they found their way back to the Greater Realm. Neither of them knew why they'd been targeted by the spell that brought them here. Perhaps these men were the ones who'd cast it. If they were after Brynne, she would fight, and Caden and Sir Horace would battle beside her.

The men broke sticks and twigs as they approached. Leaves crunched. Either they were not trained in stealth or didn't care that they sounded like approaching thunder cattle.

Near the camp's perimeter, the noises stopped. The men were so close Caden could see their dark forms beyond the trees. He crouched behind a bush. Sir Horace was as still as a statue behind him, Brynne a shadow in the east. Caden's hand twitched near his blade. With fate's favor and the camouflage he'd built, he, his horse, and the fledgling sorceress would go unnoticed.

Fate, however, was not with them this night. A moment later, one of the men pushed through the cedars and stepped into the camp. He was tall and lanky. Against the moonlight, Caden made out red hair, a dark uniform, and a weapons belt. "Whoa," the man said. "Whatta you think about this?"

The second man tromped past the evergreens. He was shorter, older, and stockier. His hair and eyebrows were bushy and graying. He, too, wore a dark uniform and weapons belt. Not spellcasters, then. City guards. Policemen, by the local tongue.

"It's organized, well hidden," the stocky one said. "Not your typical squatters, Jenkins." He circled the camp and shone his light on the shelters, on the post Caden had fashioned for Sir Horace, on the tall hiking stick Caden had whittled with his sword. "All this stuff needs to be bagged, tagged, and processed."

The lanky one, Jenkins, strode to the fire pit. He shone his light on the coals and on Caden's pot of cooked tubers sitting atop. With a nudge of his dirty boot, he tipped the pot and its contents to the ground. "Still warm."

It'd taken Caden most of the morning to collect and

prepare the tubers so they were edible. That was valuable time he'd have preferred to have spent searching for a way back to Razzon and its dragons. His hard-found dinner steamed on the cold ground. He clenched his jaw and pulled his fingers into a fist.

The stocky one squinted toward the camp's edge and toward Brynne. He shone his light around the branches, not quite seeing her but sensing her. Sometimes magic hid people. Sometimes it made them more noticeable. "Police! Who's there? Come out, now." They would find her at any moment.

Caden brushed dried leaves from his pants and stood. The peril of an unknown land was no excuse for poor grooming, and a prince always protected those in his care, even the pretty, wicked ones who didn't deserve it. He stepped from the branches. "I'm over here."

The policemen spun around and shone their lights at his face. The stocky one stepped forward. Jenkins put a hand on his weapons belt. No matter. Tall and clumsy and old and short were no match for him. Caden had his sword.

"You're not Jane," Jenkins said.

Caden didn't know who this Jane was, but he certainly was not her. "I'm Caden, prince of Razzon, eighth-born son to the honorable King Axel." He glared at Jenkins and pointed at the spilled roots that were now dirt-covered and limp in the cold air. "That was my dinner."

"Dinner?" Jenkins said. "You're kidding, right?"

"Tubers, you've ruined them."

"Lucky you." Jenkins stepped closer. "How old are you, kid?"

"Old enough."

The stocky one peered at Caden. "I'm going to need to talk to your parent or guardian or whoever built this camp right now."

Caden bristled. "I built the camp."

Seemingly stirred by the conflict, Caden felt Sir Horace fall in line behind him. His hot breath tickled Caden's neck; his magnificent presence guarded over him. The men's eyes went wide.

Jenkins frowned at Caden, at his clothes, at the sharp sword across Caden's back, at Sir Horace. "You know," he said, "the fine for having unlicensed livestock in the city limits is five hundred dollars."

To call a steed like Sir Horace "livestock" was unforgivable. He was a Galvanian snow stallion, trained by the Elite Guard, and deemed the eighth finest horse in the Greater Realm. If Caden were brasher, he would attack these guards out of pure principle.

From the east, Caden felt Brynne's amusement, even though he couldn't see her. For his part, Sir Horace flattened his ears, bared his teeth, and snapped at Jenkins's light.

"Whoa!" Jenkins jumped back. "Kid, get that animal under control."

Caden didn't appreciate the tone. He didn't appreciate these men riffling through his things and doubting his camp-building abilities. He raised his chin. "Sir Horace is justifiably insulted."

The stocky one glared at Jenkins and then motioned to himself. "I'm Officer Levine," he said. "Are you out here by yourself, son?"

"Do you see anyone else?" he said.

"You've got two shelters."

More and more, it seemed these men knew nothing of Caden or Brynne. It was possible they weren't the ones who stranded them. Still, it was smarter to be cautious. The second shelter was Brynne's, but Caden didn't mention her. Instead, he nodded to Sir Horace. "Sir Horace prefers a roof," he said, which was, in fact, true.

Officer Levine watched Caden like he knew he was hiding things. "Those look a little small for Sir Horace." It wasn't a question, so Caden didn't respond. With a soft sigh, Officer Levine reached into his shirt, pulled out a folded paper, and handed it to Caden. "Have you seen her?"

Caden kept his distance but came close enough to take the paper. When he unfolded it, a picture of a girl smiled from the page. She wore a wool hat pulled down over her ears and had straight dark hair that hung to her shoulders. There was strange writing under her image—the written language of this land, no doubt. Caden's gift of speech didn't translate the written word. He held the paper up.

"This is who you are looking for?"

"Jane Chan," Officer Levine said.

There was nothing familiar about the girl. Caden felt his shoulders ease, some of the tension in his muscles lessen. It was definitely not Brynne these men sought. "No, I haven't seen her."

Officer Levine looked away and frowned. It seemed finding this girl was important to him.

"I'm sorry," Caden said.

Officer Levine nodded, taking Caden's words as the truth they were, but he didn't leave. Instead, he walked around the camp, taking in the piled wood and the stack of tuber tops in the corner like he was calculating hours and days in his head. "How long have you been out here?"

Again, Caden told the truth. He always told the truth. Future Elite Paladins didn't lie. "We've been in the city three days."

Officer Levine took a deep breath. Beside them, Sir Horace and Jenkins were locked in some sort of man-horse staring contest. Caden patted Sir Horace's neck. No lanky city guard could stare down his steed. As if Sir Horace read his thoughts, he neighed mightily.

Jenkins was not as foolish as he seemed, for he stepped farther back. "Three days, huh?" he said with his gaze darting between Caden and Sir Horace. "Same night Jane Chan disappeared."

Caden looked back down at the paper. Suddenly, it felt

heavier. Something—or someone—had brought Caden and Brynne to this strange world. Perhaps that same thing had also taken Jane Chan. "The girl disappeared three days ago?" He hoped Brynne was listening, but there was a good chance she'd already fled.

"That's right," Officer Levine said.

He held the paper up. "What happened to her?"

"That's what we're trying to find out," Officer Levine said.

These men were searching for a missing girl. They were protectors of the city. Their misplaced suspicion of Caden aside, he felt it only proper to share what he knew. "It was dark magic that trapped me here. Three days ago just as night fell. Perhaps it also trapped her."

Neither man looked impressed with Caden's deduction, nor grateful for his help. "Evidence suggests she ran away," Jenkins said.

"Are you a runaway, son?" Officer Levine said.

Caden raised his brows at the shift to him. "I'm on a quest. I was sent by my father."

"A lockout, then," Jenkins said.

That sounded insulting. Caden narrowed his eyes. "What do you mean?"

Officer Levine stepped toward him. "Your father's not allowed to send you away."

Caden, indeed, was insulted. He pulled Sir Horace back; they moved beyond Officer Levine's reach. "He's the king, he decides what's allowed."

"No one's above the law," Officer Levine said.

"You're not grasping the concept of king," Caden said. "And I'm twelve turns. I can care for myself."

Officer Levine rubbed his brow like Caden's words made his head hurt. "You're not allowed to camp out here, and you have to have a guardian until you're eighteen." He said it as if he thought Caden didn't know these laws. Which Caden didn't—so he was thankful for the explanation.

Certainly, he jested, though. "Eighteen?" Caden said.

"That's right," Officer Levine said, and held out his hand. "You need to come with us."

Unlike Brynne, Caden always did his best to honor foreign laws. He squared his shoulders. "I'm willing to relocate farther up the mountain." And he was. Sir Horace would prefer the steeper terrain, although the sorceress would likely complain.

"I got a better idea," Officer Levine said with an annoyingly gentle tone. "We'll go to the station and Jenkins will round you up some dinner while we talk about who you are and where you came from."

"Thank you," Caden said, "but no."

"Son, that wasn't a request," Officer Levine said.

"I know," Caden said. "It was a kind offer, and I'm respectfully declining."

Officer Levine reached for Caden, but Caden easily

dodged. "Son," he said, "I already have one lost kid on my conscience."

Caden was no lost kid. He didn't need a guardian. His place wasn't to be jailed in some Ashevillian police station. He needed to find a dragon to slay and find his way back to his father. Then the king would be proud and let Caden serve with his brothers. His place was in Razzon, beside his seven—Caden paused and collected his royal self—no, not seven anymore. It was beside his six brothers, fighting for his father and his kingdom.

"I'm not going with you," Caden said.

Officer Levine looked like he was losing his patience. His expression fell, and he seemed tired and worn, like he'd had too many late nights dealing with frustrating individuals. "You don't have a choice," he said.

Officer Levine motioned to Jenkins. Jenkins moved to the left of Caden, boots crunching the dry leaves, while Officer Levine circled right. Both raised their hands in placating gestures, but Caden was not so green that he didn't recognize a coming ambush. He dropped into a defensive stance.

His sword was as sharp as a griffin's tooth and just as deadly. It was not a weapon for this combat of ignorance. He kept it sheathed and darted for the hiking stick.

Like Jenkins read his intentions, he jumped between Caden and his goal. "I don't think so," he said, reached out, and seized the stick.

Caden lunged for him, grabbed the stick's narrow end, and used the momentum to flip Jenkins through the air. Jenkins landed flat on his back, long legs sprawled, air knocked from his lungs. Caden jumped back, the stick grasped securely with both hands.

Officer Levine ran in front of the fallen Jenkins. "Stand down, son."

Caden flipped the stick so that the blunt end, the end he hadn't whittled to a sharp spear, faced Officer Levine. "Allow me to collect my things, and I'll let you go unharmed."

Officer Levine's gaze darted to Jenkins and back to Caden. He took in a deep breath. "I can't do that, son. Now, drop the stick."

Caden didn't drop his stick; he flipped it so Officer Levine faced the pointy end.

Behind Officer Levine, Jenkins rolled to his stomach and pushed to his knees. "Careful, boss. The kid's a ninja."

"An Elite Paladin," Caden corrected. Or he would be when he found a dragon to slay.

Jenkins climbed back to his feet, his hand on his belt. "You need to relax, ninja kid, and put down the weapon."

Officer Levine's expression softened. "Son, we want to help you. We'll have animal control take good care of your horse."

Sir Horace would defeat any animal control. Beside Caden, Sir Horace pawed and snorted. If he entered this skirmish, Officer Levine and his Jenkins would certainly be trampled.

Caden signaled Sir Horace to fall back and find Brynne. Sir Horace hesitated long enough to convey his displeasure, then disappeared into the trees. "Run, Sir Horace!" Caden yelled after him. Neither man followed.

Once Sir Horace's hoofbeats had dimmed, Caden put his full concentration on the men. They weren't spellcasters or trained swordsmen. They were city guards, ignorant of Caden and his world. They couldn't help Caden complete heroic deeds, fight a dragon, or find his way home. "Your help isn't needed," he said. "Now, leave me."

"That's not going to happen," Officer Levine said. "You need to understand that."

"I won't go with you. You need to understand *that*." To prove his point, Caden whirled the stick like a Korvan battle staff. If they doubted his skill in combat, that display should convince them otherwise.

The men exchanged a quick look. Jenkins pulled a strange square device from his belt. It crackled with electricity. "Kid, I'll subdue you if I have to."

The time for talk had passed. Caden charged.

4

THE FOSTER PRISON

The police station had low ceilings and cluttered desks. Caden sat on a hard wooden chair and stared at a trash bin overflowing with crumpled tissues. The castle guards would never keep their quarters so untidy. Caden told Officer Levine as much.

Officer Levine seemed amused. "Cleaning crew comes in the morning," he said. He held out a pink sugared pastry in a strange wrapper. "Why don't you eat something? Social worker won't be here for a while yet."

The food looked nowhere near as healthy as the vegan bread from the baker. Caden crossed his arms. Officer Levine frowned. He pulled up a second wooden chair and sat beside him. "Don't worry, son. We'll sort this out."

Caden didn't need him to sort this out. Matter of point, he didn't need him to sort anything out. He was an heir to the throne of Razzon, trained since he was four years old in the ways of battle and diplomacy. He sorted his own things out. The squeal of metal sliding past metal—the unmistakable sound of his sword being drawn—jerked him back to the current situation.

"This thing is sharp," Jenkins said from a room behind them. "Heavy, too." He strolled into sight and waved the sleek blade in front of him. "Where'd you get this?"

Jenkins had no right to wield it. Suddenly, the failures of this night weighed on Caden, and he fought to keep his expression even. His sword was in the hand of another man. Sir Horace was to be animal controlled. His questionable ally, Brynne, was nowhere in sight and likely had fled into the night. Caden was to be imprisoned in a strange land. He felt shame heat his cheeks. There was no honor in this night.

Officer Levine smiled and squeezed his shoulder. "It'll be all right," he said.

The next afternoon, Officer Levine drove Caden to the western side of town. No telling what terrible punishment awaited—amputated hands, a long jail sentence in a small cell far from sunlight and fresh air. Caden was in the backseat. His compass was safe in his pocket, but the police had taken his sword, and he was weaponless. He caught Officer Levine's gaze in the mirror. "What do you intend to do with me?"

Officer Levine explained it again.

It sounded like no jail Caden had ever visited. "I'm going to be given free food and lodging?"

"For the last time, it's not a prison."

Caden was trained to show no fear, no weakness, but his concern that someone might cut off his hand was strong. It was a common punishment in certain lands. He pulled his arms close to his body. "Will they try to cut off my hand? Or burn me? Or flog me?"

Officer Levine's back tensed. "No," he said quietly. He added, "Have you been subjected to those punishments?"

Caden held up his fully attached hands. "Obviously not."

"What about the burnings and the floggings?"

"What about them?"

Officer Levine drew a deep breath. "No one will hurt you where I'm taking you." He caught Caden's gaze in the mirror. "That was quite a story you told the social worker."

"She asked for the truth. I obliged."

Officer Levine shook his head. "Son, Child Protective Services wanted to send you for treatment. I stuck my neck out to get you temporarily placed. I called in favors I won't get back."

"There was no reason for you to do that."

"I want to help you."

This well-meaning man underestimated him. Caden crossed his arms, felt his seat belt pinch. "I'm well trained, smart, and determined."

"I said I wanted to help you," Officer Levine said. "I didn't say you weren't a survivor." He cleared his throat. "Rosa, the woman you'll be staying with, she's a survivor, too."

"I doubt she'd be a good warden if she were dead."

Officer Levine continued as if Caden hadn't spoken. "She's been where you are. She's a metal artist; some of her stuff has won national acclaim," he said. "She's taken in lots of troubled kids over the years. Jane was one of hers."

Caden felt for the flier he'd pocketed of the missing girl. It was folded and solid in his pocket

Officer Levine turned onto a large road. "Now stop yapping and eat your food."

A Paladin's body was his finest weapon, to be crafted of the best materials and given the most vigilant of care. Recommended dietary restrictions were clear. Caden didn't understand why Officer Levine kept pushing unpalatable foods at him. Caden pulled the crinkling, oil-stained packet from the bag.

"I can't eat this geometric meat. It's unnatural."

"The burger's genuine Angus beef," Officer Levine said. "And the fries are fresh-cut potatoes."

Caden glanced inside at the second item.

"They're tubers," Officer Levine said. "I thought you'd like that."

Caden doubted the greasy fries would pass the typical

diet restrictions of Elite Paladins. But tubers were acceptable starches in extreme conditions. "I'll try the fries."

Officer Levine grinned like he'd won a great battle.

The war, however, was not over. Caden dropped the burger back in the bag. No animal he knew had meat that formed perfectly circular cuts. "But I'm not eating round food."

"Shame," Officer Levine said. "Round cow's the tastiest."

They traveled down and up the hilly terrain of the city. The closely packed buildings of the downtown gave way to houses with big yards and tall trees. Farther out, small stalls selling junk and apples started to dot the road. They stopped on the seeming edge of the city, halfway up one of the smaller mountains.

On the slope's side stood the not-prison. It was three stories high with battered tan paint and a large porch. Behind it, the mountain was filled with evergreens and leafless oaks. In the yard, there were tall-growing winter weeds. Littered among them were all forms of oddities—cement frogs; glass suncatchers; and large, twisting copper sculptures of the sun and moon. To the side of the house, he saw metal-sculptured flowers, their petals sharp and gleaming.

Officer Levine got out of the car and opened the back for Caden to do the same.

Once on the lawn, he pointed to the metal sculptures. "Those are some of Rosa's works," Officer Levine said. "She sells her art at several local galleries."

On the slope behind the house, Caden caught a flash of white. He heard a soft neigh on the wind. Sir Horace had tracked them. Caden expected no less. On the slope near Sir Horace, Brynne peeked around an oak. With a subtle hand signal, Caden ordered them to stay. Even from so far downhill, Caden could tell it irritated Sir Horace to be idle and Brynne to be given orders.

"Son, are you listening to me?" Officer Levine said. Caden turned to him. It seemed Officer Levine hadn't noticed Sir Horace, or Brynne, for that matter. Caden's allies were masters of stealth.

Caden looked up at Officer Levine. "No, were your words of importance?"

Officer Levine sighed. "Look, Rosa will let you stay as long as you need to. I want your word you'll try to make this work."

The promise of a warm bed and warm meals was tempting, but Caden's concerns were greater than this man and this house. He would stay long enough to learn if there was a possible connection between the missing Jane Chan and the night he and Brynne were magically stranded here. But the minute he learned all he could, or found a way home, he would escape.

"I can't make that promise," he said.

Before Officer Levine could respond, a woman marched from the house. If Caden hadn't been trained to look at people as a whole his gaze would have been stuck on her clothes. She wore an ill-fitting sweater the color of mud and tight pants that were orange like firelight. Her hair was long and brown with stark streaks of gray; her eyes were a matching worn brown.

"Yes, you can," Officer Levine said. "She'll help you."

Unless this oddly dressed woman could open inter-dimensional magic portals, she couldn't help. "A prince is always gracious."

"Good," Officer Levine said, but for the first time since Caden had met him, he sounded distracted. His cheeks had taken on a rosy hue. He straightened his collar.

Caden had seen his lovelorn look before. Girls and boys often expressed it when they met his older brothers. Caden glanced at him and shook his head. "You wish to woo her," he said. "That's why you brought me here."

"Quiet," Officer Levine said. "And, no. Besides, she's ex-army. I figured you two might get along."

She approached Caden like he was a soldier in a battle line. "This him?" she said.

"Yep, and he's a handful. Knocked Jenkins on his butt."

Despite her odd dress, her stance and demeanor were like those of the Elite Guardsmen. Caden could tell she was a soldier. He stood taller, straighter, and met her gaze.

"I have rules," she said. "No back talk. No cursing."

Caden always kept his speech elegant and refined. "No cursing," he agreed.

She stepped closer. "I'll know if you curse, whether I hear you or not. Do you understand?"

"You have the gift of other sight."

The answer brought a concerned furrow to her brow. She shook her head and glanced at Officer Levine. "Just how much trouble is he in?"

"We're still trying to find his family," Officer Levine said. "Social services wanted him sent for psych eval."

A look of horror crossed her face. "They always have trouble with the imaginative ones." She looked at Caden. "You'll stay here," she said, and it sounded like an order.

"For now," Caden said.

"Call me Rosa," she said. "Had enough of titles in the service. No missus, no ma'am. It's Rosa and that's it."

"Titles are important for designating rank," Caden said. "You can call me your highness."

Rosa gave him a sharp look.

Then, to Caden's confusion, her expression softened. She stepped toward him, arms outstretched. Fast like a silver ice runner, she hugged him. He tried to pull away, but she was amazingly strong. No doubt she was gifted with strength like his brother, the second-born prince, Maden.

"You'll be sharing the attic room with Tito. He's also twelve."

Over her shoulder, Caden saw an irritated-looking boy hovering on the front steps. Tito was about Caden's build and height but his black hair was long and shiny, his face was striking and sharp-featured. His eyes were intensely dark. When he frowned, his face looked lopsided.

"He'll give you the tour while I talk to Officer Levine." Rosa turned back. "Be nice, Tito."

Tito didn't look like he wanted to be nice. He looked Caden up and down, and his frown deepened. Caden took in his sour expression, worn-looking clothes, and long hair. It seemed he would be sharing a room with a peasant. Caden, too, frowned.

With a sigh, Tito motioned him to the house. "C'mon," he said, and led him through a creaking front door. Inside, the walls were filled with pictures of boys and girls—former prisoners, or "foster kids," as Tito called them. Every table had some knickknack displayed. There was dust and clutter, but it was reasonably clean for a prison.

"These are the main rooms. Kitchen is in the back," Tito said, turning around and motioning around the first floor. "Dining room, living room, TV. Rosa's got a computer in her office, but we don't get to use it without supervision."

"What's a TV?"

Tito stopped. "You can't be serious."

"Answer my question."

Tito pointed to a flat glass rectangle about the size of a small window on a table. "Um. It's that."

Caden frowned at the thing.

"You know," Tito said, "it's a thing that shows pictures and transmits information and stuff."

Caden nodded, though he still didn't fully understand. "So it's like a Razzonian meditation disc? Only smaller and square?"

"Uh . . . sure. I guess?"

"And a computer, what's that?"

"Just how long have you been living in the woods?" Tito said. "Actually, don't tell me. First the tour. Then your issues. This way."

Caden followed him up a rickety staircase. Tito motioned to the hall. "These are Rosa's bedroom, the guest room, and the girls' room when there're girls around. It's locked now." He led him to a second staircase. "We're in the attic."

The attic room was large and divided down the center with black tape. Mismatched rugs covered the plank floor. The ceiling slanted, and two large windows were cut out of it. Outside, the mountain loomed high. Well, high for an Ashevillian mountain. In the Greater Realm, it would have been a hillock.

An unmade bed with purple pillows and purple blankets was pushed against the wall beside the door. Books were piled beside it, on top of it, and under it. The second bed was against the wall on the other side of the tape. It was draped with a pink and orange quilt.

Tito pointed toward the made bed, the pink and orange one. "That side's yours," he said, and walked to the purple part of the room. "This one's mine."

The rugs dampened the sound of Caden's steps, but the floor still groaned as he walked. He glanced at the unappealing pink and orange quilt, at Tito's challenging smile, and he sat on the bed. A prince was always polite, always honest. "I'll sleep in it," Caden said.

"Right, weirdo, that's why it's called a bed."

There was something different about the sound of Tito's voice. Caden peered at him. Tito's voice had definitely changed somehow.

Tito gave him a look and backed up a few steps. "Anyway, Rosa says lights off at ten. No exceptions." His voice was normal again.

Caden motioned around the room. "Why are we in the attic? There were empty rooms downstairs."

"She keeps the boys and girls separate."

"There are no girls."

"Yeah." Tito looked away. "But she's worried you're a flight risk. She figures if you're up here, you'll have more trouble sneaking out. I've been with her for three years. She knows I'd never leave. I'm stuck up here, you know, to help you adjust."

"I don't need to adjust," Caden said.

They fell into silence. Tito rocked on his feet. "So," Tito said, "you told the system people your father was king?"

"I did," Caden said.

"Why?"

"Because it is so," Caden said.

"Uh-huh," Tito said.

"You don't believe me."

"Don't really care." Tito scrunched up his lopsided face. "But you were stupid to tell the police. And the social worker. You're lucky they didn't ship you right off to the nuthouse. Much worse than juvie, from what I've heard."

"You think I should keep my birthright secret?"

"Yeah," Tito said, then his tone changed—the pace of his words changed, the cadence shifted. "But I can't believe I have to share a room with a nutcase like you."

Caden crossed his arms and narrowed his eyes. "Nutcase?" he said. He was certain that was insulting. "If you want to fight, we can fight."

"Right. I'm terrified," Tito said. Suddenly, his striking eyes widened. "Bro, you speak Spanish?"

"Excuse me?"

"You're speaking Spanish," Tito said.

Caden was speaking another local language. He'd never used his gift of speech without knowing it. Not until Asheville. Not until right now, and his insides twisted. It had never worked like that. Although, he'd never used it as much as he had in recent days, either.

"Well," Caden said, and shoved off his discomfort, "I speak most languages."

Tito turned his mouth back into his lopsided frown. "Huh," he said. "My advice, keep that to yourself, too."

Caden crossed his arms. "You seem full of advice."

"Yeah, well," Tito said. "Rosa told me to be friendly—I'm being friendly."

There was more to it than that. Caden could tell. He nodded toward the stairs. "You're mad at her," he said.

"So what if I am?" Tito said.

Maybe she banished him to the attic? Maybe she beat him and kept him from food and drink? "Why?" Caden said. "Is she violent?"

Tito scowled, and his voice came out furious. "Rosa's the best person you'll ever meet."

The best person it seemed Caden would ever meet called them down for dinner.

Caden caught up with Tito on the second floor and stopped him. "If she's so wonderful, why are you upset?"

Tito went still and stony. His gaze flickered to the locked girls' room. Caden followed his gaze. The flier about the missing girl was still folded in his pocket. Officer Levine had said she'd been imprisoned here before disappearing three days ago. "Was that Jane Chan's room?"

Tito flinched like he'd been hit. Caden recognized Tito's pained expression. He was certain Tito's anger covered a deeper hurt.

The king's first wife, his brothers' mother, died three years before Caden's birth. One of her portraits hung in the Grand Hall of the castle—a place of great honor. Her hair and eyes looked golden like the sun, her head was crowned in a fine silver circlet. On each anniversary of her death the castle was draped in somber dark silks. His brothers and father became sullen and quiet.

Four years ago on that dark-draped day, Caden had found his seventh-born brother, Jasan, twelve years his senior and gifted in speed, alone in the Grand Hall. His eyes were red and his cheeks wet. His tall, lithe frame, strong and ever sure, shook like he was fragile.

Caden looked at the portrait. "It's sad," he said.

Jasan's pain morphed into anger. He grabbed Caden by his shoulders. "You don't get to look at her like that."

Caden winced.

Jasan glanced down to where his fingers dug into Caden's shoulders. Immediately, he gentled. "Go away," he said with a sigh. "You wouldn't understand."

Jasan was right. There was no portrait of Caden's mother in the Great Hall, no portrait of her anywhere. The only sign she'd ever existed was Caden.

Caden might not have understood Jasan's pain, but he was good at knowing what to say to ease it. Despite his brother's words, Caden glanced up at the portrait and then back to his brother. "You look like her," he said.

Back in the present, here in the Ashevillian not-prison, Tito had a similar mix of fury and despair. What Caden didn't know was why. "You know," Tito said, "you're only going to be here a few days, so mind your own business." With that, he turned on his heel and stomped down the stairs.

Caden lingered on the second floor. Jane Chan had run

away the same time he and Brynne had been brought here. Now Caden was imprisoned in her old foster home. He reached out and tried the door to her room. It was locked, but the metal knob felt warm like it had been exposed to some nearby magic. He needed to question Tito further about the missing girl. Again, his instincts told him there might be a connection between her and Caden being stranded.

5

THE SORCERESS AND THE SAND

Caden woke to the *tink-tink* of rain on the roof. He was warm and well rested in Rosa's not-prison. There was no Brynne across the way, insulting Caden about the shelter he built and its ability to keep out the drops.

His stomach turned in a twist of guilt. His willful ally and his horse were stuck outside in the cold rain. Truly, he needed to speak to Brynne and make her aware of what he'd learned. He pushed his pink and orange quilt away and sat up.

Across the taped line, Tito was dressed in gray, shabby clothes and sitting on his bed. His hair was tied back with a band. "You awake?" Tito said.

"I get up at dawn," Caden said.

"Why aren't I surprised?" Tito said.

Caden, however, was surprised Tito was awake so early.

"Why are you awake?"

Tito put on some worn-looking shoes. Sneakers, he'd called them. "Rosa makes me run in the morning, thinks it helps me release anger or some crap like that."

"I don't know what that means," Caden said.

Tito snorted and tied his shoe. "Of course you don't."

Caden looked at the shadowed mountain out the window. Brynne was somewhere out there. Certainly, she'd be drenched and difficult already. The sooner he found her, the better. "You run out there?" he said and pointed outside.

"Up to the edge of the property and back down. Fun, fun, fun," he said, but he didn't sound like he found it fun.

Caden decided. "I'll run the mountain with you."

Tito looked up incredulously from his shoe. "She hasn't made you. You don't have to."

"Does that matter?"

"I guess not," Tito said. He looked Caden up and down and scrunched up his face. "Didn't you wear that yesterday? Did you even shower?"

Caden bristled. True, he'd first been confused by the small, closet-size room Tito had called a "bathroom." It was nothing like the baths of the Winter Castle. They were tiled in Razzonian marble and filled with hot spring water and snowmelt transported downslope to the castle by great stone aqueducts. The waters were always clear and steaming. Then he'd noticed the strange spigot and wash basin.

"I'm clean," he said. "I rinsed my clothes and person in the tiny washroom."

Tito rummaged around in his pile of unfolded, wrinkled clothes. "Here," he said.

Caden caught the wad of clothing that flew at his face. "What's this for?"

"You don't wear good clothes to run the mountain. Especially in the rain."

Maybe not, but Caden didn't wear other people's clothes, period. Nor would he wear this cheap scratchy fabric. He sniffed the clothes and frowned.

"Look, your royal highness," Tito said, "they're old but they're clean."

Caden had promised to be gracious, but he couldn't bring himself to say thank you when he wasn't at all thankful for the worn pants and shirt. His clothes were of higher quality and better fit. He rubbed the thin fabric between his fingers.

"I'll wear them," Caden said.

"Whatever," Tito said and stood up. "You coming or what?"

Caden quickly changed into the peasant's garb. The material hung loose around his shoulders. He pulled at it, but it remained poorly fitted.

Tito seemed amused. "You gotta eat more," he said. "At least try to bulk up."

Caden was tall for his age, and, no doubt, would grow

to be as tall as his brothers. "I'm the same size as you."

"Almost. But you're gonna shrink if you don't eat."

"That's nonsense." Caden grabbed his coat and traced the embroidery with his finger. Legend was that the Winterbird, the symbol of Razzon and the royal family, was one of the eight Elderkind that formed the lands and magic of the Greater Realm.

Four were said to have formed the lands. The Kingdom of Razzon, the whole of the Winterlands, was built where the Winterbird had come to ground. Razzon's great peaks were the outline of its frozen wings, Razzon's deep-blue twin lochs, its ever-watching and protective eyes.

Next was the Walking Oak, which rooted to form the Springlands. Third was the great Sunsnake, whose movements turned the sands of the Summerlands' deserts. Last was the Bloodwolf. Its red and brown fur could still be seen in the Autumnlands' great prairies and red-leaved forests.

The other four Elderkind were the powerful and fickle Elderdragons. Two of them—the Gold Elderdragon and the Silver Elderdragon—were charmed by man. In return they taught strategy, medicine, and magic to the peoples of the realms. It was said that magic with the most altruistic of motives often glowed in silver and gold in memory of their teachings.

The other two—the Blue Elderdragon and the Red Elderdragon—were angered. They punished the lands with disease, war, and dark magic. Magic of hate, magic of anger spurred whispers of their influence, destructive dragon-shaped energy that still echoed their true forms.

Tito coughed and startled Caden from his memories of myths and home. He pointed to Caden's coat. "That'll get messed up on the mountain," he said.

His coat was enchanted. It bore the symbol of the royal Winterbird. It stayed clean, always; it stayed the opposite of "messed up." "We'll see," Caden said.

"No, we won't. Rosa won't let you wear it."

Caden pulled his arms through the sleeves and grinned. "How's she going to stop me?"

Rosa was waiting on the front porch. Her clothes were layered, her outer shirt green with strange writing, her pants a bright purple. She looked Caden over with a furrow in her brow.

"He wants to run," Tito said.

Rosa paced and the porch creaked. "Why?"

Tito rolled his eyes. "Beats me."

Brynne and Sir Horace were somewhere on the mountain. Caden needed to run so he could contact Brynne, then he needed to return to Rosa's prison afterward so he could learn more about the missing Jane Chan.

Rosa walked up to him. "It's not easy."

Well, better the training then. "Good," Caden said.

"Leave your coat. You can't run with it."

"Yes, I can," Caden said.

In the gray morning light, it was hard to make out her

expression. She was either angry, amused, or both. Not that it mattered. Caden wouldn't give her his coat. He crossed his arms and waited.

"Let me rephrase," she said. "I don't want you to get your coat dirty. It's muddy and still drizzling, and your coat is wool. If you want to wear it, you can just watch with me from the porch."

Caden needed to run. The simple solution was to leave his coat. Still, he hesitated.

His sword was taken, his horse a fugitive. Brynne was in the mountains, hiding from the police. While he believed that he, Brynne, and Sir Horace would get back and that he'd complete his quest and make his father proud, at this moment, his coat was all he had of his home.

Rosa softened her expression. "It'll be here when you get back." She pulled off the green garment. Her undershirt was a bright orange and looked like a mini sun against the gray morning. "Here, you can borrow my army sweatshirt. It's special to me."

Caden didn't want to give her his coat, yet he needed to get to the mountain. Slowly he took his coat off, folded it, and handed it over. The sweatshirt she gave him in return felt nothing like it. He pretended not to care.

"The more difficult the training, the better," he said.

She tucked his coat under her arm. "If that's what you want," she said. "Run at least to the orange tape. It's the property line."

"I'll run to the peak," he said. The longer run would give him more time. And if he were to talk to Brynne, he'd need it.

"Fine," she said. "But I expect you back in twenty-five minutes."

Tito groaned, and mumbled that *he* was stopping at the property line, but Caden ignored him. Besides, running a mountain was good training. Dragons lived in rugged terrains. Well, not in Asheville it seemed, but in most other places with steep slopes, rocky paths, and fiery names.

Beyond the protection of the porch, the drizzle and air were cold. Caden's boots squelched in the mud as he dashed past Tito, into the forest, and up the path. He ran past a pine tied with orange tape, and was high uphill when he stopped. Both Brynne and Sir Horace knew the signal— two quick whistles—and Brynne certainly had used magic to track Caden and would be near.

Caden whistled, but it wasn't Brynne who answered by whistling back or Sir Horace who answered with a loud whinny. Instead, Caden heard a whisper rustle through the trees. "I'm here."

Caden froze, unsure of what he'd heard.

"I'm here, little brother." The voice was soft and strong, and sounded like his slain brother, Chadwin. It called to him like a warm fire on the coldest of days. It smelled like his father's castle. Caden felt hope blossom in his soul.

Caden had seen Chadwin bleeding with a dagger in his back, and, later, cold and still in the Winter Castle tomb. Yet, unknown magic had brought Caden to Asheville. Perhaps it had also awoken Chadwin, and he had become stranded here, too. Maybe he wasn't dead. Maybe it'd been a mistake. It could've all been a mistake.

The soft whispers turned to loud and impatient whistling. "WHEWWWW. WHEWWWW." Caden turned toward the sound. Then the whistles turned into shouting. "Caden! Get me out of here!"

Caden felt panic start to wash over him. For Chadwin to yell like such, he must be in peril. Never had Caden heard him so frantic. Caden couldn't lose him again. Like his father taught him, he stopped and took a breath. To save him, he must find him.

As he inhaled, he noticed a strange scent in the air. The woods smelled of fire and leather. They smelled, he realized suddenly, the way magic smelled when it was intended to ensnare. For Caden, that smell was his father's study, where he and his brothers would gather. It smelled like home.

The voice of his brother and the safety of the castle still felt very near, but Chadwin's voice was not real. And as he realized this, the magic around him dissipated, and something else became clear.

"Caden, I heard you whistle. Where are you?" It was Brynne calling, not Chadwin. She yelled his name again from the same direction as the whisper of his lost brother. Whatever ensnaring trap he'd found, she'd found it, too, and been caught.

There wasn't time to revisit grief for Chadwin, or to dwell on the fist now crushing his heart. His ally needed help. He darted toward her shouts and the false hope of those lost. Fir trees and leafless oaks towered on all sides. His nose itched and mud buckled under his boots. The drizzle intensified once more to cold stinging rain.

Within moments, he was at the edge of a clearing. He could feel rain soak his back, hear drops pad against the earth, and smell it. In the clearing, though, all was dry. No rain fell. No plants grew from the strange sand within it. No animals scampered across the bare ground.

Brynne was stuck in the sand and thrashed like a butterfly in a web. When she saw Caden, she reached for him. "Get me out of here!"

He was mere strides from where she was stuck waist-deep in the sand. Her hair fell in perfect waves, long enough to touch the sand, which stuck to her skin and sparkled like Razzonian diamonds. The more she struggled, the deeper she sank.

Looking around, Caden realized something else. Had Sir Horace also sunk into the sand? "Where's Sir Horace?" He'd lost his brother. He'd been stranded far from home. He couldn't lose Sir Horace.

"He's around," Brynne said. "*I'm* the one who's sinking." She was now shoulder deep. Her arms were under the surface and trapped.

Caden let out a breath. He searched for something he

could use to reach her, then glanced again at the sand. It made sense Sir Horace wasn't nearby. "Sir Horace is too clever to be caught by such a trap," he said.

Apparently, it was the wrong thing to say. Though she still sounded scared, her tone turned murderous. "Your concern for that beast is greater than for me."

"He's a true friend."

"He left you to those policemen." In a smug tone, she added, "They took you down easy enough."

"Says the sorceress stuck in the sand."

She was fury in a sandpit. "Get me out, prince. Or else."

With one hand, he grasped a prickly evergreen. He reached out with the other and stepped into the sand. He sunk, but not much. Not much at all. He frowned. "Why are you so much deeper than me?"

"I think it responds to those strong with magic."

At the rate he was sinking, it would take Caden weeks to be sucked into it. He shook some of the sand from his boots. "Perhaps it only responds to thieves with bad manners."

Brynne looked like she might bite his ankles. "If you had any talents, you'd sink, too," she said. He could tell she was trying to contain her fear and anger. "Now, get me out."

He crouched beside her. "Ask nicely," he said.

Before she could answer, before Caden could react, the sand pulled her down. Her face and nose went under.

Caden felt his mouth fall open. He let go of the prickly tree and lunged for her. The sand felt heavy on his hands as he pulled. She popped up, her hands and shoulders now freed—but he sank in the sand to his knees. Sand fell from Brynne's hair.

He glanced around, unable to meet her gaze. "I'll pull us out," he said quietly. He took off Rosa's drenched sweatshirt and looped it around a sturdy-looking fir tree.

"You should've done that as soon as you found me."

She was right. He should have helped her first, and pointed out her foolishness for getting caught second. But it had been too hard to resist. He rarely had the opportunity to mock Brynne. He said nothing as he dragged them toward the edge.

The sand was caked on his calves and feet. His legs ached as they moved. Eventually, he stepped free onto the wet earth beyond the clearing. The magical sand melted in the rain.

It washed off Brynne in glittering tears. "Water must counteract the spell," she said, and he heard the anger in her voice. "I was almost lost within the magic sand. Such traps never pull victims to easy fates, prince. Why is it here, anyway?"

It was strange to find a magic trap in what seemed to be a magicless land. No local he'd spoken to seemed to have knowledge of such things. He looked at Brynne. Her cheeks were flushed, her eyes narrowed.

To share information and distract her from being mad at him, he told what he'd learned about the missing Jane Chan, and his theory that their arrival was connected to her disappearance. He also described the foster prison and people in it.

Brynne nodded, but her anger seemed only dimmed. Then she stretched up beside him, young and elegant, and slammed her palm into his chest.

He dropped to the ground. Gnarled roots dug into his knees. He looked up at her and whatever guilt he felt for not pulling her out immediately vanished like the magic sand.

"That's for waiting to pull me out," she said.

The words were too cold and the radiating warmth in his chest was too real. "What did you do to me?" Caden said. It was surely a spell.

"You started it, prince."

He stumbled to his feet and patted his head. No horns. He reached around his back. No wings. No tail. There was nothing extra and there was nothing missing. He was wet and covered in nonmagical mud, but seemed the same as always. "What did you do?" he repeated.

Tito's voice bellowed from below. "Caden! Hey, Caden! Time's up, man."

She looked down the path and shrugged. "It should be an interesting two days for you."

He didn't want to ask. He didn't want to know. "Why?"

"You'll see," she said. "Maybe you'll learn a little humility. Meet me back here at midnight and tell me what else you find out about the missing girl. And bring me some real food."

Instead of throwing her back into the magical sand trap like he wanted, Caden nodded. "As you wish," he said.

Agreeing with Brynne. That couldn't mean anything good.

THE MATH TYRANT

*L*ater that morning, Caden waited at the kitchen table while Rosa took Tito to school, but he was certain it wasn't what he wanted to do. When Rosa returned, she ordered Caden into the large transport she called her "pickup." It had an enclosed cab with front and back seats, and a flattened bed in back. He definitely didn't want to ride in it to the market, then let her buy him ugly clothes. His body and his mouth, however, seemed to defy his brain. Brynne's revenge was obvious. For the next two days, it seemed that Caden would have to do whatever he was told to do.

That's how he found himself outside the middle school dressed in what Rosa called "blue jeans" that were so long he had to roll them up, and a collared shirt with a pattern that Rosa had called "plaid." At least his enchanted coat covered most of it.

"Follow me," Rosa said.

"As you wish," said Caden.

She paused and frowned at him. "You've gotten good at taking orders since yesterday."

Caden felt the blood drain from his face. She'd come to the same conclusion as he had—though he doubted she understood why. There was nothing he could say. He was at her mercy.

"Did your father give you a lot of orders?" she said.

Caden's father was a great man, not the tyrant these people thought. "My father gives everyone a lot of orders," he said. "It's his right."

"You believe that, don't you?"

"I know that."

Rosa touched his arm. "You don't have to defend him, not to me," she said.

He jerked away. "Apparently I do."

The school was built of stone and stood cut into the rock of the mountain. It was a gray towering building against a brown mountain and a blue sky. Inside, it smelled of mud. Caden pulled his coat tighter around the plaid shirt and followed Rosa to a front room.

"Do your best," she said.

Caden always did his best. "I will," he said and sat where she directed, at a smooth flat table of polished wood, cool to the touch.

"I'll be here to pick you up at the end of the day."

Rosa left, and Ms. Primrose, the placement counselor, tip-tapped in and sat across from him. She was small and frail and smelled like the rose in her namesake. Her shirt and skirt were covered with a blue flower pattern. Her eyes were a faded blue.

She pulled out a strange contraption, flipped it open, and set it in front of him. It whirred to life with the press of a small button.

Caden felt proud to recognize the foreign technology. "It's a television," he said.

Ms. Primrose looked at him, her eyes widening. For a moment, she studied him. Then she frowned. "No, no dear. It's a laptop computer."

Tito still hadn't explained that one.

She reached across and pushed more buttons. "You're going to take your test on it." The strange tech, the computer, flashed to life. Caden jumped, then peered closer. "It's simple, dear. Read the passage, look over the answers, and push the button that corresponds to the correct one."

It was Caden's turn to frown. The buttons matched the strange language on the screen. He understood that, but it made no difference. He leaned back in his chair and crossed his arms. "I can't complete this test."

"Caden, this is important. Ms. Rosa thinks you might place into the gifted class. Wouldn't that be lovely?"

"This tongue is not one I know."

"Whatever do you mean?" she asked, startled. "It's English. You're speaking it."

It was all Caden could take. Soft people who smelled of flowers needed to stay as far from him as possible. He stood up. "I wish to leave."

She cocked her head and studied him. "Oh, I understand." Suddenly, she seemed sharper than he'd first thought. Her faded eyes turned icy. "Many poor souls like you come to me. You're here now. You can't *leave*."

It was an odd thing for her to say. For a moment, they stared at each other. The quiet was broken only by a loud rumbling noise. It echoed in the small room like a growl. "Oh my," she said, and rubbed her stomach. "Well, it has been a while since I ate." Her cheeks were flushed, but she didn't seem embarrassed. If anything, it seemed like this was part of the test.

He cared nothing for the test. That, however, didn't mean he was impolite. He was an eighth-born prince. This small room and strange, flowery old woman would not sway his good manners. "For days my diet has consisted wholly of starchy tubers and edible winter grasses." He smiled at her. "I've heard much worse."

She smiled back but it seemed unnatural on her face, like it was an uncommon expression for her. She reached up and touched her lips, as if surprised. "You're an interesting one, aren't you?"

It wasn't the most humble thing to say, but Caden felt it

best to agree with her. "I am."

She shook her head like he was the biggest of difficulties for her. "I suppose I could read the test to you. I don't need to eat just yet," she said, and sounded sad. "No lunch today. Relax, dear. Take the test."

It was an order. Caden took the test. As soon as they'd finished, she scored his answers with pursed lips and an irritated expression.

Caden was not put in the gifted class. He was put in the special class. "It doesn't sound special," he said as he followed her through the long school hall.

"You need to learn to read and write," she said. Her manner had turned cool since his poor test performance. "After your morning literacy class, you have science, lunch, and math with the rest of the seventh graders. We have accommodations we can give you for those."

The floor was paved with unattractive tiles. Hundreds of overlapping shoeprints were scuffed atop. The walls were crowded with pale pink locked boxes. Despite the evidence that countless people usually walked these halls, it was now quiet except for the click-clack of Ms. Primrose's steps.

She squinted down at a paper in her hand. "Twelve-four. This is your locker."

Twelve-four—his age and the length of years until Brynne said the moon and sun would align such that she could attempt a spell to return them. No doubt, it was unlucky. The locked box opened with a creak. Inside were crumpled papers and stale crumbs. This was not the locked box of a well-mannered prince.

"I must decline," Caden said.

"You'll need it to store your things, dear," she said.

"It's dirty."

She raised a brow. "You're a picky one, aren't you?"

He snapped his gaze to her. "I have certain expectations. Cleanliness is one."

There was no rebuke. She closed the locker with a clank and glanced at the dirty tiles. "I'm afraid some of your peers like to roll around in the mud."

Some of the gentle dislike in Ms. Primrose's expression dimmed. He could see her struggling to keep her distance, to squash any budding affection. His intent was to be gone as soon as possible, but gaining her favor might prove smart. The time had come for a well-placed observation.

"At least," Caden said, "the halls smell of roses."

"That's my perfume, dear." She leaned down as if to tell him a secret. "It's my signature scent."

"Like your name," he said, and he could tell she was pleased.

Then she fixed him with a funny look. "Indeed."

She led him around the corner and knocked lightly on a nearby door. She glanced again at the paper in her hand. "Math's your last class of the day. No time like the present to jump right in." With a pat to the shoulder, she added, "I do hope you do well here."

Inside, he counted twenty-four desks. Students sat at all but three. Tito scribbled furiously at a first-row desk between two of the empty ones. The third empty desk was in the corner, hidden in shadow. The students looked riveted—somewhere between excited and terrified.

At the front of the room stood a man with a gray beard and bald head. One of his eyes was dark, crinkled at the side like he laughed often, the other pale blue and split by the deep scar that reached from his eye to his mouth. His pants were dark and he wore a red wool sweater.

"Don't stare, dear," Ms. Primrose whispered. She motioned in Caden's direction. "We have a new student, Mr. Rathis. This is Caden."

"Welcome, Caden," Mr. Rathis opened his arms in welcome. He motioned for Caden to join him at the front of the room. "Tell us about yourself," Mr. Rathis said.

Caden made eye contact with him and with the kids seated at the desks. "I'm new here. I live with Tito."

"Foster kid," whispered a boy in the third row.

Caden's tolerance was thinned by his racing heart and sickening stomach. "I don't like being interrupted."

The kid blinked like he didn't know what that meant.

"Anyway," Caden said. "In time, I'm certain you will like me. Most people do." He hoped he'd told enough about himself to satisfy the curse.

Mr. Rathis laughed. "Now that's the kind of confidence you don't see often."

A lesser person would be insulted. Caden's gut was too twisted for that, and he fell into silence. He was stuck in a strange land and strange school. He was cursed to do as he was told. He was at this math teacher's mercy. He was at everyone's mercy.

"Thanks for sharing," Mr. Rathis said, and his voice sent shivers up Caden's spine. There was something strange about him. Something odd in his manner. Something that Caden didn't trust. "Sit."

Caden had no choice but to obey. His magically traitorous feet were already following the order. He started to sit beside Tito in the front middle. Royalty sat in front.

"That's Jane's seat," a twangy girl's voice said. "Don't sit there."

Caden clenched his jaw. Again, an order. He was compelled to skip the front middle desk and instead take the end one on Tito's other side. This desktop was covered in scribbles. In the corner, someone had drawn a bird. It made him think of the mighty Winterbird on his coat. Thoughts of the Winterbird always made him feel braver. They also reminded him he had a dragon to slay and a way home to find.

He leaned toward Tito. "When does this class end?"

Tito looked annoyed and didn't answer.

Caden asked again.

"At three," Tito said and sounded irritated. "I'm trying to listen."

Before Caden could say more, Mr. Rathis walked to Caden's desk and tapped it. "Stop talking. Pay attention."

Caden stopped talking. He paid attention.

Mr. Rathis smirked, and the scar tugged at his mouth. He raised a hand as if to strike Caden down—and for a moment, Caden was certain he was going to hit him. Then Mr. Rathis turned and wrote LONG RANGE ATTACKS on the whiteboard. He proceeded to explain how to find the trajectory of projectile weapons. He waved his arms and guffawed as he calculated damage centers and casualty rates.

Mr. Rathis looked straight at Caden. "Fifty thousand dead." His eyes glinted as he spoke of death. For a moment their gazes locked. Then Mr. Rathis waved his hand like a performer taking a bow. "That's the importance of math!" he said, and began spouting information about fractions.

As Caden listened, a memory tugged at him. There was something familiar about Mr. Rathis. He felt that he had seen this man's face before—but not in Asheville and not in person. He fought to keep his eyes from widening, his heart from racing.

He'd seen the face in a portrait—a portrait his father had shown him that hung in the Hall of Infamy in the Greater Realm's council halls. But the man had not been painted wearing a simple wool sweater and dark pants like he wore now. His body had been draped in the red war velvets of the armies of Crimsen and the Autumnlands.

71

He bore a striking resemblance to Rath Dunn, tyrant of the Greater Realm and bringer of the red war, exiled to the vile Land of Shadow fifteen years prior, a sacrifice to the Gray Lady and her flesh eaters, doomed to fight each day for the barest of food and safety until he perished weak, alone, and humbled. His image was immortalized in the portraits so no man or woman in the whole of the Greater Realm would forget his horrible deeds or horrible fate. His image in the Hall of Infamy had looked cruel and mocking as it gazed from the portrait.

If this man was Rath Dunn, he did not look weak or humbled. Yet he was dressed in the colors of Crimsen. He had the same scar, the same wolfish grin. His voice made Caden's blood run cold.

Regardless, Caden had enough sense to know that he needed to establish he was unafraid, deserved respect, and—like all the Ashevillian boys and girls in the room— in no way suspected that the man teaching math might be a monster.

The bell tolled; the class ended.

Alive and confused, Caden moved as fast as possible to the door. He needed to think about everything. He needed to find Brynne, throttle her for the curse, and tell her of the strange Rath Dunn look-alike at the school.

"Caden. Stop," Mr. Rathis said.

Caden stopped, frozen in place, his compliance unbreakable.

Mr. Rathis settled his large hand on Caden's shoulder. "Glad to have you," he said. "You're a surprise, but I'm sure you'll do fine."

The other students hurried away. Only Tito remained, standing by the door and looking impatient.

Caden had stopped long enough to satisfy the curse. "I should leave now," he said. He did not know if this man was the villainous Rath Dunn or a mild-mannered impostor, but he preferred not to take any chances.

He had one boot in the hall when Mr. Rathis called to him again. "One last thing."

Caden raised a brow and turned back.

Mr. Rathis smiled like a wolf. "I like your coat."

With those words, Caden knew this man was no look-alike. This man was the great enemy of Caden's family and kingdom. He hadn't been banished to the Land of Shadow where he should have been; he was here, teaching math in Asheville, where Caden was stranded.

The math teacher was Rath Dunn.

7

THE WAY DOWN

Cowards fled; brave men made strategic retreats. Caden hurried from the school. Rosa's orders "Come here" and "Get in the pickup," however, kept him from fleeing to the hills.

He climbed into the pickup's backseat. He told her that Mr. Rathis was not as he seemed. He was to be feared. "He's Rath Dunn, the tyrant of the Greater Realm." He gave an abbreviated history of the man and his vile acts—the plague he'd unleashed on the land, the many dead by his hand, the rivers that ran red from the battles fought against him. "He must be stopped."

Beside him, Tito snapped his seat belt and looked confused. "From teaching math?"

"From whatever terrible deeds he has planned," Caden said.

Caden's seat rumbled as Rosa turned the truck's key and the transport engine came to life. "Mr. Rathis is a good teacher," she said. "Unorthodox, but good."

"He's a monster—his skill with math does not excuse that." He looked between Rosa in the front and Tito beside him. "We're all in danger."

Instead of pulling out onto the road and away from the terror within the school, Rosa turned back and looked at him. "Why would you say that?"

"His hands drip with the blood of good men and women."

"Math's not that dangerous," she said, a smile pulling at her mouth. She turned front, and finally drove onto the steep road. "Tomorrow will be better."

Tito shrugged. "I can help you with your homework."

Caden didn't know what "homework" was and he had no inclination to find out. He cared that he'd been taken from his land and deposited in this place; he cared that a threat walked among the backward people of Asheville; he cared his life might end far from home long before he had slain a dragon and completed his quest.

Caden's father and brothers had defeated Rath Dunn fifteen years ago, after eight years of war. Caden would study, train, and fight until he was as good a man as them, until he was strong enough to face men like Rath Dunn. He wasn't strong enough yet; he wasn't even an Elite Paladin yet. Rath Dunn—Mr. Rathis as he was calling himself—would destroy him.

With a thunk, Caden leaned his forehead against the window. "I can't stay here," he muttered.

Sadly, *that* Rosa took seriously. "You will stay," she said. "And you'll go to math class tomorrow."

Tomorrow, then, Caden would die. His father would never be proud of him. Without Caden to slay a dragon, one more would prowl Razzon, devouring hapless villagers, stealing jewels and trinkets of value, and burning thatched homes.

When they got back to the house, Caden went to the attic room and barricaded the door. He sat on the floor and watched as the light from the windows faded from afternoon to evening. He and Brynne became stranded in the land at the same time Jane disappeared. Now, it seemed, Rath Dunn—the Greater Realm tyrant—had been Jane's math teacher. Was there a connection?

At nightfall, Tito pounded on the door. "You done sulking?"

Sulking? Caden was most certainly not sulking. These were his last hours of life. He was trying to make sense of why he was here while preparing for death. He would die bravely. He hoped.

The doorframe shook. "It's my room, too," Tito said.

Across the black tape, the purple bed was unmade. Books were scattered on the floor. The rugs were covered with wrinkled clothes. Caden stood and brushed off his jeans. He turned his nose at the mess. "Then you should be able to break the defenses. And clean it up."

"Let me in before I get Rosa."

Caden wanted to say no. He wanted to say something snide about the quality of Tito's training, but it was an order. Frowning, he walked over, unblocked the door, and opened it.

Tito was a picture of steely irritation. "Rosa's decided to keep you," he said, pushing past Caden into the room. "Despite the crazy."

"It doesn't matter. I'll likely die tomorrow," Caden said.

"Well," Tito said, and flopped down on his bed. "I guess we're stuck together until then."

"You mock me," Caden said. He settled on his neatly made pink and orange bed and crossed his arms. "I'd prefer to prepare for my death in silence."

"Look," Tito said. "We need to make nice. We're stuck here together until you manage to get committed or Rosa kicks us out."

"Or we die," Caden said.

Tito threw his arms out. "All right, fine, or that. So tell me, your craziness, why do you think you're going to die tomorrow?"

"Rath Dunn—your Mr. Rathis—is the enemy of my family, my kingdom, and all the good peoples of the Greater Realm. I'm the youngest son of the man who banished him. He's killed for much less."

Caden waited for Tito to brush off his concern, but he seemed to be listening this time. Listening, however, didn't necessarily mean believing. Tito raised his brows and wrinkled his nose. "Well, he didn't kill you today."

Caden had not considered that. His heart still beat; his blood still pumped. "Your point?"

"So, maybe he won't kill you tomorrow."

It was a good point. Why had Rath Dunn let Caden walk away? When the most evil of the Greater Realm were banished, they were often sent to their deaths with a token of their deeds. According to council record, Rath Dunn had been banished with his blood dagger, magic item number forty-three. It was an evil blade. A wound made with it would never fully heal, and would reopen in its presence. He could have sliced him to wriggling prince bits where he'd sat.

Was he that flippant about Caden's abilities? Caden wasn't a match for Rath Dunn yet, but he was capable. To leave Caden with air in his lungs and fight in his heart was the worst of mistakes. From what Caden knew of Rath Dunn, he didn't make mistakes. Although, Rath Dunn was also supposed to have died horribly after banishment to the land of shadow, and not to have been in the odd land of Asheville teaching math, so perhaps what Caden knew wasn't exactly correct.

Did Rath Dunn have something to do with why Caden and Brynne were stranded? Perhaps he wanted revenge against their parents? Though, why would he grab Caden, youngest son, and not one of the others? Their loss would hurt the kingdom more. Why Brynne? As far as Caden knew, Rath Dunn knew nothing of Brynne's parents' role in bringing him to justice and banishment.

Caden shifted, uncomfortable with his thoughts. "I don't know why he let me live."

"Don't sound so disappointed," Tito said, and cocked his head. "Bro," he said, "are you upset he didn't kill you?" He sat beside him. The pink and orange quilt pulled from its tuck, and Caden tried not to let it annoy him. "He's just following school policy." Tito's face twitched like he was trying not to quake with laughter. "No killing allowed."

As long as Caden lived, he would fight. He would warn those at risk. He reached across to fix the quilt and caught Tito's gaze. "He's the enemy." Jane Chan had also been in Rath Dunn's math class. All these things could be connected. "Before she went missing, did Jane seem suspicious of him?"

Tito's mirth fell away. "Leave Jane out of your delusions."

Jane might be their best chance to find out why Caden and Brynne had been trapped in Asheville and why Rath Dunn was alive and teaching math. She was a connection to both. "Perhaps she ran away because she learned who he was?"

Like Tito couldn't contain the words, he blurted, "Jane wouldn't run away!"

The fierceness of Tito's words caught Caden off guard. He studied his new foster brother. "When I was captured, the policeman Jenkins called her a runaway."

Tito fidgeted, and the quilt came untucked again. "Her clothes and backpack are gone. The police think she ran away. Rosa does, too."

This was why Tito was angry.

"But you don't believe it."

Tito looked to the floor. "I don't know what I believe." Caden recognized the pained waver of his words and the heaviness of his tone. His father and brothers sounded that way whenever the first queen was mentioned.

Jane was Tito's friend. Tito needed to know what Caden knew. He needed to be part of the quest to find her. If Caden perished, Tito could fight the dark happenings that seemed to be going on and could protect his dragonless people.

"Mr. Rathis is Rath Dunn. He is a monster." Caden stood and nodded to the window. Maybe Jane had run away; maybe her disappearance was more sinister. He thought of the strange whispering in the woods and the trap where Brynne had gotten stuck. There seemed to be some magic in Asheville, after all. "There's a nature trap set on the mountain," Caden said. "Maybe it is related to her disappearance. That's where we should look for clues."

Tito scrunched up his face. "A nature trap?"

"An ensnaring magical clearing," Caden explained.

"Right, the math teacher's evil and magic took Jane." Tito shook his head. "Come on, bro. It's hopeless."

"Magic brought me here at the same time she disappeared. The enemy of my people was her math teacher and now is mine. You don't find that significant?"

Tito's expression became defeated, his lopsided face more asymmetrical. "I don't really believe magic brought you here or that Mr. Rathis is evil."

Caden peered out the window. It wasn't too far a climb to the ground. "You have no other leads," he said, and opened the window. "I'm right and I can prove it."

Maybe Caden's quest hadn't stalled the moment he found himself in Asheville. Maybe it was gaining meaning, gaining momentum.

They climbed out the window on the left of the room, the one with the sturdy-looking drainpipe near to it. The night was dark sky and bright half-moon. The drainpipe was cold in Caden's grasp and groaned under his and Tito's combined weights. Full water bottles hung at Caden's hip, poor Ashevillian "plastic" replacements for his sword.

"We should've snuck out through the house," Tito whispered.

"No, this is more challenging." Caden tapped the pipe. It dinged like a bell.

"Shhh!" Tito said. "If Rosa finds out about this, she'll

flip. I'm supposed to be helping you adjust, not feeding your delusions."

"You risk banishment to save your friend," Caden said. "That's honorable."

Tito's huff fogged the air. "Or stupid," he said. "I don't want to get sent away." Then more quietly, "I like it here."

Caden slid down the pipe. Tito careened into him a second later. They tumbled into the grass, side by side, dirt and stray brown blades of grass stuck to their arms and faces. Again, the drainpipe groaned. Then there was a pop, pop, pop—like arrows hitting a wall. The pipe tipped like a downed tree and hit the earth between them with a muted squish.

Caden stared at the pipe. Tito stared at the pipe. Around them, the night was quiet.

"I never should have agreed to this," Tito muttered.

Caden stood and reached across to help Tito to his feet. "I doubt we've been compromised. It didn't make much noise."

Brown leaves nested in Tito's hair. He toed the pipe with his foot. "We get caught, you're taking the blame."

Caden had no choice—not when Tito said it like that—but he cared not. He pulled a piece of wet brown grass from his cheek. "Follow me," he said.

As they hiked up the dark trail, Caden pointed out the large hoofprints near where the forest began. "He runs with the winds. He'll return soon enough." Caden then explained about his horse, the quest his father had sent him on, and the mischief that had trapped him there.

"So you have to slay a dragon?" Tito said.

"Yes," said Caden.

"There are no dragons, bro."

Caden peered at the dark woods around him. "Not here, no."

"Not *any*where."

Caden had no time to argue the obvious. "There's another thing," he said.

"There's more?"

It was a risk to trust Tito with this information, but they did share a common goal—to find out what had happened to Jane. And a room. The social workers had proclaimed them brothers, even. "Brynne cursed me. With compliance."

Tito shone his flashlight at Caden's face. "Brynne. The magical girl who comes out of nowhere and can't be trusted. Right."

Caden frowned. "For two days," he explained, "I must follow any order given to me."

Tito cocked his head. "Anything?"

"That's right," Caden said.

"So if I ordered you to be my personal slave you'd do it?"

"Not if you want to survive once the curse breaks."

Tito was far too quiet for a moment. "Bark like a dog."

Caden was going to throttle him. He opened his mouth

to say as much and a deep-throated growl emerged, followed by a high-pitched "woof, woof" that echoed in the hills.

Tito laughed.

If forced to sound like a dog, Caden would attack like one. He bared his teeth and pounced. Tito dodged. He was quick for a peasant.

"Hey, man, you can't blame me for testing it out. Once you're medicated I doubt you'll be any fun. Now, meow like a cat."

Caden lunged for him, fists clenched, hissing low and mad. "Meow, meow. Meow!"

"Stop."

Caden stopped, his fist mere inches from Tito's smiling, moonlit face. "This will wear off in a few days—you should consider that," he said. Suddenly, Caden had an idea. "You could order me not to go to school tomorrow."

"Rosa's gonna make you go."

"Order me not to."

Tito sighed, and his breath fogged the dark air. "Um. Okay. I order you not to go to school tomorrow. Feel better?"

"I still feel like I'm going to go."

"Sorry, man. I tried."

Understanding the rules of his curse meant Caden could better handle it. "Her order was first," he mused, "so it must stand."

"Yeah," Tito said. "And she's in charge, too."

They continued up the mountain. It was good to talk to Tito, even if Tito lacked faith in Caden's sanity. Since embarking on his quest, most of Caden's conversations had been with Sir Horace or Brynne.

While Sir Horace was a great steed, his replies mainly involved neighing, stomping, and, on one notable occasion, wriggling on his back in a field of magical happy flowers.

Conversations with Brynne tended to end in curses. There was something to be said for two-way conversations without the threats of tails, wings, horns, or, most recently, compliance.

Truth be told, he preferred a disbelieving ally to one who cursed him. Brynne, though, was much easier on the eyes.

THE LOST NECKLACE

Despite the earlier rain, the strange sand of the clearing remained bright under the half-moon; the firs, pines, and bare oaks were a dark fortress around it. Magic was always easier to see under moonlight, easier to avoid. Jane had disappeared when the moon was brighter and fuller. If she'd encountered the sand trap, she'd likely have noticed something was strange. Although being Ashevillian, perhaps she didn't understand the danger.

"It's weird here," Tito said, and pulled his arms to his chest. "I'll give you that."

Brynne was nowhere in sight. "Be on guard. Brynne will be here soon," Caden said.

Caden squatted at the trap's edge, noted the lack of hoofprints, and sighed in relief. Sir Horace was too wily for such a trap. He reached out and ran his hand through the dry sand. It stuck to his skin like crumbled brick.

He held his arm up for Tito. "I have only the smallest of magical talent, and it does this to me."

"It's sand. Strange glowing sand, but sand."

"Dry magic sand," Caden said.

"Dry normal sand," Tito said, and stepped into the clearing. "Watch. No magic quicksand. No nothing."

Caden watched like he'd been told, crossed his arms. "You're sinking," he said.

Tito was buried halfway to his calves. He sank faster than Caden had. Caden felt his mouth twitch in quick irritation. Even in a mostly magicless land, everyone had more magic than him.

Tito finally seemed to notice he was being pulled into the earth. "What the—" He struggled like he was stuck in the web of a Mandan death spider and dropped to knee-deep. Perhaps Tito would believe now.

Caden considered the trap. When he had found Brynne stuck, no drop of moisture seemed to penetrate the magical clearing, and the sand had dissipated as they'd stepped into the rain. Even now, in the cold crisp night, the air inside the clearing was dryer than that around it. No doubt the trap had a barrier to protect it that deflected water. He looked at the bottled water he'd brought. As the water within them was contained by dry bottles, he should be able to bring them past the barrier. He was right about that, wasn't he?

"Hey!" Tito said. "You gonna leave me in the weird

mountain quicksand or what?"

Caden snapped from his thoughts and tossed him a water bottle. "Pour it around yourself."

Tito scrunched up his nose and uncapped the bottle. "Water's gonna save me from the weird sand?"

"I'm almost certain," Caden said.

"Almost?" Tito grumbled, but he dumped the water around him. For a fleeting moment, it sat damply atop the sand. Then, with a soft glow, the water and sand disintegrated into golden smoke.

Caden threw another bottle to Tito. "Keep pouring."

All the sand vanished. Tito was left standing in a waist-deep, dry pit, which was strange. Caden was certain the trap had pulled Brynne deeper than that. Tito climbed up the side and sat on the edge. The golden smoke hung over them. The wind blew, the trees around them rustled, and the smoke furled down the mountain.

"Whoa," said Tito, catching his breath.

"Ritual magic." Caden sat beside Tito and pointed his empty bottle at the trap. "It's always attached to a place."

Shadows of branches crisscrossed Tito's shirt. His brow was furrowed; his mouth was turned down. "Okay, that was weird. But magic?"

"Your disbelief is simply denial."

Tito looked like he was beginning to doubt his own resolve. "I dunno . . . ," he said, peering into the dark grove.

It seemed odd that there was no one—no animal or

person—freed from the trap along with Tito. Few animals were as clever as Sir Horace. Certainly, some creatures should have been snared by the trap. The missing remained missing. Caden scanned the hole. There were faded marks at the bottom, scratches left in the dirt. It was possible they'd been symbols at one time. He felt his frown deepen.

Ritual magic was a magic of sacrifice and exchanges. It was the darkest of the magics. Only masters of the magic used it to much avail, but with the proper ingredients and symbols, and a lack of morals, any fool could attempt it. This trap, however, seemed to have been created by someone with skill.

In the books that towered on the blue and gold shelves of the Winter Castle's great library, there was no record of Rath Dunn ever doing ritual magic. He certainly seemed patient enough, conniving enough. But he wasn't one to dig holes and scratch symbols in the dirt. He was one who manipulated others into doing such things. Caden toed the dirt. "This seems unlike Rath Dunn."

"You think? Well, your craziness, maybe that's because Mr. Rathis isn't—"

"He's evil."

Tito shrugged and kicked at the remaining normal, nonmagical dirt. "Speaking of evil," he grumbled. "You waited long enough to help me; I'm starting to think you deserved to be cursed."

"He's a royal pain," Brynne said.

Caden took a deep breath. Again, she had caught him off guard. She stood over them. Her skin glowed with the moonlight. Her hair moved with the cold northern wind.

Beside him, Tito gaped. His mouth hung open; his eyes were big. Quickly, he recovered. "I'm Tito," he said, and stood. "Wow."

Caden didn't bother with introductions. He stood and glowered. "Remove the curse you placed on me," he said. "Now."

"I don't know," she said. "It doesn't seem you've learned your lesson yet."

Caden had learned plenty. He grabbed her by her shoulders. "There's no time for these games. Our lives are at stake."

She looked down at his hands. "Remove them," she said, "or lose them."

It was close enough to an order that Caden was compelled to obey. He took a deep breath and released her. "Rath Dunn is in Asheville."

She drew her brows together. "What?" she said. "That can't be."

"Yet, it is."

"You're making that up," she said.

"I don't make things up."

That she knew to be true. Her silvery eyes widened and she bit her lower lip. "He's supposed to be dead."

The fear in her voice made the danger feel closer, more

sinister. "He doesn't know about you," Caden said. "He doesn't even know you were born, and he doesn't know your parents were paid to fight against him."

Beside them, Tito tensed. His gaze was fixed in the hole. Before either Brynne or Caden could stop him, he jumped back into it. "It's Jane's necklace," he said, climbing out with something clenched in his hand.

Brynne looked at Tito's fist, and her interest was clearly piqued. "That belonged to the missing girl? Are you sure?"

"I'd know it anywhere. She made it."

"Let me see," Brynne demanded.

Tito hesitated.

"Jane is his friend," Caden said. He opened his mouth to say more, to tell her not to steal it, but she cut him off.

"Sit," she said. "Keep quiet."

Caden sat back down. He kept quiet.

Brynne cast him an amused look before turning back to Tito. "Let me see the trinket," she said, and held out her hand.

Tito glanced between her and Caden. "Um. You'll give it back to me, right?"

"Of course," Brynne said. "I'm not that type of thief."

Caden scoffed—like there was more than one kind.

Brynne took the necklace. She sat beside Caden on the cold earth and turned it over. The chain was interwoven wires of delicate copper and pewter, and resembled a vine. Hanging from the chain was a pendant of strange stone, black and glassy. She handed it to Caden. It warmed his hand, unaffected by the winter air.

"She never took that thing off," Tito said, and plopped down beside them.

"I suppose she wouldn't," Brynne said. "She made it?"

"Yeah, this summer."

Brynne chewed on her bottom lip like she was in deep thought. "Someone who could make something like this is very special."

"Can't disagree with that," Tito said and kicked at the dirt, his cheeks turning pink. "But, look, she bought that rock at the mall and she got the wires from the art supply store."

Brynne motioned to the necklace. "It's a protective amulet," she said. "The necklace is enchanted, and it's undocumented. No one in recent history can do enchantment or item magic like this. Not until now. Not until your Jane."

Undocumented? Caden had researched protective amulets before. This was the first he'd seen up close; the first he'd ever held. In Razzon, there were one hundred and twenty-six known magical items. All priceless. His coat was number one hundred and twelve. It seemed he held a new item between his fingers.

"Huh," Tito said. "You're supposedly a sorceress. His royal highness says the trap is magic. Why are you so surprised by an enchanted necklace?"

"Because it's *enchantment*. Look, there are three types of magic." Brynne pointed to the trap. "The magic in the pit was ritual magic. It's attached to a place." She scrunched up her nose like she was repulsed by the thought of it. "It's the darkest of magics and requires sacrifices of blood and soul—but never of the practitioner, always of the innocent." Tito paled a bit, but Brynne seemed not to notice. "With instructions and the right materials, anyone can attempt it, and too many do."

"I take it ritual magic isn't your type of sorcery," Tito said.

"Ritual magic isn't sorcery at all." She sat up straighter. "Sorcery is magic of the mind. It requires study and concentration. It's attached to people. It's one of the great disciplines of the Greater Realm and by far the most respected."

There was little respectable about sorcery. Caden couldn't speak, because he'd been ordered not to. But he could again scoff, and did.

Brynne cast him a glare but continued. "It's people magic. It takes both talent and discipline. That's sorcery, that's my magic," she said, and puffed up. "Enchantment is the third type—the magic of items."

Caden held the necklace to the moonlight. Carved into the dark stone, he saw the image of a great tree. Great trees had a special significance in the Greater Realm. While the Winterbird protected the Winterlands and people of Razzon, it was the Walking Oak that rooted in the Springlands and kept watch over the men, gnomes, and elves there. Of course, there were many trees in Asheville as well, and this might have been one of them. It might not have meant anything.

Or maybe it did.

He handed the necklace back to Tito. Tito took it quietly, put it on, and tucked it beneath his shirt. The necklace—magic item number one hundred and twenty-seven, the missing girl's amulet of protection—disappeared beneath the cotton. Things needed to be said. Caden needed to say them. He poked Brynne's shoulder and pointed to his mouth.

"What?" Her thoughtful expression turned sly. "You want a kiss?"

Even now she toyed with him. Caden blushed and shook his head. He pointed to his mouth again.

She leaned toward him like she might actually kiss him. He felt his heart begin to race and his ears turn hot. Then she laughed and pulled away. "Fine," she said. "Talk, then."

Beside him, Tito snickered.

Everything about Brynne, these people, and this situation was frustrating. Caden was tempted to kick nonmagical dirt at them both. Instead, he straightened his collar. "We thought Asheville was a place devoid of magic, but I do not think that is the case. Brynne and I were pulled here by dark magic. Rath Dunn teaches math at the school. There was a ritual magic trap in the mountains and an amulet of protection that belonged to a girl who is now missing. There is magic here—that is certain. We must find how these things are connected. Then we will know why we're here." Then, they could find their way home.

And if Jane was indeed an enchantress, and it seemed she was, there was more Tito needed to know. Jane was his friend. From Tito's reactions to her name, there was no doubt she was dear to him. Caden glanced at Brynne. She stared down at her hands, seemingly watching shadows play across her slender fingers and likely troubled by similar thoughts.

Tito glanced between them. "What?" he said.

"He's *your* peasant," Brynne mumbled. "You tell him."

"Tell me what?" Tito said.

Tito deserved the truth. Caden raised his chin. "All magics have their price. Ritual magic requires blood. Sorcery drains energy." He gave Brynne a pointed look. "More than one foolish sorcerer or sorceress has fallen to exhaustion and not awoken again."

At that, Brynne glared. "I know how to handle it."

That was an argument for another time. He turned back. "To enchant an item a person must pay the price in years of life. Enchanting even one item drastically reduces lifespan." He patted his sleeve. "It's rumored he who made my coat fell at a mere seventeen turns."

"Uh-huh, right, then why would anyone do it? Because I've got news for you, Jane's smarter than that."

Caden and Brynne exchanged looks again.

"She must have been very desperate for protection," Caden said. "Enough that she had no other choice, and the trap must have been particularly attuned to her, and powerful, when it ensnared her."

The question that hung in the air was, *protection from what?*

Tito fidgeted and looked from Caden to Brynne. "So your sorcery drains your energy, but Jane's enchanting drains her life?"

Brynne looked back at her hands. "I'm sorry, Tito. But no known enchanter has lived more than twenty turns."

"Let's say I believe you," Tito said. "Maybe Jane should just stop enchanting crap."

"That seems unlikely," Caden said.

Brynne seemed to agree. "I've never heard of an enchanter not enchanting," she said. "It's what they do."

"The bigger question," Caden said, "is why does a normal Ashevillian girl know so much about magic?"

They sat for a moment. The chill in the air cut deeper with the silence. Finally, Caden spoke. "Rath Dunn is evil," he said. "What if he trapped and took Jane?"

Brynne seemed to consider this. "If she was indeed an enchantress, she, too, might have recognized him for what he is. It would explain the amulet of protection."

"Why Jane?" Tito asked.

"Enchantment is rare magic," Caden repeated. "We will discover the reasons for his treachery. We will get her back. But we must be clever. We must use care." He turned to Brynne.

"First, though, you must remove the curse."

She arched a brow. "Ask nicely," she said.

9

THAT WITCH BINDS

Two hours later, the half-moon was covered by clouds. The temperature had dropped. The air smelled of snow, and Caden was still cursed.

"Try again," he said.

Brynne touched his chest. The burn radiated out to his arms and legs, his fingers and toes. He fell to his knees.

Caden looked up at her. "I felt something."

She nodded and looked hopeful. "Fall backward."

Immediately, Caden obeyed her order. His hope shattered as his back hit the chilled dirt. He slapped the ground with his palms. "Try again," he said.

Tito leaned against a nearby pine tree. He had his arms folded across his chest and he yawned. "You know," he said, "I don't know much about magic, but this doesn't seem to be breaking."

Curses could always be broken. "It'll break," Caden said.

Brynne looked thoughtful, then away. She was oddly quiet.

Caden got to his feet. "I'm ready."

When she turned back, for a fleeting moment she looked guilty. "There might be a problem. This curse might not break," she said.

The time she'd spelled him with a tail, she'd undone it. The time she'd turned his eyes from brown to purple, they'd faded back to normal within an afternoon. "Of course this one will break," Caden said. "All curses do."

She bit her lip and looked down at her hands. "It's your fault," she said.

Caden didn't like her guilty tone, didn't like the way she wasn't making eye contact. He especially didn't like the way her words sounded irritated but she was twisting her hands like she was worried. "What's my fault?" he said.

"My magic is strong," she said. "And sometimes my control is lacking. And you're annoying."

Caden really didn't like this. "What are you saying?"

"She's saying you're screwed," Tito said. "She can't fix you."

"I can't be stuck like this for another day," Caden said. He poked Brynne square in the shoulder. "Fix it, witch."

"I can't." She shifted and looked down. When she looked back up, she looked ready for a fight. "And if the curse won't break, it'll reoccur."

"Wait. What?"

"For two days, as the half-moon rises so shall your compliance be complete." Softly, she added, "It was an accident."

Forced obedience for two days during each waning moon for forever was unfathomable. How could he serve his father and his kingdom? He'd be a weakness. He could be used against his family, his people, and his kingdom.

"I'm sorry," she said, but Caden was in no mood to forgive her.

They trudged back to the house. Once there, Tito insisted they sneak Brynne inside, and that they enter from the ground floor window. Caden pulled through first. He landed quietly on the planked floor. Inside, the television murmured something about impending snow. He turned to help the others and froze. Leaning against the side wall, Rosa stood, arms crossed and brow arched.

Brynne dashed out of sight. Tito paled. Caden squared his shoulders and raised his chin. "It's completely my fault," he said. Rosa led them wordlessly, angrily, to the couch. Tito sat beside Caden, hunched over and quiet. A single lamp lit the space, and the fireplace glowed with embers from a faded flame.

On the television, an image of Sir Horace's magnificent rump flashed. The volume was low, but Caden heard something about "a beautiful white horse seen near the edge of

Pisgah National Forest." Caden sighed. Sir Horace did enjoy exploring new lands. Asheville and this Pisgah Forest were no exceptions, but he'd return soon enough.

"Look at me, Caden." Rosa flipped the television off. She'd said that already. She'd said other things as well, but Caden had soon lost interest. She moved in front of him, her hands on her hips. "Am I boring you?"

"Very much so," Caden said.

With a glower, she paced in front of them in a purple robe. It pooled around her feet in great velvet folds. She glanced out the window like she sensed Brynne's presence but couldn't quite latch onto it. Finally, she fixed her gaze on Caden. "What did you think you were doing?"

It wasn't an order, so Caden kept quiet.

Tito, however, seemed to be having trouble deciding if he was frightened or angry. Anger won out for a moment. "What do you care?"

"When you sneak out in the middle of the night, I care. You could've been hurt." Rosa's cheek twitched. She closed her eyes and appeared to be counting. "Explain to me what you think you were doing."

An order. "We were looking for clues to Jane Chan's disappearance," Caden said.

That seemed to drain her. "Jane ran away."

"She wouldn't have done that," Tito said. "You always believe the worst. You're no different from anybody else! You don't care." As soon as the words burst out, Tito's eyes got big and he snapped his mouth shut.

Suddenly, the purple robe looked weighty on her shoulders and she sagged beneath its heft. "I care," she said.

Tito turned away. "Right, sure. Whatever."

For a moment, the living room was as silent as a gnomish burial mound. Rosa looked between them and rubbed her brow. "We'll talk about this in the morning. Go to bed. Don't let this happen again."

"It might," Caden said. If he survived the next day, he guessed the likelihood was quite high, actually. Especially without the curse forcing his compliance. "I have to comply for now, but make no promises for later."

Rosa's expression turned to forged steel. "That's it," she said. She pushed her purple sleeves to her elbow. "You're both grounded for the rest of the week."

Wait. What? "What?" Caden said. "Grounding? You jest."

"Do I sound like I'm jesting?"

No, she didn't. She sounded the opposite. Suddenly, Tito's fear made sense. Caden paled.

Grounding was a common punishment in Gram, a small kingdom on the northern border of the Autumnlands. The guilty were staked to the dirt and left to the mercy of nature and wild beasts. Sometimes they were grounded for days, sometimes long enough that their bodies grew cold and their skin slinked from their bones. Gleaming white skeletons, patches of red fire flowers, and roving flesh-eating

Porter dogs made the Gram grounding fields look like a moving red and white corpse sea.

Caden had little hope of surviving staked to the cold Asheville ground. The dogs—or whatever horrible beasts roamed this land—would devour him, if the cold didn't kill him first. It was common knowledge royal meat was the tastiest. Truth be told, he'd rather die in hopeless combat with Rath Dunn. At least there would be honor in that.

"Can this grounding start in two days?"

"No," she said. "It starts now."

"This is why you should learn to shut up," Tito mumbled.

Tito, too, would die unless the beasts ignored him for more succulent offerings. They'd eat the untasty seconds that was Tito after they had the royal feast that was Caden.

Caden had been certain Rosa was better than this, certain she wouldn't hurt him or Tito. "Why are you doing this?"

"Your behavior has consequences."

Maybe he had to do what she said, but he wouldn't be tethered down to die in silence. He thought of the worst insult he could. "You're no better than mother goblin fodder."

Rosa blinked at him like she was thinking on the meaning. Caden thought it would have been obvious. When she said, "Make it two weeks," he decided he was right.

Tito sank down into the cushions and stared at his lap.

There was no reason for them both to perish. Caden

pushed his anger away and tried to sound convincing. He tried to use the cadence of speech that generally got him his way. "This isn't necessary," he said.

"Don't try that tone with me."

"We won't survive."

For a minute, she said nothing. When she did speak, she sounded decidedly wary. "Caden, tell me what you think grounding is."

By the time he finished, she'd pulled her lips into a worried frown. "I would never do that to you," she said. Then she looked straight at Tito and her expression softened. "And I'm not going to send you away. Either of you. But no television or computer for a week."

Since Caden still wasn't clear on the value of either of those things, that was hardly a punishment.

Caden lay in bed, staring at the dark ceiling. Tito was quiet—too quiet to be asleep. Why did he think Rosa was going to send them away? If Caden understood Asheville grounding, the punishment involved spending more hours in her home.

Caden cleared his throat. "You're mistaken," he said.

For a moment, there was no answer. Then, "About what?"

"She's not going to get rid of you. She said so."

"This isn't the first place I've been dumped." Tito sounded wrecked, far worse than the situation required.

"People say lots of things. Doesn't mean they mean it. Besides, Jane was her favorite and look how quickly she gave up on her."

"You've been here three years. Obviously, Rosa means it."

"Look, you wouldn't understand." Tito huffed and flipped over. "Nobody wants an ugly kid."

Caden understood many things. He understood what it was to not be as good, or as strong, or as trusted as his brothers. He understood what it was to be sent away by a parent. Caden leaned back and took great care with his next question. "And you're the ugly kid?"

"What do you think?"

"I think no."

Tito was silent for a moment. When he spoke again, his voice was more even. "Stop trying to make me feel better." Shrewdly, he added. "Stop now."

Before Caden could respond, he heard impatient knocking on one of the windows—the one beside the remaining, loosely connected, frail drainpipe. The same one he'd deemed unsafe to climb up or down.

"Ten bucks says that's your girlfriend," Tito said.

Tap. Tap. Tap.

The window pane rattled. Caden rushed over, pushed the window open. Snow rushed in, and he pulled Brynne inside. First, she'd fallen into a magic trap, now she risked her life on an unsafe entry point.

Suddenly, Tito looked panicked by the racket. "You know, we're already grounded. If Rosa finds out about this . . ."

"She won't," Caden said to him. To Brynne, he said, "That was reckless."

The room flooded with chilled air. Outside, the drain-pipe swayed in the wind, two loose latches clutched to the house like failing lifelines. Caden shivered as he closed the window.

Brynne brushed damp snow from her shoulders and hair and looked around the room. "I'm tired of sleeping in the cold. Besides, we're allies. We need to stay together."

Tito was looking toward the door to the stairway. When no footfalls fell, no yell from Rosa sounded, he seemed to relax a little. "Allies?" Tito said, and seemed to be forcing himself to sound calm. "Is that what you call it in your fantasy world?"

Brynne smiled. "You, too, are part of this now."

Tito seemed to consider, and his sympathy for cold, snow-covered Brynne seemed to overcome his fear of getting into more trouble. He let out a loud, put-upon sigh. "Fine." He pushed off his purple blankets, reached between two stacks of books, and pulled out a roll of shiny black tape. "I'll divide the room in three." For a moment, his fear showed once more. "But pull up the tape in the morning— don't let Rosa find you."

"She won't."

Ten minutes later, Caden sat on the mismatched rugs and tugged his coat around him. "I'm the one who's going to die tomorrow. I should get one of the beds," he said.

Brynne laughed her sweet tinkling laugh. "You agreed to this," she said.

"I would never agree to the lesser third of the room. You ordered me!"

"You're not going to die tomorrow," she said. "Tito's right. If Rath Dunn wanted to kill you, he would have already. He didn't do anything to you."

"He complimented my coat," Caden said.

"That doesn't sound threatening."

"Make no mistake, it was a threat. He recognized the Winterbird. He knows I am from Razzon, the land of his enemies."

There was a part of Caden—a logical part beneath his bravado and fear—that whispered Tito and Brynne were right. An efficient killer like Rath Dunn would have destroyed him right away if that was his intent. That didn't explain why the man lacked that intent. That didn't stop the other part of his mind—the part that was instinct and emotion—from causing his gut to churn and his palms to sweat. There was danger in the school. There were other fates as terrible as death. Maybe he needed Caden alive for a purpose more sinister than a gruesome death.

"If we want to find out how we arrived here and where Tito's enchantress is, you need to face him." Despite

Brynne yawned and sat up. Her hair was still perfect, her clothes still spotless. "I like the pink shirt—"

"Quiet," Tito hissed.

Brynne arched a brow. "Excuse me?"

"You have to be quiet until Rosa leaves for the gallery."

"Or?" Brynne said, and she sounded distinctly displeased.

It seemed Tito had no sense of self-preservation because he said, "Or else."

When Caden talked to her like that, she lashed out. Her temper was like her magic—quick, powerful, and hard to control. No good would come from Tito also getting cursed. He stepped between them. "Rath Dunn doesn't know about you," Caden told her. "It needs to stay that way."

She deflated at that, likely thinking of what vengeance he'd wreak if he knew how big a role her family had played in his capture and banishment. She snuggled down into the bed. "Tread carefully today, prince." With a forgiving smirk, she added, "You too, peasant."

"I've survived lots of math classes," Tito said, but he grew somber. He seemed unsure. "You really think he might have Jane?"

Caden folded his night clothes and put them away. When he turned back, he held Tito's gaze. "He's an evil man who is capable of great treachery."

"Do you think she's okay?"

Caden looked to Brynne for help with the question,

but she'd turned away.

"Well?" Tito said.

"If she is indeed an enchantress, then she's valuable. He'd be a fool to hurt her, and he's no fool."

Ashevillian cars and trucks lined up in the school's drive. Caden felt the engine of Rosa's truck rev as they inched uphill. The snow had left the lawn with patches of white and the building icy. In the gray morning, the school's stone walls were difficult to distinguish from those of the mountains behind it.

When it was their turn to get out, Caden took a deep breath and left the warmth of the vehicle. The chill in the air was sharp. Tito grabbed his pack and tossed Caden the one Rosa had just bought him. Caden considered his pack. It had more pockets than his satchel. The pack, at least, seemed useful.

Before he could turn toward the school and face his fate, Rosa called to him. "Meet with Ms. Primrose before classes, Caden."

Caden glanced back at her. "As you wish," he said. So far this curse was inconvenient, but it could prove deadly. Once the school's heavy double doors closed behind him, he ducked away from Tito and past the office. He'd do as told. He had no choice. He'd meet with Ms. Primrose before classes—just not right away. First, he'd scout out his enemy.

Caden was within spear-tossing distance of the math

room when the scent of roses drifted down the hall. The soft tap-tap of ladies' shoes echoed on the gritty tiles. Ms. Primrose stepped around the corner a moment later, her clothes abloom with yellow flowers.

"Caden, dear, this isn't where you're supposed to be." With a soft tsk-tsk, she shook her head and pinched her lips. "Come along, it's time you learned to read."

Without the ability to rebel, he followed her to a room in the opposite hall. She looked him over as she knocked on the door. "My, my, don't you look spiffy today."

"I look spiffy every day," he informed her.

That seemed to amuse her, and her amusement seemed to surprise her.

The room they entered was filled with computers. Three other people were inside—an older gentleman with bright white hair, a pudgy girl with overly pale skin and thick spectacles, and a boy with brown skin and a serious manner.

"Mr. McDonald," Ms. Primrose said, "this is Caden, the student I told you about."

Mr. McDonald didn't ask Caden to introduce himself. He said, "Take a seat."

Caden sat between the boy and the girl and pointed at the device. "It's a computer," he said, "not a television."

The girl blushed behind her glasses. "Y-y-yes," she said. "I know."

"I'm Caden."

"T-t-tonya," she said.

The boy said nothing.

Tonya pointed at the boy. "That's Ward. He doesn't talk much."

Mr. McDonald sighed, came over, and flipped on the computer in front of Caden. "Go at your own pace. You have any questions, hit F one." He instructed Caden on how to use leathery green earmuffs. Then he wandered back to a desk across the room and disappeared behind a thick book. A moment later a mystical voice came from the earmuffs. Caden tried speaking to it. It ignored him. He tapped the muffs, but the voice only gave him dull computer directions.

So this was the class—a boy who didn't talk, a girl who stuttered, and a useless magical voice intent on teaching letters. Caden felt his frustration grow. He needed to be among the mountains and city. He needed to bring news of Rath Dunn to his father and brothers. Still, he steadied himself and forced a warm grin for his classmates. It was always important to show grace to commoners.

His next class smelled of copper and burned wood. The back wall was full of cabinets encasing row after row of tall glass flasks like an alchemist's shop. The instructor, Mrs. Belle, was tall and thin with brown hair and warm eyes. Her shoes were scuffed and her blouse wrinkled, but she maintained an air of elegance. For someone older, she was pretty enough. Her voice was kind when she welcomed Caden.

Like in math, Tito sat in the front of the science class. Caden took the front middle seat beside him. This time, no one ordered him elsewhere. There was a picture of a tree carved into this desktop—the same tree that had been carved into the stone of Jane's amulet. Something was scribbled beside it in the letters he was learning with Mr. McDonald. He asked Tito.

Tito looked sad. "It's Jane's name," he said quietly as he set out multicolored pens for note-taking. With a shrug, he added, "When you're in foster care, you've got to know what's yours."

"It's not really her desk, though. It's whoever sits at it." To prove his point, he added, "Right now, it's mine."

Tito neither looked up nor agreed. "Don't talk again until lunch," he said.

Lunch, unfortunately, did not come quickly.

The cafeteria was down a flight of stairs. To the stairs' left was a serving station and kitchen. To the far right, the wall was made from the mountain—a speckled granite and mica masterpiece—while the wall across was filled with large windows that overlooked the leafless winter forest. The ceiling was high and the room hummed with noise—clanking forks and spoons, chairs scraping against tiles, and students talking.

To get food, he had to take a plastic tray to the serving area. Behind the counter, a withered-looking woman stood over a large metal pot. She tasted the contents and smacked her lips. An even older man hobbled from behind a partition with a tray of steaming baked bread. His cheeks were sunken and his skin looked thin. He tossed the tray on the counter with a loud rattle.

When it was Caden's turn, a third lunch attendant, a beautiful young woman, spooned stew, white mush, and a square fish onto his plate. Her eyes gleamed and her skin glowed in a way that didn't strike Caden as normal. She smiled, but Caden didn't smile back.

He hurried to the eating area. Tables were lined in neat rows. Tito sat alone at a middle one. Caden sat beside him and asked him about the witches serving the food.

"Don't start," Tito said. "The lunch people aren't witches."

"The old woman is stirring a big witchlike pot."

"That's Ms. Aggie, and her stew's delicious."

"The young one is glowing."

"She's beautiful," Tito said, gazing over at her.

Caden trailed his spoon through his delicious looking stew. The aroma tempted his tongue. "Witches are dangerous. They prey on children and the foolish. There is no telling what poisons are hidden within these temptations."

Tito swallowed a large spoonful of the no doubt poisonous stew. "They're not witches, bro."

"They look like witches."

Tito raised his eyebrows. "Ms. Jackson looks like a supermodel."

"I don't know what that is, but if you're talking about

the young one, she's obviously the leader."

"Bro, no. Just no."

At the tables, boys and girls gobbled down the witches' food. The teachers gathered at a large table near the stairs. Mrs. Belle and Mr. McDonald were there. Rath Dunn sat in the middle, at a place of little importance, and ate slowly. When his gaze caught Caden's, something cruel flashed in his eyes before he turned back to those near him. Truth be told, there was something uncomfortable about all those at the table.

Caden nodded toward the table of teachers. "There's evil here."

"Uh-huh." Tito followed his gaze. "Mr. Rathis, the lunch people, or everyone in general?"

"We'd be foolish to trust the lunch witches, but I speak of Rath Dunn." From the teachers' table, Rath Dunn grinned at him. Caden felt his muscles tighten. "And the other teachers strike me as strange."

"Relax," Tito said, turning back to his food. "You're the strange one." He opened his mouth to say more but then snapped it shut. He watched something behind Caden with the same fierce expression that Caden's seventh-born brother, Jasan, got before a parry.

If battle was imminent, Caden would fight with whatever weapon he could grab. He palmed his fork. Slowly, he turned around, fork at the ready.

He expected to see Rath Dunn, but a boy approached.

He was short and wore sneakers as white as the beard of a frost giant. "Tito nonbonito," the boy said. "Looks like you got a new girlfriend."

It took Caden a moment to realize he and Tito were being insulted. He prepared his fork. Tito darted a glance at it, and shook his head. No forking the enemy.

Very well, Caden would battle with words instead of kitchen utensils. He set the fork down, and glared at the boy in the white sneakers. "Looks like you have none, nor much hope of one."

The boy's smirk wobbled, then came back full force. "Where'd you get your shirt?" he said. "The girls' department of Goodwill?"

Caden glanced at Tito. "I assume it came from the same market as yours."

"Dude, I got this online. Special order."

"Look, Derek," Tito said. "Get lost. We're eating, and you're making us sick."

Derek snarled at Tito. "Why don't you go back to Mexico already? You can take Goodwill here with you."

Tito literally growled. "Because I'm Puerto Rican, butt face," he said.

Students from other tables were now watching. At a table near the back, a boy yelled out, "Uh-oh, you're making him mad, Derek."

Derek laughed. He raised his hands in false surrender and went to sit down with the students at that back table.

One of the girls there patted Derek on the shoulder. "Don't worry," she said, loud enough for the whole room to hear. "If you were that ugly and didn't have parents, you'd have a temper, too."

The teachers did nothing. Rath Dunn seemed amused. Caden, however, wouldn't sit while his friend was insulted. This battle had been brought to them. He started to stand.

"Sit down," Tito said through clenched teeth.

Caden sat. "I can flatten them."

"Good for you, but they're not worth it. They're jerks. That's all. Ignore them."

"They weren't ignoring us. They want a fight."

Tito pushed his tray of food away. "So? We could get kicked out for fighting. We've got more to lose than them."

It seemed to Caden that Tito's reluctance to engage grew from the belief Rosa would send them away. As Caden's father had sent him away, Caden felt he knew something about that. "Rosa would understand."

"Trust me, she wouldn't. She'd be ticked to high heck if we got in a fight." Tito sank down in his chair. "And disappointed, which is even worse. Besides, don't you already have enough enemies?"

"Sometimes," Caden said, "you have to fight."

"And sometimes you don't," Tito said. "So don't."

In math, Rath Dunn gave a lesson on the spread rates of contagious disease. Caden watched; he spent the entire class memorizing the contents on Rath Dunn's desk, the shine off his head, his clothing. His shirt was deep red and pressed—the color the same as the colors of Crimsen—and his trousers looked like they'd been sewn and fitted by the famed tailors of the lower Autumnlands.

"Pandemic is unavoidable," Rath Dunn said. With a glance at Caden, he adjusted his sleeves slightly. Under his right cuff, there was the glint of red metal.

Even partially hidden, Caden knew what it was and knew Rath Dunn meant for him to see it. It was the famed Blood Dagger, a weapon feared by all. Rath Dunn shifted, and the blade was tucked back out of sight.

To Caden's left, Tito's mouth was set in a hard line. No doubt, he was starting to see Rath Dunn for what he was. Horrific. Dangerous. Capable of killing.

When the freedom bell rang, Rath Dunn stood in front of Caden. A slow, unfriendly grin spread across his face. "Caden," he said. "Wait a spell. I'd like to talk to you."

Caden didn't like the wording: "spell." If he had his sword, he would have a chance at defeating the man. Not a good chance, but better than none, better than he had now unarmed and outmatched.

There was no use trying to resist, though. An order was an order, and he was cursed until the end of the day. He felt the color drain from his face. "As you wish," he said, hating Brynne more and more.

Rath Dunn peered at him and grinned bigger. He

seemed surprised by Caden agreeing. Immediately, Caden felt his jumping nerves start to sizzle. Would the tyrant figure out Caden was cursed? If so, he could simply order Caden to kill himself. A horrible thought occurred to Caden: Rath Dunn could order Caden to kill someone else. Someone innocent.

Around them, the classroom emptied. The other students hurried into the hall until only Caden, Rath Dunn, and Tito remained.

"Tito, I'd like a word with Caden in private," Rath Dunn said.

As Tito had pointed out, since Rath Dunn hadn't killed Caden yesterday, likely he wouldn't today. Still, Caden felt lingering doubt, and there was no reason for Tito to be "talked to" also. "Go," Caden said.

Tito backed out. "Relax, bro. It's just math." Under his breath, he added. "If you're not out in ten minutes, Rosa will come looking for you."

Rath Dunn closed the door. He looked more like his portrait now, eyes mocking, grin condescending. "I wasn't expecting you," he said. "I remember every last son of King Axel. But from that coat, it looks like things have changed since I've been banished. Well, I suppose I shouldn't be surprised he'd remarry." There was hatred in his tone. "He is, after all, resilient."

"I'm a proud son of Axel." Caden fought to remain brave. "Last I read, you were banished to a slow, painful death in the Land of Shadow, Rath Dunn."

He smiled like he was savoring a fine food. "Ahh—slow, painful deaths. I could educate you on those. I'm a good teacher." He laughed, loud and amused, and pulled out his dagger. "And now here you are, my enemy's son, served to me in a coat of enchanted wool."

"Yet, you didn't kill me yesterday."

"You know the old saying, it's the cat that plays with the rat that has the most fun." Suddenly, Rath Dunn was looming over him. "I'm in no hurry."

Caden's brothers were always underestimating him, his father never listening. Now, the great not-dead enemy of his people toyed with him. He felt his face flush hot. "Then you're a fool," he said.

Faster than Caden could move away, Rath Dunn reached out and grabbed Caden's wrist. Caden knew, at that moment, he would die. With a flash of red glinting metal, the magical dagger ripped through his magical coat, to his skin beneath it. Caden covered the cut with his hand. Blood seeped through his fingers.

It took Caden a moment to get steady words out. He'd expected his throat slit, not his arm. There was a reason he wasn't dead. "Why haven't you killed me?"

Rath Dunn sighed. "It's not allowed."

Through his fear, Caden thought that strange. He wasn't allowed? When had Rath Dunn cared what was allowed? And if he wasn't allowed to kill, it seemed unlikely he was allowed to wound. Caden heard his voice shake. "Yet you're allowed to wound me?"

Rath Dunn glanced toward the door, toward the hall. He lowered the dagger. From his careful expression, Caden suspected neither cutting nor killing was allowed.

Rath Dunn pulled a red handkerchief from his pocket. The coiled symbol of the Bloodwolf, the protector of Crimsen and the Autumnlands, was embroidered on the corner. "*She* won't care about a little blood." Forcefully, he pushed Caden's hand away and wrapped the handkerchief around the wound. "Trouble within the city isn't allowed. Outside the limits, however, you're fair game, son of Axel."

Caden pushed Rath Dunn and his bloody handkerchief away. He collected his textbooks and notebook. As he picked them up, he noticed, again, the tree carved into the desk. Rosa's house was at the edge of the city. The mountain outside, the nature trap, those were beyond her land. Caden forced himself to meet Rath Dunn's gaze, to not wince in fear or pain. "Is that why you put the trap on the mountain? You couldn't steal Jane away while she was in the city?"

Rath Dunn waved him off. "You shouldn't be worrying about Jane." He pulled a second embroidered Crimsen handkerchief from his desk, and wrapped the knife in it, still wet with Caden's blood. "That horse on the news resembles a Galvanian snow stallion. He's yours, I assume?"

There was no reason to deny it. "Sir Horace."

Rath Dunn tucked the wrapped dagger back under his cuff. It made Caden uncomfortable to think that it was still bloody. Rath Dunn smiled. "Sir Horace is the one you should worry about," he said. In a low dramatic tone, he added, "The mountains are full of interesting things."

Truly, Caden was beginning to feel like the poor rat Rath Dunn had called him. Still. "Sir Horace can take care of himself," he said.

Rath Dunn laughed. "It's amusing you think that." He stepped back, grabbed an eraser, and wiped his white-board clean. "Hide within the city limits if you want, but while you cower, the monsters of the mountain will devour your Sir Horace. They run wild, but it doesn't take much effort to direct them to a kill."

11

THE MONSTERS OF ICE

Night didn't bring darkness. The day-old snow glowed from the city lights, and as the trail moved into the woods, the snow reflected the softer silvery hues of moonlight. The icy trees shone like a crystal palace of trunk and branch. Under winter's weight, the hillside creaked. If Caden had been in Razzon, he'd have thought the mountain alive.

There were no signs of Sir Horace. He didn't come when Caden whistled. Caden didn't know who controlled Rath Dunn or what dark beasts roamed the hills, but he believed Sir Horace was in danger.

Brynne's breath clouded the frozen air. "We should have brought the peasant," she said. "He could have helped. He knows this land."

Caden's feet were chilled, his hands numb; and at the

rip in his coat, frosty air slipped inside. The only weapon he'd found in the house was a broken-off handle to a shovel. He gripped it tightly and looked to Brynne. "Tito needs to distract Rosa."

She huffed and closed her eyes. "You fear for his safety. Have some faith in him." Snow swirled down from the branches and drifted onto her eyelashes. She opened her eyes and they were the silver of the moon. "The horse is on the other side of the far peak."

The trek would bring them even farther from the safety of the city limits. If summoned, though, Sir Horace would certainly come. Caden took a deep breath and the air chilled him from the inside. "Sir Horace!"

Brynne punched him, hard, in his wounded arm. She glanced at the shadows between the trees like she expected a winter wraith to barrel out. "Hush. This is a stealth mission."

Caden tried to yell again. Nothing came out. Silently, he cursed the curse. When it broke, he would comply with no order. He glared and pointed to his mouth.

"Fine. Talk. But don't yell. Better we not draw the attention of the things that are going to kill that beast of yours, lest they attack us, too."

"You didn't have to come."

"Without my help, you'd get killed for sure."

Caden bristled. "I've survived almost thirteen years without your help and not been killed." He shifted and his boots cracked the snow. "But I'll admit you are good at finding things."

"Makes me a better thief."

Caden would not dignify that with a response.

She laughed, grabbed his hand, and pulled him up the icy path. "You're hopeless, prince."

Over the peak, the forest was darker. The trees were taller, the shadows starker. To the side of their path, hoofprints bit into the ground. Beside them, there were other, larger prints.

Caden crouched down. He ran his finger around the outline of the larger print—seven claws—and frowned at the broken shovel handle. Already, the wood had cracked from exposure to the snow and the cold. It was hardly a weapon for battle.

Brynne leaned over his shoulder. "What is it?"

He pointed his broken shovel handle at the hoof marks. His chest swelled. Hope was not lost. He wanted to jump toward the sky he felt such joy. "These are the tracks of a dragon."

Brynne wrapped her arms around her chest and frowned. "There's no evidence that there are any dragons in this land at all." With a sneer, she added, "There's hardly any magic."

"Rath Dunn is here. A mysterious *she* controls him. Tito wears an amulet of protection, and the lunch witch glows. We can assume not all is as it seems. A dragon made these prints."

Caden inhaled the chilled air. There was a dragon in Asheville. The fire dragon may have escaped him, but this Ashevillian one would not. Even in a foreign realm, he'd prove himself. He felt a slow smile spread across his lips.

Brynne looked at him and shook her head. "We should go back," she said, though she didn't make it an order. "Dragons aren't simple beasts, Caden. They aren't creatures to fight with a broken shovel handle."

Caden had studied dragons. Neither animal nor energy, they were something in between. Generated by dark magic, they embodied brutal chaos and destroyed all in their way. They were memories of the once mighty and fickle Elderdragons that taught the peoples of the Greater Realm magic and fear. "I know what they are. I'm on a quest to slay one."

Brynne's breath ghosted in and out. "That story grows old. King Axel wouldn't send you to hunt dragons alone." She was as unmovable as the mountain. "I don't believe you."

He felt blood rush to his cheeks and his anger build. "I left at my father's request." In the following quiet, the snow creaked. Caden peered at it. Beside the dragon's prints were smaller, more familiar prints. His hope became dampened with sickening worry. "These, beside the dragon's prints, are Sir Horace's marks." This wasn't as good as he'd thought. Oh no. "A dragon hunts Sir Horace." The tracks led down deep into the valley. He needed to be there to fight with his friend. "Return to the house. Sir Horace needs me. I can track him from here."

"I'm not walking back by myself."

There wasn't time for this argument. He started downhill. "Then hide until I rescue Sir Horace."

Behind him, he heard Brynne follow. "Hide?" She sounded offended—the same type of offended that had resulted in Caden being cursed. He glanced back. "What is your plan, prince?" she said. "Slay the dragon with the shovel handle?"

"My plan is to rescue Sir Horace and follow my quest. I don't wish to also worry about your safety while doing so."

Caden was good at saying the right thing at the right time—if he concentrated. That was difficult when he kept picturing Sir Horace ripped from breast to tail. If Brynne's defiant expression was any indication, he had said the exact wrong thing.

"We will face the dragon together, ally," she said.

She'd cursed Caden into following orders; she was forcing him to take her into battle. Being eaten would serve her right.

"Very well," he said. As they hurried, he took off his coat and gave it to her. She was his ally. She looked cold. He certainly didn't want her drained again. She'd be unbearable. "Here," he said. "It'll offer you some protection."

She smiled, slyly, and took the coat. "I accept the Royal Coat of Warmth and Protection."

"You can't keep it."

"I don't know," she said, keeping quick step beside him. "It seems like you just gave it to me." She looked like she was going to say more, but her gaze fixed on his arm. "What happened—"

The quiet night was split by a mighty whinny—Sir Horace's battle cry. Caden readied the shovel handle and sprinted toward the noise. "This way!"

Jagged branches, freshly broken and green inside, stuck up from the snow like a field of rough-honed goblin blades. The smells of pine and cedar grew thick. Caden slid to a stop.

In a small clearing near the lower slope of the mountain, Caden made out Sir Horace whinnying and bucking. The ground around his hooves seemed slick with ice. He was watching something with great intent. Caden tracked his gaze and felt his breath hitch, his heart race.

Facing Sir Horace, near a patch of jagged trees, was a gleaming white ice dragon. Caden stood dumbstruck. He'd seen the prints, but now he was certain. There was a dragon to slay in Asheville. He could complete his quest.

A second later, Brynne careened into Caden. She pushed him into the snow, face-first, and he heard the powerful swish as the dragon's tail cut through the air above them, the same exact place where he had stood. When he looked up, the tree trunks around them were now broken.

"Careful, prince," Brynne whispered. "That tail almost leveled *you*."

At her voice, the dragon turned in their direction. Its ice-blue eyes raked over them. Beside it, Sir Horace had fallen. A gash darkened his flank. His side rose and fell with heavy breaths. Caden's great steed, however, was not so easily defeated. He wriggled to standing, his white coat smeared with blood and twigs, and pawed the ground. He put his head down, and his ears back.

Caden jumped up. Brynne was already in a fighting stance. The dragon's nostrils flared and it cocked its head like it was deciding who to eat first—Caden, Brynne, or Sir Horace.

The chance to devour someone of royal blood seemed one the dragon could not resist. With a loud scream, it rushed Caden.

He deflected the brunt of the attack with the broken shovel handle. The wood splintered. Air whizzed by his face, cold and dry, and he flew over the sloping ground like a poorly aimed arrow.

Caden rolled head over feet. Sharp rock and icy shards scraped his elbows and knees until he stopped, sprawled in the snow and facing the heavens.

Stunned, he lay still. Sir Horace was at his side in an instant. He nudged Caden's cheek with his soft muzzle. From uphill, the dragon screamed.

Brynne.

Caden scrambled to his feet. Sir Horace looked ready to charge, but his side twitched near the gash. Caden patted

Sir Horace's neck. "Stay back, friend," he said, and grabbed what was left of his splintered shovel handle.

He ran back to the fray. Brynne stood in front of the dragon, wielding a large stick from the ground. The dragon's head was down. Its tail twitched left to right, left to right as it prepared to strike.

With broken shovel handle raised, Caden dashed behind it and jabbed the splintered wood into its tail. It did no damage, but the dragon loosed a terrible screech and spun around, its mouth a sword's length from Caden's head. Its breath was cold—colder than the mountain—and smelled of blood.

"Get back! Get back!" Brynne ordered.

Caden had no choice but to obey just as the dragon lunged for him, its jaw tearing part of his pink shirt, its teeth coming so close to ripping his flesh that he felt the cold of dragon's breath against the skin of his belly. He wished he hadn't given Brynne his enchanted coat.

Suddenly he heard a roar, and the silvery half-light around them turned warm orange. The trees erupted with flame. The forest was on fire.

The dragon thrashed. It screamed at the flames. Caden dodged its tail and then its claws as it spun in frantic circles.

Brynne ran to him. Her large stick was alight.

"What did you do?" Caden cried.

"Pyrokinesis," she said proudly. "Fire magic of the mind."

A burning tree crashed down, and the dragon jumped

farther away. It lifted its head, howled, and turned. With a flick of white scales and a spiked tail, it disappeared downhill into safety.

From the distance came an answering howl.

Caden felt his eyes grow wide, and he met Brynne's equally shocked look. *There were more of them.*

Sir Horace whinnied, and Caden's boots squelched in the slush as he and Brynne sprinted to him. The fire burned hot at Caden's back and roared like a beast. "Stop the flames," Caden yelled.

Brynne pursed her lips. She tightened her face in concentration. The large stick smoldered out, the tip dark with ash. She glanced to the red-flamed woods and jutted out her chin. "I put the stick out," she said, like it was an accomplishment. "But I don't think . . ." Her voice wavered.

"What about the rest of it?"

"Look," she said. "I can't do anything about the rest."

Around them, the fire exploded. The smoke tasted acrid and thick. Sweat trickled down Caden's brow.

Sir Horace pawed the mud and snorted. Caden's horse was of the Galvanian Mountains, a stallion born to the snow, to the cold winters and ice of the Greater Realm. Fire upset him and now it surrounded them.

Neither Brynne nor Caden were gifted with speed and they needed to escape fast before the smoke overcame them. Caden patted Sir Horace's neck. "Can you take riders?"

"Just get on the horse—don't *ask* him," Brynne said.

An order. Caden swung his leg over. Sir Horace stumbled but held strong. Brynne mounted behind Caden.

A second later, they galloped up the mountain. Sir Horace dodged and jumped burning branches, his hooves steady like a heartbeat on the slushy ground. They escaped the flames growing on the downward slope and rode toward the relative safety of higher ground. Above the smoke, the world returned to ice and snow. They stopped and turned back.

"The entire mountain's afire," Caden said.

Behind him, he felt Brynne tense. "I got rid of the dragon," she said, and let go of him to wave at the flames below. "This was an accident. I meant it to be contained."

Sir Horace took the opportunity to rear up and knock her off. Brynne glared from where she was dumped on the snow. Caden also got down. Sir Horace had been injured. He need not carry Caden's weight now that they were beyond the fire.

Caden motioned down the other side of the hill, up and down the small slopes, and toward Rosa's house. Despite his sore arm and scraped elbows, he felt a slow, hopeful smile spread across his face. "Dragons," he said. What if instead of slaying one dragon, Caden slew two? Certainly that would impress his father and brothers.

Brynne scowled at him. "Do *not* go after those dragons. And why did Rath Dunn say they would stay outside the city limits? There's no reason. They shouldn't understand things like city limits."

She was right, of course, but the dragons' odd behavior didn't change the fact that they were dragons. "They are a danger to all who might venture into the hills. It's my duty to stop them. I just need my sword back."

"Leave the dragons alone."

The quest was important. It meant everything. "No," Caden said.

Brynne blinked at him. "No?"

"No," Caden said again. His eyes widened. He looked to the sky. The half-moon was waning, the night halfway through, and the compliance curse had broken. He grabbed Brynne and spun her around, laughing. "I'm free of your orders!"

"Until next month," said Brynne, the destroyer of happiness and mountains.

A shrill screech sounded from the north. Caden grabbed Brynne's hand and Sir Horace's mane. "We must hurry."

The first thing Caden saw when they stepped from the woods into Rosa's yard was the flash of red and blue lights. Caden saw Tito watching from the attic window.

Despite the trouble, Caden felt lighter than he had in days. He could complete his quest, even while stranded in this strange land. He waved to Tito, but Tito seemed not to see him and didn't wave back. In the yard, two figures stood with Rosa, one tall and skinny, the other short and stout—Jenkins and Officer Levine.

There was no reason to hide. They needed to get warm and it was unlikely they'd sneak into the house unseen. Even if they did, Caden's absence seemed to have been noticed already. He called out to the policemen and Rosa. They turned toward him, Brynne, and Sir Horace.

Sir Horace neighed low and mean at Jenkins. Officer Levine shone his light on Brynne, then Sir Horace, and finally Caden. A moment later, the policemen and Rosa were running to them. Rosa stopped and stared at Brynne. Jenkins stared at Sir Horace. Sir Horace kept his suspicious glower on Jenkins.

The gash on Sir Horace's side looked stark and bloody in the flashing lights. Caden squared his shoulders. His horse was brave and tough. He'd recover, but he needed care. Caden peered into the concerned face of Officer Levine. "My horse requires aid," he said.

Officer Levine frowned like he didn't know what to think. Caden pulled Sir Horace into better view and pointed to the wound. "We need a medic," he said. The cold was biting, and Caden could not stop shivering. Beside them, Brynne grumbled something about injuries of her own, but she was the one warm in his magical coat. While Rosa and the police fussed and led them toward the warmth of the house, Caden felt his gaze drift back toward the hills. There were dragons in the mountains, and Caden would return to slay them.

12

THE VILLAINOUS TEACHERS

Fom the living room window, Caden could see Sir Horace tethered to the porch. Jenkins stood back while the medic—Rosa had called her a *veterinarian*—approached his steed. She was young for a healer, tall and skinny, and had a long reddish braid trailing out from her hat.

Officer Levine looked out over Caden's shoulder. "Jenkins's sister, Dr. Clara Jenkins," he said. "She works with equine rescue. She's good. Got a way with animals."

The snow called to Sir Horace; the wind pulled him. He was a blizzard incarnate. She needed to be better than good.

She sat a black bag on the porch, pulled out an apple, and set it on the planks. Sir Horace licked his lips. By the time she'd produced a third apple, he was nuzzling her palm.

"Her way is bribery," Caden said.

"A way's a way. Now drink your cocoa. We need to talk."

Caden didn't drink his cocoa. He set it on the windowsill. "About what?"

"You snuck out, set a mountain on fire, and showed up with a pretty girl. About that." Officer Levine sipped from a chipped brown mug. He nodded toward the kitchen where Rosa had taken Brynne. "I take it that other shelter was hers."

"Yes."

"You're a little young to be running off with your girlfriend."

"She's not my girlfriend." Caden's shirt was ripped, his elbows scraped. Outside, the sky and snow glowed dull orange from the fire on the nearby mountain. "We are allies; we went to rescue Sir Horace and were attacked on the mountain."

"Attacked?" Rosa came from the kitchen trailed by Brynne. "By what?"

"Maybe it was a bear," Brynne said before Caden could say "dragon." "You do have bears here?"

Rosa arched a brow. "Yes, we have bears. They don't tend to do much this time of year, though."

Brynne waved her off. "Obviously the creature was crazed. But it could have been a bear. Right, Caden?"

Neither Caden nor Sir Horace would have sustained

injury fighting some Ashevillian bear. But he acquiesced. "Perhaps," he said. "And in the mayhem, the mountain caught fire."

Officer Levine looked between them. His gaze seemed to linger on Caden's singed shirt sleeves and Brynne's ash-covered face. "And how did the fire begin, exactly?"

In some lands, the punishment for burning down a mountain would be death by flame. From what Caden knew of Asheville, it was more likely fire safety training, but he didn't want to risk either of them being tied to a pyre and burned to death.

"We defended ourselves," Caden said. "You would have found our bodies ripped and bloody had we not. Look at what happened to Sir Horace."

"What exactly did happen?" Officer Levine said, narrowing his eyes.

Caden opened his mouth to tell him. They'd battled bravely. There was no shame in that and very little in the out-of-control fire. Before he could speak, Rosa stopped him. "That's enough," she said. "I don't want you talking to Caden right now, and she's not answering any questions without her parents present."

"Rosa, there's a forest fire. I need to know—"

"They're in no condition." Rosa pulled Brynne closer and looked at Officer Levine with a glower that would make brave men waver. "Come back tomorrow. They need their rest."

Officer Levine, to his credit, stayed his ground. "She'll have to come with me while we get this sorted. We'll need to call her parents—"

"Please," Brynne said suddenly, widening her eyes and appearing an innocent girl in every way. She was a mistress of deception. "Please can I stay with Caden? My parents are away."

"Away? Where?" Officer Levine said.

"I don't . . . know!" Brynne said, and pretended to sob.

Rosa put her arm around Brynne. "That's it," said Rosa. "She's staying here."

"The side of a mountain burned," Officer Levine said. "And she's not one of yours."

"There's no evidence that she's more than a victim."

Officer Levine looked conflicted—like he wanted to give Rosa all she asked but couldn't. He turned to Brynne. "I need the name and address of at least one of your parents, young lady."

Brynne's sobs got louder. Officer Levine asked her again. Still, she cried. It seemed to Caden that this was a poor attempt to avoid the question, but after a moment, it worked. Officer Levine placed his mug on the table and turned to Caden. "Do you know her parents' names?"

Caden wouldn't pretend to sob. Also, he'd speak the truth. "They are the famed spellcasters Madrol and Lyn. They travel, but most often they stay in the Springlands."

Officer Levine rubbed the bridge of his nose, sighed,

then grabbed his coat. "I'll be back first thing in the morning."

"Bring my sword," Caden said.

Neither Officer Levine nor Rosa acknowledged him. Rosa let out a deep breath. "Thank you."

Caden followed Officer Levine to the porch. Caden spoke louder. "Return my sword."

Officer Levine turned and pulled the keys to his cruiser from his pocket. "Sorry, son, not until a parent or guardian comes to claim it."

Actually, that made things simple. "Rosa can claim it."

Rosa called from the living room. "No swords allowed."

There were dragons in the hills and villains at his school. Rath Dunn taught math and had possibly stolen Jane Chan. And Caden wasn't properly outfitted. He felt his body vibrate with frustration. "I need it to fight the bears."

"Too bad."

Officer Levine got in his car and drove off. Rosa refused to do anything about the sword. Only the horse medic showed sympathy for Caden's plight. Then Dr. Jenkins, sister of Officer Jenkins, explained to Caden that she wanted to send Sir Horace to a rescue center. "For rehabilitation."

It sounded like a prison. "Sir Horace will not stay fenced," he told her.

She brushed red wispy hair from her face. "They give the animals lots of apples." Her smile was kind. "He'll be in good hands, Caden."

Caden hesitated. "This center, it's in the city limits?"

"Yes, tucked away near the Biltmore Estate."

Sir Horace leaned down and nuzzled Caden's ear. He wouldn't be safe running the mountains, not until the dragons were destroyed. Caden wasn't certain Sir Horace would stay in a rescue center, though. "You'll have to let him run each day."

"I'll make certain."

As Caden reached to pat Sir Horace's neck, the wound on his arm hurt, and he flinched. Dr. Clara Jenkins abruptly looked at Caden like she had been looking at Sir Horace. "I can check that for you."

The next morning, Sir Horace had been taken to the horse prison, and Caden spent the hour before school answering Officer Levine's questions with Brynne. Afterward, Rosa took him and Tito to school and sent Brynne back to bed to rest.

Frustrated, Caden wiped his pink locker, cursed number 12-4, with paper towels from the bathroom. He'd had no chance to train or track the ice dragons. After the mountain battle, he missed his sword almost as much as he missed his home. He inspected the locker and polished one corner. The number might be unlucky, but there was no reason for it to be unclean.

Tito watched and frowned. "I'm surprised you let them take your horse."

"The medic recognizes Sir Horace for the fine stallion he is." He caught Tito's gaze. "Although, no Ashevillian horse prison will hold Sir Horace long."

"You sure about that?"

Caden wiped down the door. "I know my horse. Adventure calls him."

Tito rocked on his feet. "So. A bear, huh?"

Caden stopped cleaning and turned to him. Tito had been asleep when Caden was sent to bed, and Rosa had been hovering over them that morning. "Ice dragons. Two of them." He was hesitant to admit the next part, but credit should be given where credit was due. "We might not have escaped them without the untrustworthy sorceress."

"Right," Tito said. "So, let me get this straight. Mr. Rathis—the math teacher and evil tyrant of your fantasy world—sent two ice dragons to kill you and your horse, and Brynne saved you by setting the mountain on fire?"

"She lacks control."

Tito narrowed his eyes at Caden. "Okay. Let's say whatever's made you loco is catching, and I believe you. Why are we here where Mr. Rathis can find some new way to kill you instead of at home with the beautiful and powerful sorceress? Rosa would've let you stay home."

"No one becomes an Elite Paladin by hiding in his or her guardian's prison, and I don't think he can hurt us in the city. He said it wasn't allowed."

"That vet put fifteen stitches in your arm. That looks like it hurt."

Caden waved it off. "A minor injury."

"Yeah, right," Tito said. "So what do you really want?"

Caden looked at him. "I want to find out where Jane is, what Rath Dunn is up to, and who the *she* is that he's afraid of. I want to slay a dragon and find my way home." He slammed his locker. "And I want him to know he failed."

"Or maybe, you just want to gloat." The bell rang. Tito adjusted his backpack and shook his head. "Look, just stay out of trouble. I'll see you in science."

Caden placed his hand on Tito's shoulder. "Stay brave. Don't trust Rath Dunn. We will find your Jane."

Like the day before, Caden attended his first class with Ward and Tonya. He put on his green earmuffs and waited. A symbol flashed onto the screen. The mystical voice said "*A*." Another symbol flashed onto the screen. The voice said "*B*." Then another and another.

Caden pushed back from his keyboard. He had a tyrant to outwit, an enchantress to save, and ice dragons to find and slay. He'd no time for this nonsense. This information wasn't even different from the day before. He should be in the halls exploring. He should be questioning student and teacher alike. "What good is it to learn to read this language?" He said out loud. "There's evil in this school."

Tonya froze. Her fingers trembled on her computer keys.

Like she felt a crypt devil's burning breath on her neck, she glanced back. Caden followed her gaze. Mr. McDonald sat, tucked behind his book.

Suddenly, Caden felt uncomfortable. Tonya seemed scared. He realized that Mr. McDonald could be anyone. He could be a minion of Rath Dunn.

Mr. McDonald glanced up. "Eyes on your computers, people," he said.

Ward sat with his muscles tense. Tonya turned back to her work. Caden peered at his screen and hit the button called the space bar. Another symbol flashed on the screen.

"Y," said the mystical monotone.

Caden frowned. Why indeed? He lifted the muffs from his ears. In his quietest tone, he asked Tonya, "Why are you afraid? Is Mr. McDonald a pawn of Rath Dunn?"

Her brow drew up, and she blinked behind her glasses like she was trying to place the name and failing. After a moment, she looked to Ward. Caden had believed Ward was ignoring them. But after a few seconds, Ward turned. In a soft, serious voice he said, "No. He doesn't like Mr. Rathis."

Ward looked like a boy from Asheville. He looked like the keyboard was an extension of his being, like a boy of computers and televisions, who knew nothing of Razzon, magic, or the Greater Realm—nothing of Rath Dunn. Yet, he seemed to recognize Rath Dunn for who he was.

"Then why are you afraid?" Caden said. "And how is it

you know of Rath Dunn when everyone else claims ignorance of his true name and nature?"

Ward glanced to Tonya like she was his voice.

She feigned working on her lesson. Hesitantly, like she feared the man at her back, she shifted closer. "Ward's father is the janitor," she said. "He knows everything."

"About who? Rath Dunn?" he whispered.

"The t-teachers."

Behind them, Caden felt Mr. McDonald moving, heard him lumber up from his seat.

Ward motioned for Caden to put back on his earmuffs. Deftly, he reached across to Caden's computer. His fingers seemed sure as he punched buttons. "The teachers are all evil," said the mystical voice in Caden's magical earmuffs. Ward pressed more keys. "But they are scared of HER."

13

THE SPAGHETTI TOSS

र. McDonald hovered near them for the rest of class. Ward and Tonya seemed afraid to say more with him nearby and hurried away when class ended.

When Caden met Tito in science class, Mrs. Belle greeted him warmly and smiled. With her blouse buttons misaligned, it was hard to imagine her as evil or feared. Still, a future Elite Paladin was ever vigilant, ever cautious. Besides, he noticed Mrs. Belle had painted her nails bloodred. It seemed contrary to her demeanor. Maybe she was something worse than she appeared.

Caden leaned toward Tito. "Ward and Tonya believe her evil," he said.

Tito neither looked up nor agreed. "Don't talk again until lunch," he said. Although not compelled, Caden did as he said.

Lunch, unfortunately, did not come quickly.

Like the day before, Caden stood in line with a tray. His thoughts felt heavy, and his gaze drifted to the teachers at the back table. One by one, he took in their mannerisms, their appearances. Mrs. Belle had spilled sauce on her blouse. The English teacher—he'd learned from Tito his name was Mr. Frye—wore gloves as he ate. Caden could almost picture his likeness framed in the Hall of Infamy portraits, but he couldn't place him.

Another stout man, whose name Caden had yet to learn but who he thought also taught English, glowered out at the students like their existence sickened him. The others were equally odd—a long lean man who could pass for a necromancer, a woman with jet-black hair and sharp-looking features. Rath Dunn sat in the middle. He noticed Caden looking, and a slow smile crept over his lips. Was he afraid of someone at that table? Were they all villains?

Behind the lunch counter, Ms. Aggie stirred a thick red sauce in her huge pot and cackled. There was the distinct smell of tomatoes. Were they poisonous? The old lunch man, who Caden had learned was called Mr. Andre, sneered from the back. His hands trembled as he lifted the bread tray.

"Spaghetti?" said Ms. Jackson, the youngest, prettiest, and most suspicious of the lunch witches. Certainly, she might be worthy of fear. Ms. Aggie and Mr. Andre watched, their attention unsettling, their faces full of envy.

Caden wouldn't trust the lunch witches. He would trust no one at the school. Rath Dunn was here, and if Tonya and Ward were right, he was one of many to be feared. He pulled back his plate. "I don't think so."

"He's watching his girlish figure, Ms. Jackson. Isn't that right, Goodwill?" Snickering erupted in the line. A few spaces behind Caden stood Derek—the boy Tito had ordered Caden not to fight. But Caden no longer had to follow orders. At least, he didn't until the next half-moon. He pushed that uncomfortable fact away for the time being and turned back to Ms. Jackson.

"I've changed my mind," Caden said. "I'll take the food."

Ms. Jackson glanced between Caden and Derek, and piled the spaghetti high on his tray. The sauce steamed.

Caden stepped toward Derek. "I won't tolerate your ridicule," he said.

The tray grew hot from the mess of sauce and noodles—very hot. Sadly, Caden set it on the counter. His intent was to teach this commoner a lesson, not scald him.

"My ridicule?" Derek said. "When you talk like that, you bring it on yourself." He pushed past Caden, grinned at the surrounding students, and held out his tray. "Spaghetti, please."

Derek's spaghetti steamed. No doubt it was hot like the embers of the red thunder springs. Caden noticed that *his* tray, however, had cooled when he picked it back up.

The chilly air had sucked the warmth away. The red sauce looked tacky and viscous.

Caden grabbed Derek by the shoulder, twisted him around, and smashed the tray with his sticky, slightly warm spaghetti into Derek's shirt.

Derek stood frozen. In one hand, he held his tray of steaming spaghetti. The other was balled into a fist. Sauce dripped from his shirt and, with a heavy plop, landed on his too-white sneakers.

No one in the cafeteria made a sound. Then excited murmurings filled the air. Derek's face turned the same color red as the spaghetti sauce. With a scream, he flung his tray of hot spaghetti at Caden's face.

Caden ducked. The tray whizzed over his head and clattered against the granite wall.

"You really are a freak," Derek said. "My mom's a lawyer. She'll get you expelled." His sneakers slipped on the sauce and he fell to Caden's feet.

"I do not fear this mother of yours," Caden said, and crossed his arms. "And if you don't want a fight, coward," he said, "don't start one."

Derek got to his feet and wiped the red sauce on his hands on his jeans. "You'll regret this," he said, but Caden doubted it. Matter of point, Caden found this all very fulfilling.

His glee, however, was short-lived. His arm began to sting. He felt the stitches that were keeping his dagger wound closed begin to pull apart, and blood seeped through his coat, indistinguishable from tomato sauce. It was the power of magical item number forty-three: the blood dagger.

Caden looked up, and there stood Rath Dunn. His pants were a dull tan, his shirt a starched white, but his jacket was bloodred velvet. "What happened here?"

Caden raised his chin. Derek remained silent.

It seemed Mrs. Belle had also come to see the incident. She peered over Rath Dunn's shoulder and tapped one red-painted nail on the counter. "An accident, certainly."

Rath Dunn looked from Ms. Jackson to Derek's spaghetti-stained shirt, and Caden's trayless hands. "Vice principal's office. Both of you," he said.

Mrs. Belle tried to argue for Caden, but Rath Dunn grabbed Caden's injured arm. He dug his fingers into the flesh, further opening the wound. Caden flinched, but he did not cry out. That's what Rath Dunn wanted. Mrs. Belle retreated back to her table. Her attempt to help had been weak at best.

Rath Dunn led Caden to the stairs like that, his grip strong and painful. Derek followed like an angry shadow. At the top of the steps, Rath Dunn released him.

"Show Caden to the office, Derek. I expect better from both of you," he said. With a gleeful laugh, he added, "Good luck, son of Axel."

His footfalls echoed down the steps, growing fainter and farther away. Finally, Caden and Derek were alone in the long hall. Down its expanse, the messy tiled floor and the dull pink lockers disappeared into the dark depths of the mountain.

They trudged a long way down the corridor. "This better not go on my record," Derek said.

The vice principal's office was deep in the school. At the end of the long hall sat a wiry man at a metal desk. The wall behind him was a large carved door. The man's hair was slick and black, his eyes deep set. His arms and legs were long and thin, and he reminded Caden of a spider.

"Derek," the man said, and it sounded like a hiss.

Derek stepped back. "Yeah, hi, Mr. Creedly. Mr. Rathis sent us."

Mr. Creedly pointed a too-long finger to the door behind him. His sneer could have broken glass. "One at a time."

Derek went first. Before pushing open the heavy door, he paused. He slunk inside with his head down and his steps slow. His acting abilities far surpassed Brynne's. Whatever he told this vice principal would be of no benefit to Caden.

Mr. Creedly stared at Caden, and something about him jostled Caden's nerves. His stomach danced; his wound stung.

"You're new," Mr. Creedly said.

Caden was no babe. "I'm twelve."

"Not to life, to the school."

"And you're not."

Slowly, Mr. Creedly smiled. His teeth were straight, white, and looked sharp. "I've been here since near the beginning." He bent forward. "She likes you."

It was unclear whether he thought that was a good thing or not, or who "she" was. "That doesn't surprise me," Caden said.

Mr. Creedly laughed, but his face and body didn't so much as twitch. The sound pushed out harsh and unnatural. Caden kept the long-armed secretary in view while he waited.

Derek soon returned. His face was pale. The scent of spaghetti hung off him like crumpled armor. There was another smell lingering in the hallway, too.

Roses.

"Your turn," Mr. Creedly said.

The office was long and narrow like the hall, and the smell of roses grew stronger as Caden entered. The walls were filled with shelves. But instead of books, the shelves held bowls in which shiny rocks, buttons, and cheap jewelry were displayed like treasures—color sorted and polished. There were no smears on the furniture, no cobwebs in the corners, no mud tracks on the floor. There was no dust or fingerprints anywhere. The room was the cleanest he'd seen at the school, the cleanest he'd seen in Asheville. To the side, a large window looked out to a towering wall of rock and ice.

At the back was a gleaming mahogany desk. A vase of pink flowers sat on one corner and a bowl of shiny silver beads sat on the one opposite. There was no place for students or visitors to sit.

Behind the desk sat Ms. Primrose.

"I'm disappointed, Caden," she said. "Two days and you're already in my office."

He'd not expected to see her. Was Ms. Primrose the *she* who all the teachers were afraid of? Was she the one who chained them and forced them to teach middle school math and science? What was she? Was she evil? Caden was unsure. He stood in front of her desk and lifted his chin. "I thought you were the placement counselor."

For a moment she looked surprised, like she hadn't expected him to notice. Then she clasped her gnarled hands and said, "I'm whatever I choose to be, dear."

SHE WHO CHOOSES

$\mathfrak{I}$f Ms. Primrose could be whatever she chose, why would she pick an overly sweet, aged woman who smelled like flowers and worked in a school? Caden stared at her warily. She wore a spotless rose-red dress, and her hair was pulled into a tight silver bun. Now that Caden was sitting so close to her, her skin seemed to have the texture of smooth, pebbled leather.

She pulled a sheet of pink paper from her desk drawer and scribbled on it. "I gave Derek detention," she said. "But I'm willing to let you go with a note home this time." She held the note out. "Return it signed." When he didn't reach for the paper, she waved it back and forth.

With a careful nod, he took the note and tucked it in his coat pocket with his compass. What was she? Of course, he couldn't ask her. That question might offend a normal old person, let alone whatever she was. "Is that what you do here?" he said instead. "Hand out punishments?"

She reopened the desk drawer. He saw it was filled with rows of colored pens, neat stacks of the pink punishment sheets, and other neat stacks of different colored paper. With precise movements, she put the pen away. "That's the vice principal's job," she said. "Discipline."

"For students and teachers?"

"Well, no, vice principals don't discipline teachers."

"But you can choose to be something that can punish them?"

She looked at him sharply. "That," she said, "is none of your concern. You need to worry about learning to read and passing your classes. I don't like it when students don't pass. It makes me hungry."

"Hungry?" Caden asked.

"Did I say hungry, dear? I meant *angry*."

She shook her head like she was tired of explaining things and moved her gaze to the door behind him. When he didn't leave, she cleared her throat and pointed to it.

Caden held his ground. He needed her favor and he needed information. Walking out would get him neither.

From the large window, cold sunshine broke into the room. On the office shelves the bowls of stones shimmered and the plastic jewelry glittered.

Before Ms. Primrose could tell him to go, Caden motioned to the shelves. "Your collections are—" It was imperative to use the right word. Adjectives danced—"tacky," "odd," "cheap," "shiny"—but none were good enough. He had to be sincere. Any creature that could intimidate Rath Dunn deserved that respect. "Clean," he said.

Though she seemed to fight it, she puffed up a little. "Few people appreciate such things. Oh, they say this and that, but they never mean it." She ran her fingers through the bowl near the desk corner. "I spend hours polishing my treasures."

He glanced at the shelves, at the cheap trinkets glittering in the sun, and didn't understand. Nonetheless he noted her pride. She liked to collect things. There were certain powerful beings that did, and if she was who Rath Dunn feared, he had no doubts she was powerful. Also, it didn't matter if he understood why she collected what she did. He wasn't trying to exploit her connection to the trinkets. He was trying to exploit her connection to their care.

"I've wiped down unlucky locker twelve-four twice today," he said. "The other students keep smearing fingerprints across the door."

"Few understand the importance of spotlessness," she said.

Common ground established, he flashed his most charming smile. "Or honor. I believe your teachers are behaving badly."

For a brief moment, she peered at him like she would

agree with whatever he said. Then she turned her lips down and became pensive. "It's quite something, dear, that gift of yours." Then her words turned hushed and musical, "But you'd be better if you practiced more."

It took him a moment to understand what she said. He rubbed at an ache in his temple. When her meaning became clear, her comment still seemed strange. He tried to answer in the same way. The effort made his tongue feel clumsy, but he spoke the lyrical language. "I don't understand," he said.

"It seems to me you do," she said. All the musical qualities of her speech were replaced with the soothing drawl of the Ashevillian tongue. "And don't play dumb. It's illmannered." She shook her head and sighed. "Your gift of speech, dear."

"You know about that?" he said.

"Yes, and I'm impressed." She looked at him, gaze unwavering and unamused.

It felt as if she was testing him again, like she had with the computer that first day. It also seemed he'd done better this time. Caden tried to untangle his sore tongue and considered those things. The dull ache in his temple faded. She seemed to be waiting for him to speak again. "Well," he said, unsure of what had just happened. He set it in the corner of his mind. He'd think more on it. "I'm good with words," he said for now.

"I know. And you've been trying to charm me since

you walked in the door, don't deny it." She waggled her finger at him. "I wasn't born yesterday."

There was no doubt she was old. And, yes, he did want her favor, however— "What does that have to do with my gift of speech?" She didn't answer, and an uncomfortable feeling settled through his bones, like maybe he did know what she meant but had never truly admitted it. "My gift of speech lets me speak all languages." Even English and Spanish. "That's all."

She fixed him with a serious gaze.

"Oh there's much more to it than that, dear," she said. "Haven't you figured that out?"

Truth be told, Caden had figured it out. Gifts were layered. His sixth-born brother, Chadwin, had been gifted with agility. He was nimble of body but also of mind. Among all his brothers, Chadwin had been the best at strategy, the best at understanding the pieces before everyone else. Caden's gift also was layered. His skills with languages were only part of it. He was also good at talking people into things. It was a talent of conmen and charlatans.

Caden felt shame creep up his cheeks. "My father doesn't like it," he said softly.

"Then he's a fool; such a gift is a jewel, charm and tongues," she said, and waved him off. "Now back to class chop-chop."

Caden missed his father; he believed in him. His father's opinions were never foolish. He, for one, would never employ a tyrant of the realm as a math teacher. Caden felt his patience crack. "My father's a great man." The wound on his arm stung, held together only by the veterinarian's stitching. His tongue and head still ached, but he tried to speak respectfully. "Unlike Rath Dunn. I want to report him. He's my enemy. I believe he's stolen Jane Chan."

She pursed her lips like she tasted something sour. "What proof is there of that?" she said. "That doesn't sound like him."

Caden pulled off his jacket and pointed to his wounded arm, which was freshly bleeding now that the stitches had been ripped out again. "He cut me with his blood dagger."

She squinted at his arm. "Oh pish. That's tiny."

Whatever creature Ms. Primrose was, she was frustrating. He pulled back on his coat. "Are teachers allowed to steal and cut students?"

From her expression, he knew she wasn't giving in so easily. "What would this heroic father of yours think if he heard you whining about minor injuries?" she said.

He met her gaze. "My father doesn't like it when I bleed."

"Well," she said, "don't drip anything on the floor on your way back to class."

He could tell he was beginning to annoy her. At the moment, though, she seemed more like an irritated old lady than a dangerous other, and he needed to understand. If Rath Dunn was allowed to strike down those he wanted, he wouldn't be handing out detentions and trips to the vice principal's office. He wouldn't have lured Caden into the woods as ice dragon food. If Rath Dunn was allowed to do as he wanted, the halls would run with blood and Caden would be dead.

He stood tall. "You didn't answer my question," he said.

Ms. Primrose straightened the bowl on her desk. She sighed long and loud like Caden was the worst of headaches. "No," she said, "teachers aren't allowed to wound students. Not in this enlightened time."

As he'd expected. "I demand justice."

For a moment she stared at him. Then, like it was the most tiring of tasks, she reached under her desk and pushed a button. "Mr. Creedly?"

The wiry secretary appeared immediately. "Yes," he said.

"Call Mr. Rathis to my office, please."

Two minutes later, Rath Dunn arrived. He'd buttoned his red velvet jacket shut. In the sun, with the scar splitting his face, he looked almost as dangerous as he was.

Ms. Primrose took a yellow sheet from her drawer. She scribbled away with the same red pen from before. "You're not allowed to do harm to students, no exceptions. No corporal punishments and all. You know how ridiculous the city can be."

Rath Dunn smiled. "It was just a nick," he said.

Caden's arm stung. With Rath Dunn so close, the

wound reopened. "The veterinarian put in fifteen stitches."

"Veterinarian? How appropriate," Rath Dunn said. He turned to Ms. Primrose. "Is this necessary?"

Rosa had gone white when she'd seen Dr. Clara Jenkins sewing up the slash. Ms. Primrose seemed to find the wound trivial. "He leveled a complaint," she said with a huff. "And rules are rules."

Rath Dunn met Caden's gaze. "His father was always a bit of a whiner, too," he said.

The statement was so absurd Caden ignored it. He pointed to the math tyrant. "He's involved in Jane Chan's disappearance. Certainly, the school has rules against kidnapping."

For his part, Rath Dunn gave him an odd, appraising look. Before Caden could read much into it, Ms. Primrose stood up.

"You can quit now, dear," she said. "I'm already writing the reprimand." She turned to Mr. Rathis and walked to a cabinet beside the window. "This is going in your employee file. Don't harm the boy again."

"Or my horse," Caden said.

"Snow stallion is delicious," Rath Dunn said.

For a moment, Caden was too shocked to react. Rath Dunn had threatened to eat Sir Horace. He swiveled to face Ms. Primrose. "I demand protection for my horse."

"Lesser animals aren't my concern, dear."

"Sir Horace is no lesser animal."

Rath Dunn chuckled and licked his lips, like he was thinking of the most scrumptious of foods. "See you in class, son of Axel." He patted Caden on the shoulder and walked out.

Caden watched after him and turned back to Ms. Primrose. "That's it?" he said.

"Child, I've done as you asked. The write-up goes in his employee file," she said. "Permanently."

Caden felt his cheeks heat, his blood rush. "He took Jane Chan."

"Nonsense," she said, and sat back behind her desk.

He was taken aback by her denial. Rath Dunn was a villain. He'd threatened to eat Sir Horace in front of her. She'd seen Caden's bloodied arm. Caden placed his palms on her desk. "He's a tyrant. He let loose ice dragons on the mountain. Innocent Ashevillians could have perished."

Ms. Primrose fixed him with a chilling stare. "Dragons?" she said, and arched a brow.

Caden leaned forward. "I'm talking about magic, ice-breathing, mindless dragons." He paused on the word "dragon," giving it weight. "We were almost killed."

Even before he finished speaking, he knew something was wrong. He felt the office grow cold. The window iced from the inside and blocked the breaking sun. Ms. Primrose's expression shifted from impatient but charmed old lady into something much older and more dangerous.

She peered at him, the faded blue of her eyes unnatural

looking, the pupil too small for the dim light. She sat statue still. Caden waited; he listened to his loud breaths as he inhaled and exhaled.

"It's time you leave, dear," she said, as cold and sharp as the ice outside.

Caden walked back down the long hall and listened to the echoing of his steps. The air tasted stale and damp. For the moment, he was alone in the hall. His father and brothers were a realm away. Whatever powerful beings and terrible forces had brought him here, his family was a realm away. He felt the unsettling and familiar feeling of being lost.

When he was seven turns, Caden's cat had bounded into the dark catacombs of the Winter Castle. After waiting for her to return for long hours, Caden made his way to his father's strategy room. Nine Elite Guards and three of Caden's brothers—Jasan, the seventh-born; Chadwin, the sixth-born; and Maden, the second-born—were crowded into the small ornate room. He slinked around Paladin after Paladin until he found the Winterbird-embroidered, dusk-colored coat of his father, the king.

His father turned and frowned down at him. "You're supposed to be asleep."

"Windy is missing," Caden said.

His father didn't seem to recognize the name and looked to Jasan for clarification.

Jasan's hair and eyes shone gold in the low light. His

frown mirrored their father's frown. "His wind cat, father."

Caden nodded. "I came to notify the guard."

His second-oldest brother, Maden, chuckled. Gifted in strength and the size of a small frost giant, he had a gentle broad face and hair the color of straw. "Caden's pets often require assistance," he said. "They are a troublesome group."

Chadwin reached down and touched Caden's shoulder. He had the same kind eyes as the portraits of the late queen and hair so light it could pass for white. "Wind cats can take care of themselves. She'll be all right."

One of the Elite Guards whispered above Caden and into the king's ears. "The gnomes are refusing to attend the council. The people of Crimsen may also back out." The king's face became graver; his shoulders seemed to become heavier. He looked back down at Caden like an after-thought. "Your brothers and I have business. Go to bed. You can search in the morning."

He said it in a low, firm voice, and there was no mistaking the order. The discussion was over; the king's commands must be followed. Even at seven, Caden believed that. He lived that.

He stayed in bed until the late night bell tolled that signified the end of one day and the beginning of the next. With morning official, Caden went to the catacomb entrance.

The thick stone walls were cold to the touch; torches

on them gave off faint light and fainter heat. He followed the sound of screaming winds and gentle breezes down stairs and around corners until he found Windy. She sat on a crumbling tomb, silver fur whirling in her wind, fire rodent dead in her jaw like a piece of limp coal.

"I've come to save you," he said, because that was what future Elite Paladins said.

With a slow, leisurely stretch, she dropped from the tomb and settled to eat on the stone floor. Only when she was done did she stand and rub against his shins like a gentle breeze.

With her cradled in his arms, he walked back, but the only stairs he found led down, deeper into the ground, and to darker passageways. Not knowing which way to go, Caden sat under a torch and closed his eyes.

He awoke to the sound of yelling. "He's here!"

In moments, Caden was blinking up at his father's stoic face. Jasan stood back, looking weary. Maden towered behind him and let out a soft sigh. Chadwin seemed relieved.

"He'll be fine," their father said, and wrapped Caden in his embroidered coat. "Keep this, and it will keep you warm."

Maden, Jasan, and Chadwin looked surprised, envious even. Around Caden's shoulders, the coat was warm and soft. As soon as his father said it was Caden's, the fit became perfect; the fabric soothed his freezing skin.

After they were back to the castle proper and the medics and magicians had deemed Caden cold, foolish, but otherwise unharmed, his brothers returned to regarding him with—in order of birthright—amusement, sympathy, and irritation.

If their father noticed, he ignored them. He turned to Jasan. "Make sure your brother gets back to his room," he said.

Once Jasan and Caden were beyond earshot, as Caden followed Jasan up the spiraling staircase of the western tower, Caden heard him mumble, "Half brother."

Five years had passed since then, and the weight on his father's shoulders seemed to get heavier and heavier; the strategic meetings more frequent; the whispered secrets among his brothers and guards increased. The country was in turmoil. No one had told Caden outright, but he knew. He'd seen his brothers increase drills with the Elite Paladins and castle guards. He'd watched men and women ride to the castle in the dead of night, wounded, and carrying important messages. He'd seen his brother die.

The memory of his home made his heart ache, but the memory of Chadwin felt like a chain squeezing his chest. What new problems would arise when Caden didn't return home?

Caden tugged his coat tighter. The magic was strong: the fit was comforting and the wool always warm. It couldn't, however, bring back his dead brother Chadwin.

It couldn't even reunite him with his surly brother Jasan or giant brother Maden. What it could do, however, was remind him he was the eighth-born son of King Axel. He was a future Elite Paladin. He must be brave and noble in the face of villainous teachers and powerful old ladies.

15

THE LAND OF THE BANISHED

aden scrubbed his locker until it shone. He forced away the memories of his home and his dead brother. Tito leaned against the adjacent locker, twelve-three.

"You've got some issues," he was saying. He hadn't stopped talking about the spaghetti incident since Caden had gotten back from Ms. Primrose's office. "But, hey, if you weren't nuts, you might not take down bullies with pasta." For someone who'd prevented Caden from fighting the day before, Tito seemed thrilled with Caden's spaghetti toss. "You should have smashed it into his face, though."

Caden took out his math book. "The goal was to humiliate, not to injure."

"Goal achieved," Tito said. "But Rosa's gonna kill you." Caden felt his eyes grow wide, and Tito laughed. "Not literally. She just doesn't believe in humiliating people."

"He insulted us first," Caden said, and shut the locker door.

"Rosa won't care 'bout that, and I've met Derek's mom. She's totally scary. But, hey, it was worth it, right?"

"I wouldn't have done it if it wasn't."

In the math room, the students murmured quietly, some laughed, some flipped through their texts. The woody scent of pencil shavings mixed with the smell of wool that was still damp from the snow outside.

Caden sat and prepared to face his enemy.

Rath Dunn entered like he was walking onto a stage. With a flourish, he turned off the lights and flipped on the projector. Grisly scenes and bloody battlefields flashed on the board. It was a lightning storm of gore and death.

"Today, we learn to calculate percentage," Rath Dunn said, and flipped back on the lights. "Case study—percentage dead from battle."

The room filled with nervous energy and the sound of writing implements scratching paper. Caden sat and listened. He could not read this English nor write it, and there was nothing he wanted to learn from a tyrant who stole enchantresses and threatened to consume Galvanian snow stallions.

Halfway through the lesson, Rath Dunn stalked to Tito's desk. "Out of five hundred fifty soldiers, one hundred twenty perished. Percent dead?"

Tito blinked. "Uh . . . like twenty-two percent?"

"To be exact twenty-one point eight one repeating. But close enough. Smart boy."

Tito looked down and smiled. Caden kicked him. Tito must not forget that Rath Dunn was the enemy. Too many others had suffered horrible fates by letting down their guard, by letting the man use his keen insight to force his way into their trust.

Rath Dunn moved in front of Caden. "Caden, what percent survived?" His eyes took a curious glint and his voice a challenging lilt.

Despite fighting hard to learn nothing and keep Rath Dunn's lesson from inching into his head, Caden knew the answer. All he was required to do was subtract Tito's answer from one hundred. Seventy-eight tickled his tongue.

Caden swallowed down the number and hardened his gaze. "Too few," he said.

"Interesting." Rath Dunn leaned close. Caden braced for the stretching of stiches, the sharp pain of a cut, but his wound remained intact. The stitches didn't pull. "Although, that depends on your perspective. Mathematically, though, it would be seventy-eight point one eight"—he punched to the air and raised his voice dramatically—"repeating!"

When the freedom bell rang, Rath Dunn blocked Caden and Tito's escape. Caden scowled at him and at the place under his velvet jacket where Caden knew he'd had the blood dagger earlier.

"Why don't you have your weapon?" Caden said.

At that, Rath Dunn curled his lip. He looked like the largest of the Winter Castle wind cats, the smug cat that came to Caden's knees and had fur the same silver as steel. All he lacked was the giant fire rodent wriggling in his teeth.

"I put it away, as a reward."

"For what?" Caden said.

Rath Dunn chuckled. "For humiliating your enemy and showing no mercy for a boy you know nothing about."

Whatever this was about, it was not Derek. "I know he started it," Caden said.

"And you finished it, then quite adeptly charmed Ms. Primrose," Rath Dunn said, and motioned to Caden's hurt arm. "Hence, I decided to spare your arm my blade. Ms. Primrose does approve of rewards. Best to keep her happy."

Tito moved closer and, for a brief moment, reminded Caden of the hovering presence of the Elite Guard—alert and ready to protect. "C'mon," he said. "Let's go."

As they stepped through the doorway, Rath Dunn called out. "It was my impression," he said, and Caden could hear the knowing grin curl his lip, "that you boys wanted to find dear little Jane Chan."

Caden stopped, surprised but not. No matter what Ms. Primrose believed and said, Rath Dunn was connected to Jane's disappearance. Something between validation and despair battled within him. He feared what might have happened to her.

Tito spun around. "Where is she?"

The rage in his voice was new. Caden had heard his friend annoyed and frustrated—the normal emotions people seemed to express before they gave in and did what Caden wanted. This was the first time he'd heard Tito sound dangerous.

Six months prior, Chadwin had been slain. Caden thought of the pain and guilt he felt for not being there to save Chadwin, for the pain and guilt he knew his brothers and father felt, too.

For Tito, this wasn't about honor or about proving he was brave and capable, it was about saving someone. "Where is she?" he repeated.

Caden could do nothing to bring back Chadwin, but he could help Tito find his friend. "Tell us," Caden said.

Rath Dunn motioned to them like they were hissing kittens. "In a few years, you two might be threatening," he said, and shrugged. "I don't have her."

Tito's face remained stretched in a snarl. His fist was clenched at his side. He inhaled deeply like he was on the edge of control. "Then who does?"

"Good question. Like I said, smart boy. I might know something."

Tito remained furious. "What do you want from us?"

Rath Dunn nodded slightly, like he approved of the question. "That's why you're good at math. You're good at getting to the point. I have no use for you, though. I already possess that skill."

Caden snorted. "You are hardly getting to the point."

"You, though, son of Axel," Rath Dunn said, and turned all his attention to Caden, "you may yet be useful. You have talents and information I don't."

"I must decline."

Rath Dunn's gaze lingered on Caden's wounded arm. For a second, he seemed to be disappointed, and Caden again thought of how carefully Rath Dunn had saved his blood before encouraging him to die on the mountain.

Rath Dunn paced the room. "Axel would have had you gifted like your brothers. Let's see," he said. "Valon in leadership, Maden in strength." He paused after each name like he was cataloging Caden's response, like he was seeking answers to some question. He continued. "Lucian in stealth, Martin in accuracy, Landon in fortitude, Chadwin in agility."

Caden flinched at Chadwin's name, at the memory of him pale and lifeless on a stone bier, and his throat felt tight. "My brothers are none of your business," he forced out.

Rath Dunn continued as if he'd learned what he needed. "And Jasan—favored seventh son—gifted in speed . . . and *more*."

Caden glared. "All loyal and brave men."

"You think so? Maybe, maybe not. There were whispers of dissent among them even before my banishment."

Tito's cheeks turned red, and his shiny hair fell into his face. "Caden's dysfunctional family can wait. Where . . . is . . . Jane?"

The distance between Tito, loyal and brave foster brother, and Rath Dunn, the releaser of the devil blight, was too close, too dangerous. "Get to your point," Caden said to the tyrant.

Deliberately, Rath Dunn turned to him. "You show up here—that's curious enough."

He glanced again at Caden's arm, near the spot where he'd wounded him, and sighed. It seemed whatever he'd meant to accomplish had not been accomplished. Caden lifted his chin. That was good. And Rath Dunn had also been written up by the mysterious collector of shiny things and school vice principal, Ms. Primrose.

Rath Dunn continued. "You speak English, not such a feat really. There are spells and tricks and charms that can accomplish that." His gaze went to Tito and back to Caden again. "Then I hear you speaking Spanish with your little friend here. Two new languages, fluent at the same time, that's more curious, and there's the illiterate part." He paused and chuckled as if he found that especially amusing. "What is your gift, prince?"

"You seem to already know," Caden said.

"Tell me."

"Tell me about Jane Chan."

Rath Dunn spread a huge, catlike grin across his face. "The perfect reply!" he said, and laughed. Then, more to himself than anyone, he added, "Gifted in speech. Axel must love that. You need to practice, though, if you want to bring it up to your potential. You may still be useful. I'm glad I didn't try harder to get you killed."

"You tried hard enough."

"If you think so, your father has sheltered you too much."

Beside Caden, Tito fumed. "Are you going to tell us about Jane or continue to torture us with your theatrics?"

Rath Dunn was in front of Tito quicker than seemed possible. "If I was torturing you, you'd be screaming." Slowly, smile in place, he caught Caden's gaze. "Maybe Caden could charm me into telling. Ms. Primrose seemed quite charmed by him."

"Maybe I could charm her into getting rid of you."

"Doubtful," Rath Dunn said, and sounded not in the least bit concerned. "You've barely developed your skills. But the fact that you can charm her at all is of great interest to me."

Caden was good at knowing what to say to get what he wanted, but it didn't work all the time. It wasn't like his compliance curse. His gift never forced anyone to do anything. People could choose to say no and, often enough, they did.

"I can't make anyone do anything," Caden said.

"I know. You can do something better: you can convince them to choose to," Rath Dunn said. "Well, you could if you practiced." His eyes were bright. "I could use someone of your talents. Here's the deal, son of Axel. I want a vial of Ms. Primrose's perfume. Use your gift to convince her to give it to me, and if you do, I'll help you find the girl."

Caden rubbed his arm near the wound. Rath Dunn had wanted Caden's blood. That Caden was certain about. Now, he wanted something from Ms. Primrose, the "she" who seemed to keep the other villainous teachers in line. "Why do you want her perfume?"

Rath Dunn cocked his head. "I have my reasons."

Whatever they were, they were certainly evil and vile. "No, I won't help you."

"No?"

"We have no reason to believe you didn't kidnap her yourself," Caden said.

Rath Dunn feigned offense but seemed to be enjoying the bargaining. "If I kidnapped her, would I be offering you information?" he said. "You can trust me. I'll tell you what, I'll give you a hint, free of charge and obligation. As a show of good faith."

"Free?" Caden said at the same time that Tito grumbled out, "What's the catch?"

Rath Dunn looked at Caden and then at Tito. "The catch is next time, it won't be."

The statement was like the web of a Korvan spiderbird, sticky and full of bloodsucking traps. Once Caden and Tito entered his web, fighting their way out would be almost impossible. Caden pushed Tito toward the door. "We'll find her without your trickery."

Rath Dunn reached out and grabbed Caden's arm. He wrapped his other hand tightly around Tito's wrist. "Believe this, boys, you won't find her without my help. And if you don't find her before the next new moon"—he paused and his eyes widened dramatically—"she'll be dead."

Caden doubted his truth, meaning, and usefulness. "Why should we believe you? You sent your dragons to devour Sir Horace."

"They're not mine," Rath Dunn said. He dropped his voice low and confident. "And it's unwise to call them that. You'll insult her." He glanced out his window to the winter sky. "Here's my information; think on it carefully, son of Axel," he said. "The locals call Asheville the Land of the Sky." He looked at Caden. "But I and the other teachers, we call it the Land of Shadow, the land of the banished."

Asheville was not the Land of Shadow. It couldn't be. It was a quaint city with small mountains, colorful cars, and artists selling wares on each corner. It was not a dumping place for the Greater Realm's worst villains.

Caden took a deep breath. It was important to breathe. "This isn't the Land of Shadow."

"I'm afraid it is. I'll admit," Rath Dunn said with a dramatic arm flare, "it's nicer than advertised. One of the better prisons I've known. You worry about me, but there are twenty-four others banished here just like me."

The room fell quiet. Rath Dunn stood in front of them,

unmoving, his red velvet jacket glistening under the harsh indoor lighting.

"The new moon's only four days away. Bring me Ms. Primrose's perfume, and I'll help you find Jane before she's dried up and empty. Or don't," he said with a shrug, "and she'll die screaming and alone."

16

TRUTH AND CONSEQUENCES

Outside, the sky was blue and the air crisp. The hills cracked with shifting ice. Caden's enjoyment of it, his respite from his heavy thoughts, was short-lived. The new moon would bring about an end to Jane Chan. Then the half-moon would reinvigorate his curse. Both his fate and Jane's were tied to the moon phase. He was so lost in thought, he almost didn't dodge Tito's poorly aimed fist. He did, though, and it swished past his shoulder.

Caden looked at him. "What are you doing?"

Tito lowered his arm and glowered. "Rathis says he'll tell us how to find Jane and you decline? Bro, we're doing what we have to do to find her. Period."

Caden replayed the conversation. The dragons didn't belong to Rath Dunn. Don't call them dragons. Most ominously, Jane would die by the new moon. He watched the

English instructor talking to a parent. He saw Mrs. Belle stumble on the sidewalk as she walked toward her car. Ward and Tonya said they were evil. Rath Dunn claimed they were banished like him. If they were all villains, any of them could have taken Jane Chan. As hints for a missing enchantress went, those were weak at best, designed to confuse at worst. "Falling into his trap will not bring her home."

"Finding out what he knows might."

Rath Dunn had wormed his way into the trust of men older and wiser than him and Tito. Their path was becoming twisted, their journey treacherous. The ground beneath his feet felt slick like the ice on the side of the road.

"He can't be trusted, even if he speaks the truth," Caden said, to remind both Tito and himself.

Tito rubbed his wrist, the one Rath Dunn had grabbed, and looked to the sky. "I don't care." There was iron in his voice, and he kicked at a nearby bench. The metal structure echoed with the force. Ice broke from it and landed whole on the hard ground. "He said she'd be dead soon."

The kick, in Caden's opinion, showed more promise than the punch. Maybe the bench with its stationary, unconcerned manner was just a better target. Tito had power and some natural fighting ability but he lacked finesse. With practice, he'd improve. His height and build were similar to Caden's, and Tito looked fit enough. Caden had an idea.

Tito narrowed his eyes. "Stop looking at me like that."

Caden would start Tito with the Korvan battle staff. It was easier for a beginner to wield, and unlike the sword, mistakes rarely resulted in lost fingers, arms, or feet. Besides, Caden's sword remained confiscated by the police and a battle staff could be forged easily.

"I've decided to teach you the ways of the Elite Paladins," Caden said.

"No," Tito said.

"It's a great honor."

"No."

"It will help us in finding your Jane," Caden said. Tito's bad mood would pass. Once Caden had assessed Tito's skills, he'd plan a training schedule and revised weapon list. "We should not rely on the villainous tyrant's help. We face enemies of great evil." He placed a hand on Tito's shoulder. "We must be prepared."

Tito huffed, sat on the icy bench he'd attacked moments earlier, and glared at the icicle on the ground. In the parking lot, cars pulled in and out, their roofs covered in thick hats of snow. Student after student got into white-tipped red cars, black trucks, and blue vans. The drive emptied and the flood of cars became a trickle. Rosa's shiny truck was nowhere.

"Your guardian is late," Caden said.

Tito peered up and toward the road. "*Our* guardian."

Caden was well trained, clever, and the son of a king. He needed no guardian and accepted none. Those arguments, however, seemed lost on Tito. Truth be told, they seemed lost on Brynne as well and she better knew of Caden's skill and birthright. He sighed, straightened his stance, and revised his list of suspicious people at the school.

Five minutes later a familiar silver and black police cruiser pulled into the drive. The window descended and Officer Levine smiled at them from the driver's seat. "I'm off duty this afternoon. Get in. I'll drive you home."

"Where's Rosa?" Tito said.

"Delayed."

"Delayed why?" Tito said.

Grudgingly, Caden decided Rath Dunn was right. Tito was good at getting to the point.

"She took Brynne shopping," Officer Levine said, but he didn't elaborate.

He should tell them everything without prodding, and he should stop demanding that Caden sit in the back. Royalty belonged in the front. Officer Levine would take neither point seriously, though. Caden calmed himself, climbed in the back, and smiled charmingly at Officer Levine.

Tito looked at Caden, exasperation clear on his face, and climbed in beside him. "What are you going to do now?" he whispered in Spanish.

"He investigated Jane Chan's disappearance. I'm going to ask him for information," Caden said, and motioned to the front. "Distract him. He'll say more that way."

"Sure," Tito said, but he sounded skeptical.

The rearview mirror reflected the intensity in Officer Levine's eyes. "You speak Spanish?" he said to Caden, demonstrating unexpectedly good hearing and no mastery of the Spanish tongue.

Like many questions he'd asked Caden, it felt heavy with meaning. Before Caden could answer, Tito leaned forward. "Yeah, man, I'm fluent."

In the rearview Officer Levine's eyes crinkled a bit, and Caden got the impression he was fond of Tito. At the moment, Caden was also fond of Tito, as he seemed good at being distracting.

"And your foster brother there?" Officer Levine said.

"Him?" Tito stuck his thumb at Caden in a gesture that was considered obscene in Razzon. "His royal wordiness speaks many languages."

"That so?" Officer Levine said. He pulled out of the school drive and started up the hill. "What other languages can you speak, Caden?"

"I suppose I can speak them all." With a sly grin, he added, "Rosa doesn't know. It would be a reasonable excuse for you to speak with her."

Officer Levine looked straight ahead, Rosa likely prominent in his mind. Beside Caden, Tito scowled.

Caden looked back to the front seat. "She needs comfort," he said. "She's distraught."

That brought Officer Levine's attention back. "You think?"

"She doesn't understand why Jane ran away."

Tito watched. His discomfort with the conversation was evident in his expression, in the tight pull of his muscles.

"She told you that?" Officer Levine sounded justly suspicious. Rosa did not seem the type to burden others with her worries, especially people like Caden who were quite unnecessarily put in her care.

"No," Caden said, "but I'm observant and it would be easier if she knew the truth."

Officer Levine exhaled, slowly. "And what's that?"

"Jane did not run from her. She was taken."

"The state police deemed otherwise."

"But when we met, you were looking for a missing girl."

"A runaway girl."

"Jenkins said runaway. *You* said lost."

"Get to your point, son," Officer Levine said, and Caden suspected that his gift of charm might not be working.

The next words were important. Caden needed to say the right thing, something that would get Officer Levine to see things his way, something to get him to investigate the school so that Rath Dunn was not their sole source of information. He concentrated. It seemed he did need practice.

While he was thinking, however, Tito leaned forward and peered toward the front seat like in his mind the puzzle pieces had already fit together. "You don't think she ran away either."

At that, Officer Levine stopped the car beside the metal sun sculpture and they got out. "I don't know what to think." His voice turned kind. "But it's not your fault she's missing."

"No, it's your fault for not finding her. It's Rosa's fault for thinking she'd ever run away," Tito said.

"Rosa's doing her best, Tito." After a moment, he glanced between Tito and Caden. "The two of you really believe she was taken?"

"Yes," Caden said. "And we believe someone at the school knows by who."

"Okay," Officer Levine said, and started toward the porch.

Rosa met them at the door with a weary expression. Caden gave her Ms. Primrose's note and her brow wrinkled further.

"Already?" she said.

"My hand was forced. Derek called Tito 'Tito nonbo-nito.'"

Rosa's mouth thinned. Officer Levine motioned Tito to the kitchen. As soon as they'd disappeared through the door, Rosa opened the note and read it. "You threw spaghetti," she said, and didn't sound nearly as happy as Tito had when he'd found out.

"It seemed a good solution."

She held his gaze. "Throwing food is not the way to solve a problem."

"Respectfully," Caden said, straightening the blanket on the couch. "I disagree. Derek will rethink before he insults me or Tito. And when he does so, he'll smell tomato sauce."

She tightened her jaw and glanced toward the kitchen. "This Derek, he makes fun of Tito?" she said. "I don't get that. Tito hasn't said anything to me."

"It's his problem, not yours."

"It's my problem, too." Her expression turned fierce, and her mismatched clothes did nothing to distract from it. "And no one at school does anything about this name-calling?"

Caden considered his next words carefully. He needed to convince her that his actions were not only justified but honorable. "I did something."

"And now I'm going to do something," she said, and he imagined her with a sword, charging the school and demanding justice. "I am calling this boy's mother and you're going to apologize. After that, I'll discuss his bullying and name-calling with her."

Wait? What? Caden was speechless for a second. That was not the outcome he expected. He clenched his fists. "I'm not apologizing. I'm not sorry."

He was playing on her temper, but antagonizing her would not get him anywhere. He took a calming breath and smiled.

Rath Dunn was right about one thing—the gift of speech was a blade Caden had yet to sharpen. He needed to practice with persuasion like he now practiced with his fighting stances, like he'd once had to concentrate really hard when speaking other tongues. If Caden was to direct her away from such foolishness, he would need to work at it.

Before he could speak, she held up her hand. "That's enough. If you wanted to talk your way out of this, you should have done it before you threw the food."

Suddenly, her demeanor felt familiar. She'd learned he was clever of word, so she was refusing to listen to him. It wasn't the first time a shrewd person had used this approach. He felt his charming smile falter.

"I'd like to explain—"

She held up her hand. "The discussion's over. You're apologizing."

Whether Caden said what he said next because he was frustrated or because it was true, his hands shook as he said it. "My father never lets me explain either."

Officer Levine and Tito came back at that moment. Obviously, they'd also had a frustrating conversation. Officer Levine patted Tito's shoulder, but Tito shrugged him off. Rosa walked out with Officer Levine to his patrol car.

Tito spun on Caden as soon as they were out the door. "What's your problem? My issues with Derek are none of Rosa's business, and definitely none of Officer Levine's.

Don't go telling them. Not cool, man. Not cool at all." He pointed at the door. "And what's with the matchmaking?"

"One," Caden said, serious and irritated. He raised a finger. "If Rosa knows the details of our interaction with Derek, she will understand my actions."

Suddenly, Tito seemed to be having a hard time staying angry. His twisted expression twitched and a laugh burst out.

Anger wasn't useful, but laughter wasn't appropriate either. "This conversation doesn't require giggling."

Finally, Tito calmed. He reached out and pushed Caden's finger down. "Don't use the middle one, bro."

Caden ignored him and pulled away. "Two," he continued and raised the middle finger plus one. "He's agreed to investigate the school."

"He didn't agree to investigate," Tito said.

"He'll investigate," Caden said. He tried to think back to the phrase Jenkins had used in the park. "No stone unturned."

"He won't tell us what he finds out."

"True," Caden said, "but he might rattle whoever is involved. If nothing else, Brynne with all her wicked ways makes for an excellent spy. We can ask her to snoop about. She would be thrilled to do so."

At her mention, Tito glanced around the room. "Where is Brynne?" he said.

Caden heard knocking upstairs, as if someone was

tapping their foot against the floor. He headed for the stairs and toward the direction of the sound, toward where he suspected he'd find Brynne. "Up to no good, no doubt," he said.

THE FUTURE ELITE PALADIN OF ASHEVILLE

The girls' bedroom was now unlocked, and Brynne was staying in it. The walls were sunny yellow, the ceiling was high, and the large window was framed with billowy curtains. A bunk bed was pushed against the side wall, and both the top and bottom beds were covered in pink and white quilts.

Brynne was hunched over a small desk. Her long dark hair hid the top. She turned when they walked in. "Did you discover anything about Jane?" she said.

She still looked like a sorceress, although her clothes were Ashevillian—dark jeans and a long silvery sweater. She'd thrown a steel-gray coat over the armchair. Surrounded by the rustic charm of the room she looked like a sleek dagger lost among the kitchen knives.

Suddenly, Caden's moss-green shirt felt scratchy. His

jeans seemed thin. He was certain Brynne's expensive-looking clothes came from the same market as his colorful yet cheap ones. "You've magicked yourself," he said.

Beside him, Tito was frowning, but he wasn't looking at Brynne and her magically enhanced clothing. He was staring at the walls like he expected to see another person in the room. Quietly, he said, "Mr. Rathis says Jane will be dead by the new moon."

Brynne looked alarmed. "So it is Rath Dunn who took her?"

Caden shook his head. "He claims he only knows something about who did." He inspected the room more closely. There wasn't much in it other than the furniture and Brynne's things. He ran his hand along the bed frame. There, carved in the wood, was another tree. Truly, it looked like the Walking Oak; and the room had a comforting feel. He pointed it out to Brynne.

"I saw it," she said. "And she is an enchantress. For answers, we need to find her."

Caden nodded. "There's more," he said. "Rath Dunn called Asheville the Land of Shadow and said the other twenty-four teachers are those banished like him."

Brynne drew her brows together and frowned. "This is no realm of eternal torture and death."

"Yet Rath Dunn is here." Caden continued and explained the events of the day—the encounter with Ms. Primrose and later with Rath Dunn. "Ms. Primrose controls him, and the other teachers, too, I think."

Brynne turned to Tito. "Could *she* have taken your Jane?" she said.

It was a good question, and Caden didn't know the answer. What type of being would make Rath Dunn teach children math? His reputation for malice was unequaled. Caden sat on the bottom bunk and sighed. The same type of being that would put witches in charge of school lunch, he supposed.

"She didn't seem interested in Jane's disappearance. I'd have thought a kidnapper would have behaved differently, but I don't know." Caden smoothed the pink quilt. "I don't know what she even is."

Brynne scrunched up her face. "Maybe she's a sorceress?"

"I don't think so." Caden shook his head. "You're a sorceress, and it's clear you do magic all the time. I didn't get that from her." Caden thought hard. "When she got irritated the room turned cold. She felt bigger than she looked. I don't think she's human."

Brynne stood and walked over to him. "But she looks human? She can take human form?" Her eyes grew wide with worry. "Maybe she's a swamp doppelgänger? Or a fright demon. Cold follows them."

"She smells of roses, not sulfur. She's not a swamp doppelgänger. And fright demons don't talk. She talks like a stern old lady and collects trinkets." He paused.

"Sometimes, I think she has silver and blue scales."

Brynne frowned. "So, maybe she's one of the lizard people?"

"The lizard people look like people-sized lizards. And they live near fire and flatlands."

Tito had been quiet, solemnly lurking around the room and staring at the bed, then the window, then the desk. Suddenly, he froze.

"Have you found something?" Caden said, and stood up.

Tito nodded. He reached behind the desk lamp and reverently pulled out a blue device Caden recognized as a cell phone.

"Oh," Brynne said, and she sounded proud. "That's mine."

Tito gaped. "Rosa let you get a phone?"

"Not exactly." Brynne picked up her coat and reached into pockets hidden within and pulled out two more cell phones. "I got three."

"Rosa let you get three?" Tito seemed to be growing rightly suspicious.

"Isn't it obvious?" Caden said with a sigh. "She stole them."

Brynne beamed and looked from Caden to Tito. "Indeed, and it was no easy feat. Your guardian is of strong mind and sharp eye. I swiped them from the market while she spoke to the shopkeeper."

Tito went still like he awaited a lashing. "Did you cast a spell on her?"

"I wouldn't do that to Rosa."

Tito motioned at Caden. "You did it to him."

She looked away for a second as if hit with a wave of guilt, but when she turned back she said, "He deserved it."

Tito looked pensive. "Yeah," he said, "I can see that."

Did they not understand what such a curse meant to someone like Caden? It could ruin his life. It could end it. He felt his face flush, and his musings on lizard people and powerful old women faded away. He clenched his fist at his side so as not to hit either of them.

With much control, he stood and turned to Tito. "Perhaps I should have pulled Brynne from the trap sooner, but I deserved no such curse. If Rath Dunn finds out . . ."

Caden shook the words away. Rath Dunn wouldn't find out. Then something else occurred to him that made his stomach churn and his heart sink. If the teachers were all villains, what would happen if any of them found out? Or Ms. Primrose? She seemed to like to keep villains as schoolteachers, and that didn't bode well for her morals.

He jabbed Brynne's shoulder. "You will find a way to break the curse."

For a moment, he thought she would again say it was impossible, or tell him she was about to break his jabbing finger. Instead, she held out one of the phones—the pink one—like a peace offering. "Of course, I will," she said with a dazzling smile. "Besides, I brought you a phone, prince. It's like a communication spell without all the blood and phoenix feathers." She pointed to one of the buttons. "Hit this one and you and I can talk."

Instead of taking the phone, he stepped back. "I know what it does."

"Take it," she said.

"It's stolen," he said.

Tito held up the blue phone and peered at it. "You have to pay to activate and use these."

"They're prepaid, peasant," she said.

Caden could stand no more. What did Brynne mean by "prepaid"? He waved his hands around the room to capture the extent of the strange land, strange people, and strange tech, to emphasize that Brynne was as much a foreigner as him. "What do you know of prepaid phones?"

"Bro, relax," Tito said. "You look like a helicopter."

Caden didn't know what a helicopter was but he was certain he looked nothing but regal and appropriate. Also, he would not relax. "No," he said, and pointed to Brynne. "Tell me how you know about these things."

She put her hand on her hip like she actually found him frustrating. "I'm starting to regret stealing you a phone, Caden." She attached her phone to a white cord and plugged it into the wall. "Listen," she said. "Sorcery takes study and training; understanding the tech of this world takes study and training. Sorcery takes inner power." She motioned to the wall outlet. "This technology requires outer power."

Caden saw little resemblance between the sorceress and the square phone. "You claim this tech is similar to your magic?"

"The tech is the magic of Asheville, and I'm good at magic." With a snotty tone, she added, "If you had any magic at all, you'd understand."

Caden couldn't do magic, but he had studied it. "I understand that magic drains, and you've cast a lot of spells lately."

Even the most practiced sorcerer or sorceress would fall if he or she used too much magic at once or without proper rest. He peered at his wicked friend for a moment. She'd set the mountain ablaze the night prior. Her spells to understand seemed to work well, but they weren't curses. He had no idea how often she had to cast them. Weekly? Daily? More than that? Under the beauty and attitude, she looked a bit thin, a bit frailer than usual.

"Don't overdo it," he ordered with all the authority that came with his birthright.

The words seemed to echo in the tall room. Her silvery eyes shone with outrage, but she said nothing. It was possible magic overuse already affected her.

"I mean it," Caden said. "You'll make yourself ill."

She looked down, tapped on her phone, and smoothed her sweater. When she finally finished fixing her perfect clothing—and she certainly should not be using magic to enhance her appearance—she'd mustered up enough indignation to project only that.

"If you don't want the phone, don't take it," she said. "If I need to contact you at school, I'll text Tito." With a shrug, she added, "You wouldn't be able to read it anyway."

Tito glanced between them, then at the phone in his hand. "You know, Brynne," he said, "Rosa's going to make you go to school, too."

"No one's going to make me do anything," she said, and gave Caden a piercing look to make sure he understood that included him.

Tito looked doubtful and stuck the stolen phone in his back pocket. "We'll be able to communicate better this way. The phones aren't ideal, bro, but they might help."

Caden did not take a phone. An Elite Paladin shouldn't condone stealing. An Elite Paladin's allies shouldn't include thieves. Above all else, Elite Paladins were honorable. He stomped out, slammed the door, and tried not to think about how disappointed his father would be with his choice of friends.

Annoyed, he went to search the house for a Korvan battle staff. He needed to practice and focus. He needed to lead Tito on the path of the Elite Paladin before he was further corrupted by Brynne. Soon, he suspected, she was going to try to teach Tito some magic. Yes, Tito's Paladin training needed to start right away. Rummaging in the kitchen pantry, he found a good-weighted broom.

The broom needed to be cleaned, but he took it to his attic room. He didn't even bother to remove the broom's bristles before he swung it around in battle formation four. When he'd worked his way up to formation eleven, Tito sulked into the room. He sat on his bed between his piles of books. "Hey, thanks," Tito said, and didn't sound grateful at all.

Caden paused. "For what?"

"Rosa spent the last hour telling me how striking and handsome I am."

"She believes that." Caden returned to his practice.

He was annoyed at Tito for taking the phone, and he missed his brothers and father. They'd know what to do in this situation. They'd know the honorable way to act. He turned away so he could see out the window and twirled the broom above his head. The mountain looked cold, the ice on the trees sharp. Jane had been kidnapped out there; she remained missing among the snow and dragons. She was an enchantress lost among villains.

"You know," Tito said, "Brynne said there's no way your father sent you on a quest alone."

Caden flipped the broom back into the air. Brynne knew nothing about Caden's father. She and Tito had no right to talk about him. He executed a forward strike with the broom and ran his pillow through. The pillow mushed in defeat. "She's wrong."

Tito made some small talk, but Caden ignored him.

Finally, he heard Tito sigh—a loud and exasperated sigh. "So," Tito said, and motioned to Caden as he performed attack formation eight, "you gonna teach me to do that or what?"

Caden felt some of his anger drain. Of course, he'd known that Tito would agree to train. He turned and nodded. "Your journey begins here," he said. "One day, you will become a great Elite Paladin."

"Uh-huh," Tito said. "Just teach me to twirl the broom."

He reached for it, but Caden pulled it away.

"I have to knight you first," Caden said. "Those who choose the path are given a title."

Tito scrunched up his face. "So you're a knight already? I thought that's why you wanted to slay dragons."

For one so smart, Tito could be quite dense. Caden spoke slowly. "I'm a prince. That's my title. The honor of Elite Paladin can only be earned." Caden readied the broom. "Now, kneel, peasant, so I may knight you."

Tito looked skeptical. "You're going to use that?"

"The police stole my sword," Caden said. Tito remained standing. He squinted at the bristly end of the broom. Caden was doing his best here. He raised the broom like a ceremonial sword. "Stop being fussy and let me proclaim you Sir Tito of Asheville."

"I'm not fussy, bro, you're fussy," Tito said.

Caden pointed to the floor. "Kneel," he said.

Tito glanced to the floor like it was a giant fanged

mucus slug. "You know," he said, "if you can use a broom to knight me, you can knight me while I'm standing up."

If Caden needed to practice with his gift of speech, this seemed the time. There were many reasons for Tito to kneel. But they only had four days. Chadwin couldn't be saved, but Jane could. Caden touched the broomstick to Tito's shoulder while Tito stood and looked uncomfortable. "You will make a noble Paladin," Caden said. "And for your first task on that path, we will save your Jane."

"Darn straight," Tito said. "And then we'll find out why you're stuck here."

With the broom's handle, Caden tapped Tito's left shoulder, then right. "We will, indeed"—Caden lifted his chin and smiled— "Sir Tito of Asheville."

18
THE TEACHER KEEPER

Caden awoke and dressed in his boots and training clothes—the sweatshirt Rosa loaned him and the worn pants and shirt Tito had given him. Out the window, the trees dripped with melting ice. The sun was rising into a cold, clear sky. He used the broom handle to poke Tito. "Time to train," he said.

Tito groaned and mumbled something that sounded like "No."

"You did it the other day."

"Rosa gave me today off. So." He turned over and pulled the covers over his head. "Sleep." Tito didn't move.

Caden poked him harder. "We must train."

With a huff, Tito sat up. His hair stuck out at odd angles. He threw off the covers and pointed at Caden with the exact middle finger he had advised Caden not to use.

They practiced fighting forms three and five before adjourning for breakfast. Rosa plunked a bowl of suspiciously round grain in front of Caden and patted Tito on the back like she was especially proud of him. "Eat your cereal," she said. "We leave in twenty."

Tito motioned to an empty chair at the kitchen table. "Where's Brynne?"

"Asleep," Rosa said.

"Not getting ready for school?"

"She's not feeling well." Rosa's tone was soft. It wasn't one Caden had ever imagined her using, and it wasn't one he suspected was used much by anyone with regard to Brynne. "The police can't find any record of her or her family. She needs to rest. I'll enroll her Monday. Now, hurry it up. I want you there on time," she said, and went outside to deice her truck.

Tito pointed his spoon toward the ceiling, milk dripping from the handle to the table. "Your sorceress won't get away with playing sick for long," he said. "Rosa will see straight through that soon enough."

Caden raised a brow. It was true. Brynne's deceptions were easy to discern. Caden glanced at the ceiling with a slight feeling of worry. Rosa seemed sincerely concerned. "There is another possibility."

"And what's that?"

Outside, the truck revved. Caden picked up his spoon and made a point of avoiding the floating grains as he spooned up milk. "Maybe the magic has finally gotten to her."

In Caden's first class, the mysterious voice in the computer taught him to read "cat," "hat," and "bat." Ward seemed to be playing a computer game. Tonya peered without blinking at her computer and mouthed words.

On the other side of the room, Mr. McDonald leaned back, entranced by another of his thick books. Caden cataloged his face, his mannerisms. Nothing about him seemed familiar. Caden didn't remember a portrait looking like Mr. McDonald in the Hall of Infamy, but many had been banished over the years, and not all the portraits were as impressive as Rath Dunn's.

Suddenly, music blared. Mr. McDonald jumped. His book fell to the ground and flopped open. To Caden's left, Tonya's eyes were wide behind her glasses. To his right, Ward scowled at Caden's backpack. Caden was confused. He took off his earmuffs and the music was even louder.

Ward pushed back his red earmuffs and said in his soft, strong voice, "Your backpack is ringing."

Mr. McDonald stomped over, stooping to pick up his book on the way, and said, "No cell phones."

Caden pulled his backpack to his lap. "I have no cell phone." The front pocket of his pack seemed to pulse with each music beat.

Mr. McDonald's snow-white hair glowed against the

ceiling lights. He reached into the front pocket of Caden's pack, pulled his brows into a deep furrow, and dragged out a pink-bejeweled cell phone. The music stopped.

Tonya looked as confused as Caden felt. Ward glanced at the phone with what seemed to be mild amusement. Mr. McDonald looked bothered.

"That's certainly not mine," Caden said.

"It's in your pack." He pointed to the phone. "This is your name in pink crystals."

"As I can't read or write, it's highly unlikely I put it there."

Mr. McDonald nodded like he could relate. "You've been framed," he said, and flipped the phone over. He squinted at the phone's display and handed it back. "Tell this Brynne to stop calling you at school, then report to Ms. Primrose for punishment."

"Punishment? I'm innocent; you've agreed to as much."

Mr. McDonald's shoulders sagged. "When has innocence ever mattered?"

"It always matters," Caden said.

Mr. McDonald pointed to the glittering letters. "Show her the phone and argue your case, you'll see it really doesn't."

In the long hall that led into the mountain, the phone again played music. The display flashed letters—"b" and "r" and "y" and others—and Caden had no doubts they spelled Brynne. Maybe his earlier concern for her was warranted? He pushed buttons on the shiny pink device until Brynne's voice filled the empty hall.

"I need to talk to you." She sounded quite healthy.

He should make sure, though. He held the phone in front of him, unsure of what to do. "Hello?"

"Push the green button and put it to your ear," she said.

Caden did as she said. "Are you well?"

"What? Yes, of course." Her voice no longer echoed down the hall. "I need—"

Caden didn't let her finish. Sometime in the night, she had snuck a stolen device into his possessions. He wanted to throw the phone across the hall. He told her how angry he was, how wrong her actions were. In the middle of his rant, the phone started playing music again. He pushed buttons until it stopped and put it to his ear.

"Don't make me hang up on you again," she said.

"I'm in trouble because of this phone," he said. "It rang out loud music in class!"

"I set it to vibrate." On the other end of the phone, she was quiet for a moment. Then she said, "You must have knocked it."

Brynne was so frustrating. "I didn't know I had it," he said. "Ms. Primrose won't be happy. Another note to Rosa is a real possibility."

"Oh. You've been sent to see Ms. Primrose?" She sounded nervous. "Are you with her now?"

He was tempted to say yes—if for no other reason than

to see what she would say—but he didn't. He glanced down the hall. It seemed to lead into shadow. "I'm alone," he said.

"Well, that's good," she said, and definitely didn't sound sick at all. She sounded sharp and well rested. "Look, I've been thinking about *her*, about Ms. Primrose," she said, and he heard her take a deep breath, "about what she might be."

"And?"

Brynne seemed to hesitate. "To control the villains of our world, she must have great power. She's no normal magical being. Maybe she's a being of legend—like the Elderkind, or maybe she's something of this world we've never encountered."

Perhaps she wasn't feeling well after all. Caden traced the sleeve of his coat and remembered the myths of the beginnings. "With the possible exception of the great Winterbird," he said, "the Elderkind don't exist. They're just stories to explain our world."

He heard Brynne huff. "The Ashevillians believe magic, gnomes, and the Greater Realm are myth. You, prince, are a hypocrite."

Caden was not a hypocrite. He was practical. "Why would a great and powerful being live here?" Truly, why would anyone pick quaint Asheville over the magnificent and magical lands of the Greater Realm?

"How should I know? Maybe she's a mystical being of this world?" Brynne said. "Does it matter? The villains behave. Rath Dunn behaves. She must have great power to make them do so, no swamp doppelgänger could manage that. The Elderkind could take human form."

"She appears like an old woman who smells of roses. She runs a school in a city of small mountains and limited magic. She's no being of legend."

"I fear you're wrong. And if she's one of the Elderkind, we need to figure out which one."

Caden leaned against the wall and considered. Could Ms. Primrose be an Elderkind? A being of great power. Well, she must be powerful to keep the villains in their teaching jobs.

Still, she was certainly no Winterbird. Despite the many trees carved into things, he immediately dismissed the idea she could be the Walking Oak as well. One, spring was said to follow the great tree. Two, unlike the others, the tree always was said to appear as a big talking tree. He doubted she was the Bloodwolf or Sunsnake either. They were protective and wise; they were said to have become one with the Greater Realm.

The Elderdragons, though, were known to be fickle. And Ms. Primrose had been strangely angered when he'd called the ice dragons, well, *dragons.*

Could Ms. Primrose truly be an Elderdragon?

Perhaps Brynne's opinions had merit, perhaps not. He peered at the flashing letters on the phone then brought it back to his ear. "Why didn't you tell me this morning?"

There was a pause. Then, "I was asleep."

That wasn't it, though. Something Brynne thought so important, she'd have told him immediately. "You've drained yourself," he said. "I knew you'd done too much."

"Just be careful," she said, and hung up.

As he trudged down the long corridor, Caden thought about dragons. Elderdragons of the myths, powerful and ancient, and also of lesser dragons like those he needed to slay. It was difficult to picture Ms. Primrose as an Elderdragon. But she did seem powerful.

He dismissed the idea she could be the protective Gold or the vicious Red Elderdragon. When they were rumored to take human form, they'd always been described as male. If she were any type of Elderdragon, she was the Silver or Blue. They were rumored to take the form of beautiful young women. Ms. Primrose wasn't so young, but those myths were also millennia old. It seemed more likely, however, she was something that actually existed.

At the corridor's end, the slick-looking secretary, Mr. Creedly, was half-hidden by his desk. He stood, unhurried, and uncurled his long limbs like a predator.

"Back so soon?" Mr. Creedly said, and looked happy in a cruel, terrible way. "Oh, but she's in a mood today."

If he and the rest of the school staff were villains, any of them might have taken Jane. Mr. Creedly smiled like a spider, and Caden moved him up on his list of suspicious people. He put him above Mr. McDonald, who seemed to believe himself unjustly here, but kept him below the lunch ladies and lunch man. He didn't trust the lunch witches—not with their geometric meats, their hungry expressions. Caden kept Rath Dunn at the top. It was wise to remember he'd once almost destroyed Razzon and Caden's family; he had threatened Sir Horace and wounded Caden with the dagger.

Mr. Creedly kept his chilling smile as he opened the door. Inside, Ms. Primrose stood beside her ornate desk. The rose pattern on her suit was dark purple on a dark background. Without careful inspection, the suit looked black.

She was frowning at one of her beads, turning it over in her hand like it was a thing of mystery and disgust. "Not right," she muttered, "not right at all." With a narrowing of her eyes and a shake of the head, she crushed it to fine dust.

Caden doubted if his second-oldest brother, Maden, gifted in strength, could have crushed it so completely. "You're stronger than you look," Caden said.

She turned and he could see the delicacy of her patience. "I thought we'd already established that. Why are you here?"

He glanced around her office. She did seem to like collecting things. That was dragonlike, though regular dragons spawned from dark magic tended to go with items of greater value. He tried his most charming smile as he held up his phone. "I've been framed," he said.

Her gaze traveled between his face and the bejeweled

phone, pausing for a moment on the pink crystalline letters. Soon, though, her appreciation for the shiny parts was replaced by an expression far too shrewd for Caden's comfort. "Framed by who?"

"A friend," Caden said.

"Dear," she said, "friends don't frame you."

"It's complicated."

"Is it? Give me the name of this friend."

He looked straight into her icy blue eyes. Was the color indicative of her identity? She was a punisher of students and villains. Could she be the Blue dragon, bringer of destruction? Her hair was silver, though, and she ran a school. If she was an Elderdragon, perhaps she was the Silver, who taught the Greater Realm magic and architecture. Truth be told, though, Caden was finding it hard to think of the powerful old woman as an ancient dragon of legend.

It was better to keep Brynne unknown and safe until they knew exactly what Ms. Primrose was. "It's no one you know," he said.

Obviously, it was someone she wanted to know. Her mouth thinned into a tight line. "Is that so? No matter," she said with a dismissive wave. "The rules are firm—no cell phones on campus, no exceptions. You'll have to face the consequences."

He clasped his hands in front and felt his skin itch with irritation. He was innocent. Whether dragon or not, she shouldn't punish him. "Will you send another note to Rosa?"

"Yes," she said, and tutted about like a prim old lady. "And you're also serving detention, dear."

Detention sounded worse. Caden envisioned the great prisons of the desert lands, cut into the sands, the time shaded from the hot suns varying from cell to cell, by the seriousness of each occupant's crime.

Ms. Primrose smiled her cold, polite smile. "Monday to Wednesday," she said. "Mr. Rathis will monitor."

"I'd prefer Mrs. Belle."

"Your preference is noted," she said, "and denied. Mr. Rathis is on detention duty. He volunteered. He'll oversee you."

An afternoon alone with Rath Dunn made the idea of the hot desert suns more appealing. Detention was a punishment given to more students than him. It didn't seem so bad. Truly, none of the punishments he'd earned in this land seemed that bad. However, Derek would also be in detention. With a local in the room, perhaps Rath Dunn would be less brazen. Somehow, it seemed unlikely. Still, he'd prefer not to be alone with his people's greatest enemy.

The phone on her desk rang. She looked at it as if she might crush it like she had the bead. "Since your little food-throwing spat, Derek's mother has been calling me nonstop." Her tone turned icy, her expression furious. "Dreadful woman."

He looked between her and the phone and was confused. "You control Rath Dunn and villains of great evil. You are as you choose, yet Derek's mother is a problem for you?" he said, and raised his brows. "I find that hard to believe. Can't you just make her stop?"

"No, I can't 'just make her stop.'"

Perhaps Caden should fear Derek's mother. "Is she more powerful than you?"

She looked at him as if he'd asked if the mountains were flat. "Certainly not," she said. For a moment, she was quiet. Then, through gritted teeth, she said, "She's a lawyer." She sat and took great care in opening her desk drawer and pulling out a purple detention form. She cleared her throat. "It's in her nature."

It sounded as if that were important. "It's in my nature to find those lost, protect those in danger," he said.

The room went silent. The air felt cold and damp like that of a cave. From the window, sun broke. Ms. Primrose's buttons, beads, and baubles shimmered. Her arm gleamed in the sunlight and, for the briefest moment, it looked iridescent with striking silver and blue scales. Her size remained unchanged, but Caden had the uncomfortable feeling he was in the presence of something huge.

Her gaze remained icy and the corner of her lip turned up. "Dear," she said, "you are one of the lost, one of those in danger—especially as you stand before me now."

19

SPEAKING IN TONGUES

aden felt small before her, even smaller than he did when he stood beside his father and his brothers. Facing her now was nothing like facing the ice dragons on the hill. If she were a dragon, the similarity was in name only. Her stare didn't waver, and Caden knew he best speak carefully.

Good Ashevillian words danced in his mind. Suddenly, he knew how to respond. He squared his shoulders. "I don't fear danger. I know where I am and what I seek. I'll complete my quest and—" He paused.

She narrowed her eyes and looked straight through him. "And you'll what?" she said as cold and inhuman as he'd heard her.

He kept his chin level. Don't call them dragons, Rath Dunn had said. Caden smiled. "And I'll slay a lizard."

Ms. Primrose blinked, once, and he realized he hadn't seen her do it before. Then, with an amused twitch of the face, she said, "Is that what you princes do these days? Slay lizards?"

"We rescue those taken and we protect those in need." He felt his confidence building. "The lizards prowl beyond the city limits. They attacked my horse, they put the locals in peril. Already, I fear for the mountain animals."

"The mountain animals?" she said. Her chair creaked as she leaned back. "Oh, my, but you do tickle me."

Caden's purpose, however, was not to tickle. It was to learn about Ms. Primrose and, if possible, find why he and Brynne were here and Jane Chan was missing. Caden remembered the respect Rath Dunn gave Ms. Primrose, the way he'd buttoned his coat in her presence. He might just be able to charm her into revealing what she was. "I owe you an apology," he said.

"Oh?"

"Never again will I confuse the vile beasts that terrorize the hills with one as proper, nice-smelling, and powerful as you."

"Is that so," she said, and tapped her fingers on the dark mahogany desktop. "Then, tell me, and consider your answer carefully, who is it you think I am?"

The word "dragon" tickled his tongue, but it felt more like a "what" than a "who," and he remained unsure if he was right. Anyway, he doubted that would impress her.

"I believe you are what you choose, and you choose to be a placement counselor and vice principal." He glanced around the spotless office. "You choose to be a collector of treasures."

She peered at him for a long minute. "And keeper of those banished and lost from other realms." As she said it, she looked so like one of his castle tutors—proper, unyielding, and unafraid to discipline a prince—that Caden was taken aback. She seemed so human at that point. She added, "Like your Mr. Rathis."

Rath Dunn wasn't his. "He's nothing of mine but an enemy."

"He's your math teacher," she said.

"Isn't that the same thing?" Caden placed his palms on her desk and leaned toward her. "He's Rath Dunn, the Crimsen demon of the Greater Realm. He's a danger to us all." He was a danger to all he encountered. "Including you."

At that she looked up. "You think he's a danger to me?"

"A terrible one."

For a second time, she blinked. "Oh my." She laughed and wiped her eyes. "I haven't had a delight like that in a while."

The old flowery woman was frustrating. He stood back and crossed his arms. "He most certainly plots against you. It's in his nature to conquer and destroy. He wants a vial of your perfume."

Her cold smile warmed further. "Does he, now?" she said.

"It's for no good reason. I'm certain."

"A danger, indeed," she said, and giggled. Then her manner turned strange, her eyes curious. "You are precious, aren't you?" Despite the meaning, her words had a harsh, guttural quality, and as simple as the statement was, it took a moment for him to understand.

His head pounded. "I'm going to save her," he said, but it felt like his tongue split as he spoke.

Her face went soft. "My ears have forgotten such sounds. For the second time, you've understood one of the forgotten tongues. With minimal harm, it seems. Even before they were forgotten, few could speak such powerful words, and no spell could be used to teach them.

Forgotten languages? Two? He thought back. The soft, musical words that hurt his head—those she'd spoken yesterday—that had been the first. The harsh tongue-splitting words she'd just said, that was the second. Could they really be in forgotten languages?

She collected trinkets and spoke tongues that hurt him to hear and speak. He considered those things and shifted on his feet. She seemed to be waiting for him to speak again. He kept to non–head splitting Ashevillian English. "It seems you know them quite well."

"And for that, and for being concerned for my safety and lifting my spirits"—she leaned forward and the silver of her hair shone—"I'm going to reward you. I do reward those who please me."

The words registered quickly and he did not hesitate to say what he wanted. "Tell me where to find Jane Chan."

"Oh, pish," she said, and still seemed amused. "Dear, there's no proof anyone took her. If there was proof, there would be consequences. Besides, you don't get to choose your reward."

Caden straightened back up and stood with his arms at his sides. Perhaps she wouldn't help him because she was the kidnapper after all? Perhaps she had Jane all along? Weren't there ancient beings that devoured girls and boys? Since she seemed pleased with him, he dared the question. "Did you take her, Ms. Primrose?"

She waved him off. "No, certainly not. Now enough of that. Do you want your reward or not?"

Caden thought saying no would insult her. "Yes, ma'am."

"Good choice," she said. She produced a key from around her neck, opened the desk drawer on the left, and like a librarian handling a rare book, pulled out a leather box. "Now, for giving me a giggle," she said, and held up a finger—although, he noted, not the middle one, "I will grant you aid. I will help you with your time here." She handed him the box.

It was heavy. It had to be a great weapon or charm. Despite himself, he felt excited. He opened it with shaking hands. A gift from an Elderdragon—or whatever she was—would be powerful. Inside, there was a stack of papers. The top page was filled with neat black type, as were the many pages below it. It looked like homework.

Ms. Primrose beamed. "It's a copy of my standard employee contract."

"I don't understand." He took it out of the box. Whatever reward he expected, the heavy paper contract wasn't it. A being capable of controlling the villains of the Greater Realm could produce a better reward than paperwork. If not missing Jane Chan, at least a gleaming sword or a protective ring. "I can't read this."

"That doesn't matter," she said, and sat back at her desk. "And perhaps it will give you incentive to learn."

Talking to her was somewhat like talking to a castle wind cat. Basic reasoning seemed lost, and his words seemed to blow around her without weight. He turned his attention to the contract. Whatever she was, whatever her nature, he did believe she meant the contract to help him in some way. "All your employees sign one of these?"

"In blue ink and life blood. I also have them notarized."

"In blue ink?" he said. He ran his thumb along the stack of papers and flipped through them. It was more than a hundred pages thick. He looked up at her. "What happens if an employee breaks his or her contract?"

She winked at him. "I gobble them up, dear."

Slowly, he picked up the thick stack of papers. Did she

jest? For the first time, it dawned on him. She was capable of killing. "Do you do that often?"

"Oh my," she said. "More than you'd think. I'm still short a gym teacher since my unfortunate dinner with Ms. Halliwell last month."

Caden remained still, unsure of what to think.

"Don't look at me like that," she said. "I was hungry, dear, and she was rude."

Like someone who says the exact wrong thing at the exact wrong time, the phone rang. A little green light flickered on its face. Ms. Primrose's good mood flickered. "The lawyer again," she said, and something in her voice sounded ravenous.

It was Caden's duty to protect commoners. That included ones he didn't like. "May I request you eat neither Derek nor his mother?" he said.

She shrugged in a noncommittal way. "I rarely eat locals. It's bad manners."

He tucked the thick papers into a large pocket hidden in his coat's front flap and gave her back the box. He spoke as calmly as possible. "Generally, I'm against eating people," he said.

"Well, if everyone is polite and does his or her job, you'll get your wish." She looked Caden up and down. "School is your job now."

His job was to protect the realm, become an Elite Paladin, and serve king and kingdom. His job was to find kidnapped and missing Jane Chan. When in the presence of those with more power, it was still important to stand one's ground. "I'm not one of your villains," Caden said. He patted the papers in his pocket. "I've signed no contract."

"Of course not," she said, and sounded sincere. "They're part of my prison; they're here for life. You're part of my youth program. As long as you get good grades, you won't be removed, and you'll be free to go in five years."

Caden planned to leave as soon as Brynne could magic them back. To Ms. Primrose, he said, "I see." He asked no details about how students were removed. He feared the answer would upset him. "Thank you for the favor," he said politely.

"Off you go," she said.

There would be time later to convince her he was neither one of her baubles nor her future food. It was more important that he keep his arguments inside. They needed to find Jane by Monday. It was Friday. For now, that had to come before the puzzle of Ms. Primrose. An Elite Paladin always prioritized.

20

THE EXPLODING DOOR

As science class ended, Caden dragged Tito into the hall beyond Mrs. Belle's earshot. Her bumbling manner and red nail polish likely hid a dark core. She was one of the banished. It seemed likely all the teachers were. Caden trusted none of them. In hushed tones, he told Tito about his morning phone call from Brynne, his visit to Ms. Primrose's office, and his encounter with the creepy secretary.

Tito leaned against a pale-pink locker and nodded. "Dude's creepy," he said. "Creepy Creedly."

"He's high on my list of suspected kidnappers."

"How long is that list?" Tito said. "It's no help if everyone is on it."

"No one can be ruled out. Not now. Anyone could be one of Ms. Primrose's prisoners cast out from the Greater Realm." Caden looked at his friend and kept his expression serious. "If it makes you feel better," he said, "you're at the bottom."

"You're at the top of my weirdo list."

Students for the next class began to file into the room. Ward and Tonya were in their midst, walking side by side like two small soldiers. With a nod, Caden tried to show his solidarity. They walked past him. He watched as they sat at two desks in the room's dead center—a strategic choice if ever Caden had seen one.

Tito nudged him toward the cafeteria. "Lunch."

Those of the first lunch group were back in their classrooms and tucked away. The students and teachers who had second lunch were in the cafeteria, devouring the lunch witches' questionable food. More important, Rath Dunn was in the cafeteria.

Even if Rath Dunn hadn't taken Jane, he knew enough about her disappearance to offer Caden help—should he choose to trust the villain and help him in return. Plus, the twenty-four other villains were in the cafeteria or in classes. The more he thought about the list of possible suspects, the more he feared Jane's fate.

Ms. Primrose, possible Elderdragon and speaker of forgotten tongues, didn't seem to care about Jane. Caden, however, did, and he would work to find her. He scanned the halls. "You go to lunch without me," he said. "There is something else I must do."

Tito fumbled with his backpack. "They'll notice."

"Not if you distract them."

They separated, and Caden hurried to the math room. The door was locked. This was unusual, as doors to class-rooms were never locked. He kicked it, pushed at it, but it didn't budge.

He pulled out his pink, bejeweled, stolen phone. Bringing even a legal version was against school rules. Ms. Primrose, however, had given it back to him when she'd given him the purple detention note. She must have known he might need to use it. He tapped the Brynne button.

"How do I get into a locked room?" he said.

"Hi to you, too," she said. There was a worried pause. "It's not Ms. Primrose's room, is it?"

"No."

"Oh, well, then you pick the lock, or, if you had any magic talent, I suppose you could just magic in and out, or—"

"I need to get in now."

Another pause. "Isn't patience one of the ten virtues of the Elite Paladins?"

Patience was a virtue he must practice, sure as he must practice his sword and his speech. Not today, though. "Patience in battle, not in door unlocking."

"So you say," she said, and laughed. "Actually, I have an idea. I'm going to try something I've been thinking about since acquiring the phones."

He didn't like the sound of that. "What?"

"Remote telekinesis."

"That sounds made up."

"Sorcery requires creativity. I'm going to unlock the door using the phone connection and a spell."

"So you did make that up," he said.

"Shush, prince," she said. "I'm concentrating."

He stood, looked left to right, and rocked on his feet. The door was a solid obstacle in front of him, the handle a sphere of unturning metal. "Nothing's happening."

"It's not like hitting something with a stick, Caden. It," she said, "takes skill."

He could almost hear her mind working over the phone. Five seconds later, the lock clicked open. Another second after that, the door went flying from its hinges. Caden dived to the gritty tiles. The door barreled past him. It slammed into the pink lockers of the opposite wall, exploded, and made a resounding boom.

"Did it work?" Brynne said, breathless and excited. "It sounded like it worked."

From every direction, Caden heard classroom doors opening. There was little time to hide and no place to run. He jumped to his feet.

"Wait," Brynne said. "It's not Rath Dunn's room? Because that would almost be as foolish as the dragon's room."

The pink lockers were crunched. The metal seams were

broken and sprouted torn textbooks. The splintered pieces from the door were impaled in the lockers.

"Caden?" she said.

He heard people coming from both directions. Soon the empty hall would be full of gawkers and investigators. He needed to find out what he could, then hide. "I must go," he said, and pushed the off button.

He bolted into the math classroom. Instantly, he felt a sting in his arm. The skin pulled against his stitches. Rath Dunn might have been at lunch, but his dagger was not.

There were no cabinets in the room. There was no closet. The only place to stow blood daggers and secrets was the desk in the front corner.

Caden crouched in front of it. The top was smooth and was supported by wooden pedestals, each with three drawers. Small pegs kept the pedestals off the dirty floor.

Caden tried the drawers. None would open. He considered calling Brynne back. She could remote telekinese them open. Of course, then the desk would explode, and that seemed both dangerous and beside the point.

From the hall, he heard the murmur of voices, the tap-tap of women's shoes. He had but one chance to get inside the desk before ducking for cover. His arm stung the most when closest to the bottom left drawer. With all his power, he kicked the bottom left drawer's lip. Like a slow-wheeled catapult, it rolled open.

The scent of roses tickled his nose. Outside, he heard

Ms. Primrose scoffing at the destroyed lockers. Caden crawled between the two wooden pedestals and peeked in the drawer.

The contents were tidy and few. The blood dagger lay on a white satin cloth, clean of Caden's—or anyone else's—blood. The image of the Bloodwolf—the symbol of Crimsen and the Autumnlands—was embroidered on the cloth's corner. Caden dared not touch such an evil blade.

Beside it lay two open glass vials and one sealed one. Caden picked up the sealed one. The cork was burned with the image of the wolf. In sharp-looking handwriting, it had been labeled in a language he could read, that of Crimsen, as "Tear of Elf." He set it back down and peeked at the empty ones. The second said "Magical Locks," and the third "Blood of Son."

Caden picked up the "Blood of Son" vial. Was that why Rath Dunn had so carefully saved the dagger? The vial was empty though. Perhaps Caden's blood wasn't strong enough. He was unsure how that made him feel. His blood should be plenty good for whatever reason. There was more noise from the hall. Quickly, he put the vial back.

As he did, he saw another empty vial. It was further back in the drawer, like it had rolled as the drawer had opened. It was labeled "Essence of Dragon." Caden was staring at it when he was startled by Ms. Primrose's irritated voice. "There you are!"

The empty vial slipped from his hand. It landed on the

satin cloth with a soft thud but didn't break. He held his breath.

"Mr. Creedly," he heard Ms. Primrose say, "did you hear me? Get these students back to class."

She was only talking to her assistant. She hadn't seen Caden. With a slow exhale, he propped his body and legs between the desk pedestals so he wouldn't be visible. Also, it kept him off the dirty floor.

"Oh my," he heard Ms. Primrose say. "Such a mess."

Charming as Caden could be, blowing a door off a classroom seemed an eatable offense. He stayed as quiet as the dead. The legends said the Elderdragons were powerful and fickle. Nothing said they were all knowing. There was no reason to believe she'd sensed his royal presence.

The next voice he heard wasn't one he expected. "Does this type of thing happen often?"

"Certainly not, Officer Levine," Ms. Primrose said. "Exploding doors are not a common occurrence at my school."

Caden heard Officer Levine moving around the room. "No other damage, though," he said. "The rest of the room looks untouched."

"I allowed you here to interview my faculty, nothing else." She tap-tapped around after him. "You're here to investigate the girl." She sounded furious. "Without any evidence she's more than a runaway, I might add."

"Your janitor says he saw a pink backpack in the cafeteria

Dumpster the day after Jane disappeared, thinks it might have been hers."

"You interviewed my janitor?"

"Yep."

Officer Levine's heavier boot-clad footsteps stopped in front of the desk, and it creaked and shifted under his weight as he sat on it. The open drawer slowly and silently rolled shut. Caden felt the soft click of the lock.

Officer Levine returned to pacing. "It looks like a bomb detonated. That's definitely police business."

The room grew cold; there was the sense of something powerful nearby. Ms. Primrose's voice was the sharpest ice. "If you say bomb, I'll get calls from parents. From the news station."

"Ms. Primrose," Officer Levine said in his calm, placating manner, "my job is to protect your school and your students. This may have been rudimentary and not very powerful, but it's still an explosive. And if someone's setting explosives, I need to stop them."

The chill crept from the room. The sense of something powerful dimmed. "It's in your nature. It's in your rights." It sounded like that irritated her beyond measure. "Fine, investigate what you will. But my people know better than to do anything to tarnish the reputation of my school. It's my prize jewel."

"Thing about people," Officer Levine said. "Knowing better doesn't always mean they do what they should."

From the door, the overly dramatic voice of Rath Dunn rang out. "What's happened?"

"Keep him out," Officer Levine said, and from the way he said it Officer Levine didn't like him. "Follow your lock-down procedure until my people are able to process the area."

Ms. Primrose's noisy shoes tapped, tapped, tapped back toward the hall. "Let the man do his job," she snapped. The room remained chilled. "Everyone, get where you need to be chop-chop." In the hallway, her footfalls faded.

Caden heard Officer Levine exhale as he paced around the room, stopped by the window, then the door. When he walked near the desk, he sighed. "You wanna come out now?"

21

ONE IS SILVER AND THE OTHER BLUE

Caden unfolded, lowered to the ground, and crawled from under the desk. His knees were covered in dirt and pencil shavings. "I'm innocent of this destruction," he said.

Officer Levine raised his brows. "You just happened to be hiding under the desk when the door blew off?"

"I took cover to avoid being blamed."

"Uh-huh?" Officer Levine inhaled, and his nostrils flared. With a shake of the head, he said, "Go wait in the hall with Jenkins for now."

"I don't want to wait in the hall."

Apparently, what Caden wanted mattered not. Jenkins stayed with him in the hall. "My sister won't stop talking about that horse you found," he said.

"I didn't find him. Sir Horace is a kindred soul."

"Well, she thinks your kindred soul is getting out of the stable and jumping the fence at night. Always comes back the next day, though."

This was nothing Caden didn't already know. "A Galvanian snow stallion cannot be fenced."

A moment later, Rath Dunn stalked around the corner. He looked surprised when he saw Caden. If Rath Dunn hadn't suspected him initially, he had suspicions now. "Caden," Rath Dunn said in a voice like daggers, "why are you outside my classroom?"

Caden wanted to ask him about the vials, demand to know their purpose, but perhaps it was better Rath Dunn not know Caden had found them. He stepped closer to Jenkins.

"Boss is driving him home in a few," Jenkins said.

It was a futile attempt to protect Caden. It was noble enough in its way, and Caden mustered some gratitude. For his part, Rath Dunn didn't acknowledge Jenkins at all. He kept his gaze locked on Caden.

"No matter," Rath Dunn said. "We'll have lots of time to talk during detention next week." With a cruel grin he turned his back and peered at the twisted lockers.

Jenkins moved toward him. "Sir," Jenkins said, "you need to leave."

Rath Dunn ignored him. He inspected the splintered pieces of door and the crushed lockers, and ran his finger along the sharp edge of the torn metal. "Powerful," he muttered.

He switched from his leisurely pace so quickly that neither Caden nor Jenkins had time to react. One moment he was looking at notepaper sprouting from pink metal, the next he was pushing Caden against the wall and hissing in his ear.

"This seems beyond your skill set," Rath Dunn said. "Very interesting, indeed."

Then he let go and was moving on. He slowed as he passed the broken door of his classroom and looked inside as if he was memorizing everything. After a moment, he walked down the hall and around the corner. His laughter echoed in the halls. Long after the fact, Jenkins put his hand on his weapon. His hair was frizzy like an odd red halo, his mouth contorted into a confused line. "What was that about, kid?"

This was not the time to explain interrealm travel to Jenkins. There might never be a time for that. Caden, however, would not lie. "He is enemy to my people," he said.

School was released early, and Officer Levine did drive Caden and Tito home. He stopped the car beside the metal sun sculpture. Brynne ran out from the house. As soon as she saw Caden, relief seemed to come over her in waves. Rosa followed her out.

While Rosa talked with Officer Levine, Caden, Tito, and Brynne huddled on the porch.

"You turned off your phone."

Yes, Caden had. He could learn this tech, too, but he'd

no time for idle talk. He told them about the vials in Rath Dunn's desk. He told them of Ms. Primrose and her office. He told them of the forgotten languages she claimed to have spoken.

As he spoke, Brynne's expression became more and more concerned. "Forgotten languages?" she said. "What's that mean?"

Truthfully, Caden didn't fully know. He crossed his arms. "Languages that hurt the head to hear and the tongue to speak. One sounded musical, the other abrasive."

"That sounds like the tongues of power, spoken by the Elderkind." She peered at Caden for a long while. "And you said Rath Dunn had a vial marked 'Essence of Dragon'?"

"Yes."

Tito, too, was frowning. He and Brynne looked at each other like their thoughts were aligned. Tito spoke first. "One of my foster mothers wore a perfume called 'essence of desire.'"

The perfume. That's why Rath Dunn wanted it. It was part of the ingredients he was collecting.

Brynne twisted her hands together. "She really is an Elderdragon, isn't she?" That realization had slowly been building in Caden's mind, too. And if that was the case, it was likely her perfume was a powerful spell component.

"Dude," Tito said, not seeming to realize the weight of this realization, "you're not slaying Ms. Primrose."

Caden frowned. "I doubt I could."

"Well, good. Then don't try it."

Brynne looked pale. She paced across the porch. "She could kill us all," she said.

When trying to save a stolen girl, one must expect to encounter anything, even enemies and Elderdragons. Caden considered Ms. Primrose's silver hair and iridescent skin. Like Rath Dunn, she hadn't killed them. "I'm certain she's the Silver."

The tension and worry in Brynne seemed to lessen slightly. The Silver Elderdragon was known for much more mercy than the vicious and chilling blue.

Caden looked out at the sculptures. Ms. Primrose did seem to want to eat someone. "Either the Silver or the Blue."

Brynne widened her eyes. "She can't be the Blue," she said, but Caden was unsure.

22

TIME IS SHORT

Brynne bit her lip and looked fearfully around. "The Blue? Are you certain?"

After a day of dragons and explosions and an aching arm, Caden found her response amusing. The dragon wasn't on the road or hiding in the woods. "She wants to meet you."

"What?" Brynne said. Her eyes narrowed and her cheeks turned red. "What did you tell her about me?"

Perhaps it was better to be kind. He set his hand on her shoulder. "Nothing," he said. "I told her nothing."

Caden was saved from Brynne's then-building wrath by Rosa. She came back to the porch while Officer Levine drove away, then gathered them around the small kitchen table. She stared at Caden for a moment. "You look pale."

"I'm fine."

Caden could have sworn that she did have magic of the mind, for she said, "Show me your arm."

"I already did," Caden said.

"Again," she said.

Reluctantly, he removed his coat. The large contract Ms. Primrose had given him hung heavily inside as he leaned it over his chair. The purple detention sheet crinkled from the other pocket. Rosa looked only at his wound. The color drained from her face. She grabbed a cloth, knelt next to him, and wrapped it around his arm.

He fidgeted away from her tending. He had no mother, and he didn't need one. "An Elite Paladin ignores his pain, he concentrates on his duty, he fights the—"

She held up her palm. "I want you to stop that."

"Stop what?"

"Stop Razzon. Keep your answers confined to this realm." She squinted at him and, after a moment of silence, she said, "I can see the appeal of a world of kings and magic. This world can be gut wrenching."

"In one of the lower kingdoms, the penalty for desertion is to be split open across the belly. That's gut wrenching."

"This realm of yours seems violent."

"Yet, you don't believe it exists," he said.

She gently taped the bandage. "I want you to face what's happening here and now." He let her fuss for a moment. His arm did feel better wrapped and tended. It occurred to him it was a good time to give her the detention slip. While she worried, perhaps she wouldn't get mad.

He reached for his coat and pulled out his detention slip and pink-bejeweled phone. "I need you to sign the form," he said. He smiled and pushed it and the phone to her. "Ms. Primrose was adamant."

Then again, maybe she would get mad. Rosa turned as red as an elvish firestone. She took the phone and seemed to scan through it. Brynne quietly left the kitchen. Tito started laughing.

Rosa turned her full military gaze at him. "Tell me, Tito," she said, "do you also have a phone?"

Tito stopped laughing. He, too, went pale. "I wouldn't swipe a phone, Rosa," he said.

"That's not what I asked, and you're listed in Caden's contacts," she said, and she said it quite astutely in Caden's royal opinion.

They were grounded yet again.

"I don't see how this is punishment," Caden said.

He rested back on his ugly pink and orange quilt. The attic room felt cozy, but it was difficult to get comfortable. Today was Friday. The new moon would rise Monday night. He released a breath and let the events of the day play through his mind.

Tito was also ill at ease. He huffed and turned into his pillow. "No computer, no TV, no phone."

"Brynne will steal the phones back. Lest you forget,

she's a thief and a magic user."

Tito seemed unpleased by that. He turned around enough to glare in Caden's general direction. "That's a bad idea. Rosa's already irked," he said. Tito flopped back on his bed. "Rosa's mad and we're one day closer to losing Jane for good. I shouldn't have taken that stupid phone."

Caden thought about Rath Dunn. He was connected to Jane's disappearance. Caden was almost certain. But how? And what was the purpose of the vials? "Rath Dunn is up to some evil plot. I'm sure of it."

"With the vials?"

"Maybe they're spell ingredients." Caden closed his eyes. Rath Dunn wanted Ms. Primrose's perfume—that was the essence of a dragon. He'd taken Caden's blood. It seemed it hadn't worked, but that partially explained the "Blood of Son." What about the "Magical Locks" and "Tears of Elf"?

Caden opened his eyes and looked at Tito. There was something he'd forgotten. "There's more. I heard Officer Levine speak to Ms. Primrose." He told Tito about the janitor and the backpack.

Tito was visibly troubled. "That sounds like Jane's pack."

"I know it's worrisome," Caden said. "She disappeared at night, no doubt snared in the magic sand trap of the mountain. Why would her backpack be disposed of at the school?"

"I was more concerned about what it means about Jane."

"We have until the new moon to find her."

"That's only three more days."

Caden held Tito's gaze. "We have the contract Ms. Primrose gave me—she meant it to help us in some way. Jane yet lives. We'll find her."

Tito leaned forward; his hair fell over his face. Bent and hunched, he looked as if he'd been punched in the gut. "She's been missing for over a week," he said. "If she's okay, why'd someone throw away her stuff?"

Caden worried over the conditions in which Jane was being kept. He didn't voice his worries to Tito. "We need to interview the janitor. Maybe he knows something more. According to Tonya, he's Ward's father, and he knows the teachers are villains."

At that, Tito shook his head. "The janitor's like seven feet tall and he doesn't speak to anyone, especially students."

Caden was confident he could get this janitor to speak, and what did the janitor being seven feet tall have to do with anything? Caden's second oldest brother, Maden, was over seven feet tall and Caden spoke to him all the time.

"He speaks some—he spoke to Officer Levine," Caden said.

"Like I said, I'll try anything." Tito sounded defeated and certain. "But we'd have better luck just asking Ward, and he doesn't talk either."

"Ward talks to me," Caden said. "He'll help us."

"Bro, he thinks you're nuts."

"Quiet!" Rosa yelled up.

Tito looked down at his hands like he was lost.

Caden's father often said, "A prince serves his people. A prince is compassionate." Caden needed to show compassion now. Tito needed it. "Rosa will not kick us out," Caden said. "Not for the phones."

Tito looked unsure. He glanced at his stacks of books and traced a finger along a purple thread on his ugly quilt. "Maybe, maybe not," he said.

Caden got up, crossed the taped line to Tito's messy side of the room, and sat beside him.

"What are you doing?" Tito leaned away. "You've got the same freaky look you had when you knighted me with the broom."

"My sword was taken," Caden snapped. He took a calming breath and placed a hand on Tito's shoulder. This was a serious matter. Proper decorum was important. "Dear foster brother," he began.

Tito groaned. "Whatever you're going to say, please don't."

Caden ignored him. "If we are kicked out, which is highly unlikely," he pointed out, "you may live in the woods and eat tubers with Sir Horace, Brynne, and me. After we find Jane, she may live with us as well."

Tito looked surprised, still somber, but surprised.

"I will show you how to build a shelter," Caden added. "It's a needed skill for an Elite Paladin."

"No offense," Tito said, and scooted away, "but I'm not living in a shelter in the woods and eating tubers. Neither is Jane. We're not rabbits. Go back to your side of the room. You're invading my personal space."

Caden knew of no rabbit that ate tubers, but perhaps Ashevillian rabbits weren't carnivorous. He stood back up. "You're picky like a rabbit," he said.

Tito's shoulders still slumped, his voice still sounded weary. Caden supposed he could sacrifice his food preferences to reassure his friend.

"Fine," Caden said. "If you do not wish to eat tubers, I suppose you could just eat rabbit. You must understand, though, it upsets Sir Horace when I hunt."

Tito blinked at him. Some of the heaviness weighing on him seemed to let up. "Bro," he said, "I don't believe for one minute you'd kill a rabbit."

"I've hunted with my father and brothers for years."

"So you're telling me, you've killed a rabbit?"

Truly, Caden was insulted. He was a soon-to-be Elite Paladin. He challenged dragons and despots. His goal was to slay a dragon—or lizard—or whatever he was to name the vile beasts. He didn't like hunting much when it involved the small and furry, but that was beside the point.

Caden crossed his arms. "I'm trained to survive."

"I bet you cried like a baby."

Caden went back to his clean side of the room. Tito was grumpy and irritating. If Tito wanted to eat rabbit, he would have to hunt for his own. He stretched and began his evening exercise regime. "Elite Paladins do not cry like babies," he said, and turned away. "They cry like men."

THE SORCERESS AND THE NAP

Caden dreamed of the Winter Castle, of his father and his brothers, of Chadwin alive and the world as it should be—draped in the dark blues and sparkling silvers and golds of Razzon. When he awoke all was wrong. His bed was small. The room smelled of dust, must, and wool. Even in the faint light his quilt was unmistakably orange and pink.

"Go back to sleep," Tito said.

For the briefest of moments, Caden wondered how Tito got to the Winter Castle. Then he pushed off the warmth of his quilt and sat straight up. He was not in his childhood room. He was in Asheville, land of the banished, and Tito was awake on the other side of the room. Caden's family was a realm away, and Chadwin was six months buried. He blinked and rubbed the ache for home from his face.

From Tito's side—across the tape barrier—came the sounds of swishing papers and the flashes of stray light beams. Sounds and flashes that had pulled Caden from his dreams of family and home.

He was about to ask Tito what he was doing, why Caden's sleep was being disturbed, but when he looked over he understood. Tito was propped up in his bed. His hair was pulled back from his face. He'd converted one of his book stacks into a makeshift desk; his flashlight was in his right hand lighting up the area, his blue pen in his left.

The contract was on top, split into a read pile and an unread pile. His red and green pens lay beside them in easy reach. Tito flipped through the pages with impressive speed and marked them like the pages in one of his school notebooks.

"What have you learned?" Caden said.

Tito paused, looked to the window, and twisted his mouth into a lopsided frown. "Nothing yet," he said.

Outside, the moon was a mere sliver. However, there was no reason to dwell on things they couldn't change. He and Tito had no control over the movement of time. Nor was there any reason for Caden to let his memories of home deter him from his duty. The empty sky of the new moon would come with or without them, as later would the half-moon and his curse. They had to concentrate on the most pressing matter—finding Jane, and finding her soon.

He shook off the homesickness and turned on the lamp

beside his bed. If Tito was to spend the night working, Caden would provide him with proper lighting. He shielded his eyes as it washed the slanted walls in a warm, yellow glow.

Tito grunted and flipped off his flashlight. He switched to his green pen, underlined some text, and set another page into the read stack.

"How can I help?" Caden said.

"By going back to sleep."

Although that was what he said, it wasn't what he meant. Caden narrowed his eyes and extracted himself from the bed. "You wish me to be silent."

"It's almost Saturday. We're running out of time and I need to concentrate. The only time you shut up is when you're sleeping."

"You say that as if I talk constantly."

Tito's response was a pointed look. He stared for a moment. "You look weird. Well, weirder. You okay?"

Caden's sadness must have shown on his face. He squared his shoulders and smiled. "Of course," he said. It was best he focus on the here and now. He reached under his bed. While Tito watched, his expression growing ever more suspicious, Caden hauled out spare sheets, towels, and fabric scraps he'd collected while exploring the house. "I, too, have things to do."

Already, he'd tied some of the sheets together. Once finished, the patchwork would make a fine escape rope. The knots needed to be unyielding, though, the braiding taut.

Tito directed his pen at the burgeoning escape rope as if it was something smelly. "What's that?" he said.

"We need to be able to sneak in and out of the room."

"Yeah, okay." Tito turned back to the contract. "I'm not climbing down that. If we need to leave, we can sneak out the front door."

"That would be expected." Caden tightened the first knot. "And we were caught coming back in that way."

With a derisive snort, Tito shook his head.

"You'll see I'm right," Caden said.

"Sure, whatever you say, your chattiness."

For a moment, they worked in silence. Caden, however, could not let his friend's veiled insult go unanswered. "I am not chatty," he said.

"No?" Tito didn't look up. "I still hear you."

"I'm defending my character."

Tito let loose an exasperated sigh. "If the moon was half full, I'd order you to shut it," he said.

"The moon is quite near the opposite, so you're out of luck."

Early the next morning, Rosa knocked on their door. Caden stuffed his escape rope beneath the bed. Tito covered the contract with his purple quilt.

She peeked inside. "You're awake, good," she said, and tossed Caden her army sweatshirt. "You've got cleaning to do."

Truly, they had no time for housework, but Rosa gave Caden no opportunity to argue. These were the punishments as so decreed by her, foster mother and house warden: Caden was to clean the bathrooms, Brynne the kitchen, and Tito the living area. There was to be no television, no computer, and no other like distractions.

Caden's brothers also remained in his thoughts. If they knew he was doing the work of servants, their ridicule would never end. He had more important tasks to complete. Before Rosa turned to the stairs, he found a break to speak. "My maids usually do that," he said.

Rosa turned and her face had hardened to iron. "Are you trying to aggravate me?"

Caden considered. "I suppose not."

"Stop it then," she said. "Be down in five. Brynne's already up." She closed the door, and he heard her stomp down the steps.

Tito walked over and, with surprising force, smacked Caden on the arm. Tito's eyes were rimmed red from overuse, and there were dark circles beneath as proof of how little he'd slept. "Just do what Rosa says," he said. "We need to get this done as quickly as possible."

Caden pulled the army sweatshirt over his head. "Royalty doesn't clean houses. That's the way it is."

"So? You like to clean. I saw you sweeping the room with the sparring broom, don't deny it," Tito said as he dressed into his dark sweat clothes with impressive efficiency.

Truly, if he could learn discipline, he would one day make a fine Paladin. "Look, it's better than being staked to the ground and left for the dogs to eat, isn't it? And she's leaving for the day. We'll plan after she's gone."

Tito had a point.

"You have a point," Caden said.

"Uh-huh," Tito said. On the top of the steps, he paused, his dark eyes concerned, his expression etched with sleeplessness and worry. "I finished reading it," he said.

Caden stopped and focused on him. "You found something?"

"Maybe," Tito said.

Downstairs, a disgruntled-looking Brynne waited for them. Her hair was pulled back like Tito's. She wore sparkly sweat clothes, purple sneakers, and the surly expression of a career criminal. For her part, Rosa was a quiet fury.

Rosa motioned them to stand by the sofa. They stayed at attention while she put buckets, mops, lemony smelling cleaners, and rags at their feet. "I expect it spotless." She set the full force of her gaze on Tito. "When I get back I will ask if any of my rules were broken. Understand?"

Tito looked down. The question seemed to worry him. "Yes, Rosa."

She placed a fond hand on Tito's shoulder and softened her voice. "The gallery closes at five. I'll be back soon after." She grabbed her keys and coat, and went outside to load her truck bed with welded metal sculptures.

They watched from the window as she revved the truck twice and carefully turned it onto the muddy road. Once the pickup was gone and its engine noise faded, Caden refocused on his friends. He motioned them to follow him into the kitchen. He poured three bowls of rounded, hollow grains, and handed out cut fruit. While they ate, he recounted what they knew. Sometimes connections were clearer in the morning. He hoped a clue to Jane's whereabouts would become evident.

Brynne just wanted to hear about the door. "Tell how it exploded again," she said, and looked quite pleased.

Tito, also, seemed to notice her happiness. "Look, Miss Destructive," he said, "it's not a good thing."

Her smile grew. "My spell did more than move a bolt," she explained. "That relieves me."

Caden looked at her disapprovingly. From her continued pallor and tired eyes, it also seemed to have drained her more than moving a bolt would have. She blew doors from hinges and set mountains afire. She'd cursed him for life by accident. Caden wished to reach out and shake her. "You need to learn control," he said instead. She would be no good to them comatose, and the new moon was closer and closer.

She waved him off and leaned over her grains to look at Tito. "What of the contract, Sir Tito?"

"It's long," Tito said with his mouth full of mush.

Neither worry nor fear seemed to dampen his hunger. "It's like reading a warranty, and there're rules for everything. Like everything. Eating, sleeping, what clothes to wear."

Brynne made a noise of disgust.

Tito nodded and wiped his mouth with his sleeve. Caden pushed a napkin his way. Tito looked at it, ignored it, and continued. "All employees have to live within two miles of the school. No one's allowed to leave the city limits without permission."

The sand trap was beyond city limits—not by much—but by enough. Ms. Primrose had called the city her territory. Was that why the ice dragons didn't enter the city? Could they sense her somehow? He swirled his spoon in his milk and grains. "How does one get permission?"

"With a formal, confidential request."

Out the window, the mountain looked cold. "We find who left the city limits, we find who set the trap. We find who set the trap, we find Jane."

"Yeah, easy breezy," Tito said gloomily. "It took about fifty pages to get to that." He reached in his sweatshirt and pulled out a crumpled white page of the contract. He'd written on the back in green pen and he read them his notes. "Also, they must follow the laws within the city, and show excellence in their discipline."

Caden frowned. "Who decides what excellence is?"

"Ms. Tiamathia Primrose," Tito said. He pulled out

another sheet and showed where she filled in her name in red-looping letters.

"I see," Caden said.

Brynne seemed to approve. "If she's an Elderdragon, I'd wager she'll honor the contract, too. If she doesn't care that Jane was taken, it's because whoever took Jane stayed in the bounds of his or her contract."

"They kidnapped her," Tito said.

"They took her outside the city limits." She reached over and thumped the paper. "They only have to follow the laws *within* the city. It says so."

"Except she's still missing. I'm pretty sure keeping her captive is illegal in and out of the city," Tito said.

"Then she's being kept outside the city limits," Caden said. "The teachers only have to obey the laws of the contract in Asheville proper."

"It would seem so," Brynne said, but her attention now appeared to be elsewhere. She peered for a long moment at Caden. Then she stared off into space, her expression full of wonder, as she slowly stirred her milk and grains. With a slow, careful manner, like she was tasting her words to see if she liked them, she said, "Ms. Primrose wanted to meet me?" she said. "I think perhaps I want to meet her, too."

"No," Caden said without hesitation. Truly, he wanted to shake her. Earlier, she'd wanted to hide from the Elderdragon. Now, she wanted to chat with her. "You meet her and she'll make you part of her youth program. You'll annoy her and she'll eat you. I think she's the Blue dragon."

"Or the Silver," Brynne said, and ran her fingers through her long hair. "And she didn't eat you." She glanced at Caden's expression and grinned. "Relax, prince, I wouldn't do anything to get eaten." Her smile was dazzling and mischievous. She reached into the pockets of her sweatshirt and pulled out a pink phone and a blue phone. "And, look," she said in an obvious yet effective change of subject, "I stole your phones back."

She said it as if it was a good thing, and maybe it was. They needed any advantage they could get. Communication was always helpful. Caden took the pink bejeweled phone. He was beginning to see the value in the devices.

Tito hesitated. He stood up and brushed crumbs from his pants. "I think you should put them back," he said.

"What?" She, too, stood. "No, I worked hard to get them. Rosa had them locked up in a safe box."

They bickered for a few minutes, but Caden paid them no mind. They seemed to be becoming friends. Brynne could be rash at times, but on the curses front, she'd learned her lesson, even if it was Caden who had paid the price. This new desire of hers to meet the dragon, however, made his stomach turn. He pushed away the rest of breakfast.

"All I care about is finding Jane," Tito was saying. If Brynne could annoy him, she would certainly annoy Ms. Primrose.

"Then take the phone," Brynne said back. "I put your name on it and everything."

True, Sir Tito's blue phone had sparkly blue letters. Caden recognized several of them—the *T*s and the *S* at the beginning. No doubt, they spelled Sir Tito. Brynne held it out to him. Tito put his hands in his pockets.

Caden stood up between them. He held his phone to the early light shining in the kitchen window. The pink letters sparkled. "Would the school janitor have one of these?" he said.

Brynne looked unsure.

Tito shrugged. "Most people have some sort of phone."

As Caden had thought. Good. "How do we contact him?"

"We need his number." Tito hesitated. His gaze still lingered on the sparkly blue phone. "We could find it on the computer, but Rosa's got it locked and she'll know if we try to get into it. She's got a sixth sense or something." He took his hands from his pockets. "I guess I can use the phone to get his number. We might get the network outside."

Caden placed a supportive hand on his friend's shoulder. "We need information, we need to communicate, and the sparkly stolen phone is useful," he said. "Take it."

With a slight shake of the head, and hesitant hand, Tito did as Caden told him. Tito rocked on his feet and glanced toward the driveway. "If Rosa finds out we have them again—"

"She won't," Brynne said, and stretched up like a cat. "I made certain."

Tito's sharp eyes darted to her. "What does that mean?"

"It means don't worry about it and go call the janitor," she said and walked into the living room. He and Tito followed. She plopped onto the sofa and curled into an attractive lump.

"After that, we're doing our chores," Tito said and fidgeted. "We're doing what Rosa tells us."

"I'm taking a nap," Brynne said.

"No," Tito said slowly. "You're cleaning the kitchen."

She'd closed her eyes but cracked one open in a lazy scowl. She looked haughty, a little like how Sir Horace looked when Caden tied him to a tree. "We'll see," she said. She sounded haughty, too, but Caden was mostly all right with it.

Tito, it seemed, wasn't. He twisted his mouth into his lopsided frown. Caden spoke first. "Let her rest while we call," he said. "She's still drained."

While she rested, Caden pulled Tito out to the porch. The sky was clear and blue, the air cold. Tito held his phone up. In a mere moment, he'd found the janitor's contact information. He turned his phone so Caden could see. "You call. You're the talker."

Caden pulled his pink phone from his pocket. Quite proudly, he punched the numbers into it and hit enter. "I've learned to work this tech."

"Yeah, you're a wizard," Tito said.

Nonsense. Caden frowned as they listened to the phone ring and ring. "If anyone is a wizard, it's Brynne."

"Just put it on speaker," Tito said.

On the fifteenth ring, someone picked up. "Hello."

The direct approach seemed best. "I must speak with the school janitor."

For a moment, there was no answer. Then, "Caden?"

There was a familiar terseness to the voice, a recognizable smoothness to the tone. Fortune smiled. Caden knew to whom he spoke. "Ward. Greetings, ally."

Ward said nothing.

"I need to speak with your father," Caden said.

There was a pause. Caden waited. Ward seemed to need time to think before answering. "Why?" Ward said finally.

Caden explained about Jane Chan and about Officer Levine's statement that the janitor had seen her things in the cafeteria Dumpster. He listed potential evildoers—Rath Dunn, the spidery secretary, the evil lunch people, the crazy science teacher, most everyone else.

"Pa's not here," Ward said. "He won't want to talk to you."

"I see," Caden said. It was the smallest of obstacles. While Caden was not gifted with resolution like his great father, he'd watched him enough to know the power of persistence. It would be easier if Caden could see Ward's expression, read his body language. He continued on sheer instinct. "Convince your father to speak with me. That's all I'm asking."

Even over the phone, Caden could tell Ward was thinking hard on it. He'd help if he thought the danger real, if he believed Caden could stop it. Perhaps Ward needed to be reminded of their school's reality.

"You know the teachers aren't as they seem. You know they're dangerous," Caden said. "If I'm wrong, the price is an awkward conversation for your father. If I'm right, the reward is a saved life."

Caden could tell by the way Ward exhaled into the phone that he was going to agree. "I'll ask him," Ward said unsurprisingly. Before hanging up, he added, "but he doesn't like you," which was much less expected.

As Caden had never met the janitor, he felt rightly insulted. He fidgeted on his feet, crossed his arms, and kicked at a plank. "He's never met me."

"Bro, not everybody's gonna like you."

Whether true or not, that did not explain why this janitor didn't like him. "I don't see why not."

"To tell you the truth," Tito said, "I only tolerate you."

Caden was halfway through mopping the kitchen floor when Tito skulked into the room. Dust was stuck in his hair. In his left hand he held the sparring broom. In his right, he had the dustpan. His shoulders were slumped. "Has Ward called back yet?"

"No."

Tito took a slow look around the kitchen. "So, you're

doing Brynne's chores?"

"I told you, she's drained."

"And that means what, exactly?"

Caden turned away and wiped down the counter. "It means she needs to rest."

"Bro, I swept her off and she didn't so much as blink." When Caden looked, Tito was smiling, but it seemed forced.

Caden played along. "You swept her with the broom?"

Tito brought out the phone he supposedly wanted only to save Jane. "I got a picture," he said. "It's my new screen saver." There on the phone was an image of Brynne, mouth open, eyes shut tightly, dustpan balanced on her head like a strange helmet.

"Show her that and she'll kill you," Caden said.

"Nah," Tito said. "We've got a no-kill, no-curse understanding." He pushed some buttons. "There, I sent her a copy for when she wakes up." He glanced back toward the living room and scrunched up his nose. "She's okay, right?"

Caden returned to the counters. "She blew up the door," he said. "Her energy was still low from setting the mountain on fire." With an irritated sweep of rag over Formica he added, "Low from cursing me for life. As long as she rests now, she'll be fine."

"And if she doesn't?"

The countertops were beginning to shine. Caden put down the rag. Brynne might have a no-kill, no-curse understanding with Tito, but she and Caden had no such pact.

Their relationship was more complex. "She'll get worse." He sighed. "Understand, I've known her since we were small. My father sometimes hired her parents. She and I would play in the Winter Castle gardens when her parents were on contract." Caden washed his hands. "When we were six, Goram assassins broke in and attacked. They killed my guards. Her nurse, too."

It was not a memory Caden liked to relive—the white snow shrubs splattered with blood, Caden's guard, Luna, pushing him and Brynne into the labyrinth as a poisoned arrow stuck through her breastplate, three Elite Paladins and Brynne's nurse all dead.

"Brynne screamed. They flew away from us and smashed against the garden wall," Caden said. "They didn't get back up."

"Like ever?"

Caden nodded. "Telekinesis magic. It's a rare spell for someone only six turns." He dried his hands and turned to Tito. "After, her eyes rolled back and her body convulsed. By the time the guards got to us, she'd stopped shaking, but she didn't wake up for a long time."

"And you think that will happen again if she gets worn out?" Tito said.

Tito was a friend to him and to Brynne. One day, she might need Tito's help. Caden lowered his voice. "It's happened already. Powerful magic pulled us here, toward the spell's caster, but Brynne deflected us. She collapsed right after. I fear she may again be drained and not telling us."

"That's stupid," Tito said.

Caden disagreed. "In the Greater Realm, it is unwise to show weakness."

"If Brynne's having secret seizures or passing out, she needs to tell Rosa."

"That's not our decision," Caden said. "That's hers."

As the day progressed, Tito seemed to be having a harder and harder time keeping still. He kept looking to the sky and watching the sun pass the time like it made his heart hurt. He kept asking Caden to check his phone.

Rosa returned at exactly half past five when the sun was low and the mountains cast long shadows. She inspected the bathrooms, the kitchen, the living area, then set her keys on the table and her coat over a chair. "Everything looks good."

"We've cleaned as instructed," Caden said.

Rosa raised an eyebrow and looked from him to Brynne and Tito. "No rules broken?"

Tito looked down. His hand twitched near the pocket that contained his sparkly blue phone. For a moment, Caden feared Tito would tell their secrets, but he stayed quiet.

Rosa watched Tito rock on his feet and Brynne fidget. "Go run the mountain before it gets dark. You can burn off some of that restless energy."

Tito nodded. Brynne scrunched her nose. Caden

clapped happily. Running would help them think. If Ward didn't call back soon, they'd need to track him to his home. Rosa checked that they had on warm enough clothing and guided them outside. "Twenty minutes up, twenty down," she said. "Stay together." From the porch, she watched with her feet planted a short distance apart, her arms crossed, and her expression hard.

Near the beginning of the trees, Caden saw the unmistakable hoofprints of Sir Horace. He'd visited in the night. The prints were at the bottom of the hill and led back toward town. As long as Sir Horace continued to stay within the city limits, he'd be safe. He was back at his horse prison eating apples by now. No doubt, he'd return to Caden come nightfall. Caden made a mental note to leave him treats and instruct him to keep to town. Then he sprinted up the mountain.

The rush of the race made his blood pump and his muscles burn. Above him, the sky was the deep blue of thick ice. The ground was crunchy under his boots, a combination of melting ice and wet earth. The air smelled of cedars. With each breath, his lungs stung from the cold.

He stopped halfway up near the orange tape that marked the edge of Rosa's property and the city limits. He sat on a fallen log and waited for Tito and Brynne. They arrived minutes later. From their leisurely pace and unwinded look, they'd not run as fast as they could have run.

"Elite Paladins must always push themselves, Sir Tito."

"Look," Tito said and collapsed on the log beside him. "I practiced with that stupid broom last night," he said, "and I did some of your weird exercises this afternoon. That'll have to be good enough."

Brynne sat cross-legged on Caden's other side. "I'm going to teach him magic," she said. "It's more fun."

"Tito is on the path to being a—" Caden didn't get the chance to finish. With no warning, his pocket began to buzz. He pulled his phone from it, tossed the phone to the crunchy ground, and jumped away. The phone quaked— shaking and bumping like it was a dying crater wasp.

Tito and Brynne just watched. The phone continued to buzz. If there were any animals Caden truly disliked, they were wasps. Always, they stung him. "What new mischief is this?"

Carefully, Tito reached down and grabbed the phone. "Dude, it's set to vibrate. It's just a text."

With caution, Caden returned to his spot.

Tito showed him the message. "Ward says his dad will meet you Monday before class."

"Ward knows I don't read," Caden said.

"I could cast a spell on you," Brynne said.

He scowled at her. "I'll learn on my own."

"You're just making it harder for yourself. Am I not right, Sir Tito?"

Tito shrugged, either not caring or too smart to answer, and typed into Caden's phone. He paused, frowned, then typed some more. "Ward says Monday morning, no sooner." He looked up. "That's the last day we have to save Jane. We're cutting it too close—we have to see him sooner."

There was a reason patience was one of the ten virtues of the Elite Paladins. In battle, in rescue, in all things noble, waiting was often necessary. They couldn't make anyone else hurry. Caden put his hand on Tito's shoulder. "If we push, I fear he'll back out," he said.

Tito visibly swallowed. "Yeah," he said. With a slump of his shoulders, he stood up and returned the phone to Caden. "I just hope that's soon enough."

Brynne also stood. She put her arm around Tito's shoulder. "It will be," she said. Then she beamed at Caden. "Caden's gifts are great. He can make almost anyone talk."

Tito nodded. "And no one can make him stop," he said.

"You aren't funny," Caden said.

"You do talk a lot," Brynne said as if it was a revelation. Suddenly, she got quiet and her cheeks became rosy. She twisted her hands together. "I like that though."

Caden felt his own cheeks heat. Before he could respond, Rosa's voice echoed from below, calling them to return to the house.

Brynne fidgeted like she was embarrassed. "Best we go back," she said. Then she turned and ran down the path.

Tito patted Caden on the shoulder. "Now I see why you cleaned the kitchen for her. Nice." He sprinted after her.

Caden stood on the hillside a minute longer. He took

a few breaths of the cold air to cool his cheeks and calm his mind. He felt they were close to finding Jane; he felt his father would be proud of that. Then he ran, dodging branches and jumping roots, to race down the mountain to the house.

24

THE REPENTANT LIAR

The next day, Sunday, sped along way too fast. It was a blur of housework and training. Tito was quick to learn fighting stances and attacks. He didn't seem to need the endless practice that Caden had needed. Like Caden's brothers, Tito had natural ability, and the clear skies and bright sun gave them hope. Sparring with broom and mop, however, was not the same as the clink of metal on metal from the sharp blades of swords or the thump, thump of sturdy Korvan battle staffs.

By Monday morning the hope and clear skies of the weekend had given way to anxiety and heavy clouds. It was difficult to tell dawn from day. Caden stood on the porch and looked at the sky.

"A bad omen," Brynne said.

She was dressed in jeans and a fuzzy white sweater. Her coat was the color of pressed steel and fitted to her. Everything she wore looked rich, yet her clothes came from the same sale racks as the too-long jeans and too-big turquoise sweater he wore. It was a frivolous waste of magic.

"You should save your energy for something other than fashion," he said, and pulled on his magical coat to hide his hideous sweater. The day would be cold and dark; at dusk the sun would set. The new moon would rise into a dark sky. "We must find her today, bad omens or not."

Brynne nodded and adjusted a pack on her back.

Caden pointed at it. "Why do you have that?"

"I start school today."

Caden clenched his jaw and looked away. "That will complicate things."

"You need me, prince."

Caden didn't deny it. She was vital to saving Jane. "We need you alive and well. We need you to prepare while we're at school."

She put her hands on her hips and narrowed her silvery eyes. "I'm not going to sit at home and do nothing. Not when there are Elderdragons to meet."

Caden couldn't believe what she was saying. "You were terrified of Ms. Primrose not three days ago. And we still don't know if she's the legendary Silver dragon or the infamous Blue."

"She must be the Silver. She runs a school," Brynne said.

"Where the teachers are villains."

"Who teach math, science, and reading," Brynne said. "They haven't ripped you apart. Certainly, they must want to. Most people do."

Caden resisted the urge to rub his bandaged arm. "Tomorrow," he said. "Stay out one day more, that's all I ask. You're our unknown advantage. Gather supplies, prepare for the fight. With luck, the janitor will know where Jane is." He hesitated. "And I need you to bust Sir Horace from his cell."

Brynne scrunched her nose at the mention of Sir Horace. "That beast can jump the fence."

"He still needs to be summoned," he said. "Please."

With a huff, she pulled off the pack. "Rosa wants me to go. What do you want me to do, put her under a spell?"

That's when Caden felt inspiration. He felt the tingling feeling of accomplishing two things at once. "Tell her of the shaking," he said. Using a weakness to an advantage was different than showing it accidentally. "Use it to get your way."

Brynne looked scandalized. She glanced left and right as if to make sure no one had heard. "No."

Caden looked straight into her silvery eyes. "You live here, Rosa will likely find out." He nodded back to the house. "And I doubt Tito will keep it quiet for long. He thinks you should tell her. He thinks she can help you."

"Tito knows?"

"He needed to know. Perhaps Rosa does also."

Brynne's embarrassment and anger zeroed in on the closest target—Caden. "I can't believe you told Tito," she hissed, and stomped inside. "You just wait until the half-moon, prince."

That angered Caden. She should be working at removing the curse, not using it to threaten him. "Do as I say, sorceress, or I'll tell her myself."

Brynne slammed the door. During a tense breakfast, however, she did take Rosa aside for a talk, and Rosa hugged her tightly afterward. When it was time for school, Rosa told Brynne she could stay home another day.

"How'd you work that one?" Tito said, after he and Caden were dropped at school.

The grass on the lawn was stiff from the cold and crunched as they walked. Before them, the school looked like a gray castle in front of a dark mountain in front of a stormy sky. It looked like the home of a dragon.

Caden stepped onto the sidewalk. "I told her to tell Rosa about the shaking."

Tito looked relieved but only for a minute. He reached in his pocket and pulled out his phone. "She says she'll get the beast? What does that mean?"

"It means she'll collect Sir Horace. If we need to cover distance, he'll be essential." First, though, they needed to find where Jane was hidden. He surveyed the steps leading to the school. "Where am I to meet this janitor?"

"Behind the gym."

"After, we meet in the boys' restroom."

Tito looked to the dark sky and nodded. "Right," he said.

For as small as Ward was, the janitor, his father, was the opposite. He was as tall and sturdy as Caden's second oldest brother, Maden. He clutched a plastic bucket of sawdust and within his grip it looked deadly. His hair was braided and he wore a blue jumpsuit.

When he spoke, his voice was deep and soft. "What do you want?"

Caden wanted many things. He wanted to slay a dragon. He wanted to return home and have his father be proud of him. More than anything, he wanted Chadwin to be alive. Right now, though, he just wanted to save someone. "To find Jane Chan."

"Is that it?" the janitor said. His voice was the type that belonged to a commander of armies. "I think you seek honor, you seek fame and fortune." He shook his head. "Leave the girl for the police, boy."

As he moved, underneath his sleeve, Caden glimpsed the colorful tattoo of the great Sunsnake—the markings of the Summerlands' desert people. He stepped back and peered up at the man. He was like the others, then—a villain banished from the Greater Realm and collected by Ms. Primrose for her school.

Ambassadors from the desert peoples were rare in Razzon, but Caden's father, King Axel, welcomed them. His father traded weapons and wares for their books and their knowledge. Their battle strategies were unequaled.

Though limited, Caden had had enough contact to speak their flowing tongue. He used it now. "You're of the desert peoples," he said. Caden studied the janitor's face, his tattoos. This man had been a villain. "You're like the others. You were banished."

The janitor peered at Caden and answered in English. "Long before your time." He swept a hand out to encompass the area. "Most people who fall from there to here, she eats. Those she likes, she lets teach. The teachers and staff you see are a wretched bunch. I was one of them. Given an undeserved gift, but through it, I've seen the error of who I was." He looked down like he was ashamed. "My life is one of penance now."

Hearing his words, Caden spoke softly. "If you seek penance, find it by helping me find Jane Chan."

He shook his head. "What I seek will never be in my reach. So I work and humbly accept the gift of my prison. I can't be involved beyond my job and my son. I can't trust myself." He turned as if to leave. "These police are good men, capable men. Let them find the girl."

They had so little time. Caden had to be bolder. If the janitor sought redemption, better he work for it than hide behind his cleaning bucket. "Good, capable men of this land won't find her. I will. She was stolen by dark magic. I know of magic; they don't. And her life will end by tonight's new moon if I don't find her. The villain of the math room told me so."

The janitor flicked his gaze to the building, somewhere in the direction of the math room and Rath Dunn, and his frown deepened. He clutched the bucket and it made a crumpling noise. When he spoke again, his voice was softer. "You're a child, and a foolish one at that, to trust one like him."

"I don't trust him," Caden said. "But I think he knows who took her. Don't make me bargain with him for her life."

The janitor turned back to Caden, blocking the sky, a crumbling tower of a man. "My life is one of quiet reflection and simple work. I don't get involved."

If this man had done such bad deeds as to be banished, if he'd learned such guilt as to be sorry, he should help. "You told Officer Levine you saw her things. You are involved."

He looked as sad as someone so large and seemingly dangerous could. "I lied, child."

The statement was so casual, so easy, that Caden stepped back. In Razzon, honesty was upheld. Caden's father and brothers, the men and women of the Elite Guard, all lived and died by their words. So did the peoples of the neighboring kingdoms. Even Brynne's people with their twisting speech, their thieving, and their mischief were mostly truthful about it. People of the Greater Realm told the truth. People of the Greater Realm held lies as heavy, serious things.

"You're surprised," the janitor said. "You can imagine how it served me, the only liar in a world of truth tellers." He looked to the side with an expression of pure shame, "and even now, humbled and aware of my atrocities, when I try to help, I return to my sordid ways."

"I don't understand."

"I want the girl found, so I lied about her backpack."

"How does your lie help find her?"

"Hearing my story, a good policeman would eventually question the cafeteria staff. I saw them watching her days before she disappeared." He bent down to pick trash from the ground. "Be careful," he said. "They devour youth and suck life force. That is what they want to steal from Jane."

When Caden arrived at the boys' restroom, Tito wasn't there. In his place was a stern, somewhat hungry looking Ms. Primrose. Her suit was printed with white and black lilies, and she looked out of place beside the urinals. "Why aren't you in class, dear?"

Caden kept her in his sight as he glanced under the stall doors. "I'm trying to save a life. Where's Tito?"

"I sent him to English. I like you well enough, but he's one of my shining stars. His grades better not drop because of you."

Caden turned to her. She definitely looked hungry. "Ms.

Primrose," he said, and used all the respect he could muster. "I believe I know who took Jane. The lunch witches—"

Before he could finish, she waggled her finger at him. "You must go to class. You need to do your job, and your job is school. My tolerance of you has its limits."

Though small and old, she somehow seemed to fill the bathroom. He felt as if they were crammed inside, him and the massive thing that she was. Though she stood several paces away, he felt her cold breath near his cheek, and worried that unseen teeth were close to his flesh. Against the tiled walls, her shadow looked a shocking blue color.

Caden felt his heart flutter and his stomach turn. The Blue dragon was said to be ravenous. "Will you eat me if I miss class? Even if I do so to save a lost girl?"

In the dull bathroom lights, her skin started to take on the same bluish tint as her shadow. "Oh my, but you can be blunt. Yes, I will." Her hunger seemed to flare; her anger, too. "Like my teachers, you can do what's in your nature. Search for all the missing girls you want." The room grew colder. "But do not miss class. And if you think someone here took Jane Chan, you best prove it. First it's Mr. Rathis, now it's the lunch witches. Your baseless accusations on the matter are making me cranky. I get hungry when I'm cranky."

"I see."

"And don't embarrass my school."

It seemed the school and her collections were all she

cared about. "I won't," he said cautiously. He added one more thing because he thought it important. "If I find Jane and unmask her kidnappers, it will be they who bring shame upon the school and I who bring it honor." He forced a polite smile. "Not only that, but if my suspicions are correct, they are greater in number than me. They would make a much better dinner."

Ms. Primrose took his arm and walked him out and toward the computer room. Her skin felt like smooth, soft hide. Her shoes tip-tapped on the tiles. "Well, you do amuse me," she said. "I'd prefer to eat someone less interesting."

"I'd prefer you eat fruit."

"Fruit gives me gas, dear," she said. "But, Caden?"

"Yes?" Caden turned back around.

"If you are wrong in your accusations, it won't matter to me if you are interesting or not."

It wasn't until science that Caden got to speak to Tito. Tito's relief was palpable when Caden scooted into the desk beside him. "Ms. Primrose bust you, too?" Tito said.

"She's hungry."

Tito looked like he was in shock, like he was beginning to truly understand that there was a dragon at this school, and she was collecting villains like baubles. "Yeah, she told me if my grades fell, she'd eat you."

"That's hardly fair."

"Yeah." Tito nodded. "And she'll eat us both if we skip

class. Bro, her stomach was rumbling." He held his green pen and flicked it back and forth, back and forth. "I don't think we can get out of here before the end of the day."

For Caden, though, the final bell would not mean freedom, not today. Today was Monday. "I have detention this afternoon."

"Dude, if Rathis is right, we have to find Jane before moonrise tonight," Tito said. Though he acted mostly normal, Tito's fears were beginning to show more and more. His voice had an edge. He kept flicking the green pen back and forth. "Get out of detention," Tito said.

"I can't," Caden said. He took a deep breath and squared his shoulders. "But I know who has her. We just need to find out where." He explained the janitor's statement about the lunch witches, and hoped the janitor was right.

Tito took it as truth. At lunch, he stood in front of the mashed food tray and demanded to know where Jane was. "Where is she, Ms. Jackson?"

Ms. Jackson, her smile radiant, her skin glowing, laughed. "Brother, Sister," she called. Decrepit Ms. Aggie and Mr. Andre shuffled over. "Tito is looking for someone. Who was it?"

"Jane." The fury in his voice was startling.

From behind Ms. Jackson, Ms. Aggie let loose a low cackle. "No need for anger," Ms. Aggie said.

Mr. Andre clattered the bread tray against the counter and smacked his lips. "No need at all," he echoed.

Ms. Jackson offered Tito an extra large scoop of food. "Don't make a scene, Tito," she said, and grinned. "We'd hate to have to report you to the vice principal."

Their guilt seemed as thick as their stew. Caden had to drag Tito away then; he had to spend the rest of the lunch talking him down while other students insulted their brotherhood and Caden's sweater. The lunch witches weren't going to talk. They had no reason to do so. None. They'd taken Jane without conscience or caring. They wouldn't give her up now.

"Look," Tito said, "instead of using your talky, talky on *me*, why don't you go back and get them to spill."

"I can't make someone do or say something. I'm just good at getting my way. Their silence benefits them too much. There is nothing to be said."

"And what? We're supposed to just let her die?"

"No," Caden said. "Find out where the lunch witches live, how they have permission to leave the city. It may help us find Jane."

Tito stirred his potatoes. His new hatred for the lunch witches didn't seem to translate to their food. He contemplated his carrots. "The cafeteria's all organic. They get food from local farmers."

"Where are the farms?"

Tito swirled his spoon in a big circle. "All around. Some are outside the city limits, I'm sure." Suddenly, he dropped the spoon and it made a startling clink. "How are we going to find her by tonight?"

Caden nodded toward the teachers' table. "We have another source of information."

Tito's eyes followed his.

"Do you think Mr. Rathis was telling the truth? He knows where she is?"

"I do," Caden said, and his stomach turned at the words. "I'll go to him. We've no other option."

25

THE ELF'S TEARS

Detention was held in the math classroom. Caden sat in the middle front desk—Jane Chan's old desk. She'd etched a tree into this one as well. For his part, Rath Dunn was gleeful that Caden wanted to deal. "Let us come to terms, son of Axel."

Caden feared the wolfish smile on Rath Dunn's face, the amused sound of his words. Whatever Rath Dunn asked for, it would come at greater costs to Caden than charming a dragon. Caden thought back to the strange vials in Rath Dunn's desk. The only thing Caden thought they could be were ingredients for a spell. Perhaps Brynne could figure it out. Magic could be strange at times.

Caden looked up at Rath Dunn. "What are your terms?"

"Well, well, well. What do I want? I still need that perfume. And I'm quite curious about your brothers. About

Chadwin, in particular."

The name spoken aloud was a worse sting than the blood dagger. Caden was assaulted by memories. Chadwin happy. Chadwin laughing. Chadwin lying still with a dark blade sticking from his back.

His fears were replaced with hot anger, and he pounded the desk with his fist. "My brothers are none of your concern, tyrant."

Derek, who had been successfully ignoring them to this point, looked up from his notebook. His mouth hung open. His pencil was gripped tight in his hand.

In front of Caden, Rath Dunn had gone still. He looked ready to strike out. For a moment, Caden feared he would do just that, but Rath Dunn was not one to do anything rashly. With jaw tight, he straightened to standing. "Watch your manners, prince," he said. "If you don't want to tell me about dear Chadwin, you can get me the perfume. Or just let the little enchantress die. I'm giving you lots of options here. The choice is yours, but time is ticking by."

As Caden considered, he knew he couldn't aid the infamous villain in the creation of any spell, and trying to charm Ms. Primrose when she was so hungry seemed foolish. But telling Rath Dunn anything current about his family and their tragedy felt like a betrayal. Caden's stomach felt heavy and his chest tight. Rath Dunn was an entire realm away from Caden's family. The danger to Jane Chan was near, was soon.

"Have you made your choice?"

Caden looked down at his desk. He looked back up and squared his shoulders. "What do you want to know about Chadwin?"

Rath Dunn stalked in front of him. He placed his palms on the desk and leaned into Caden's space. Likely remembering Caden's flinch at the name, he said, "Chadwin's dead, isn't he."

Caden's throat felt tight. He nodded.

"Tell me how and who and when." He leaned in close and grinned. "I want details. And, in exchange, I'll tell you who took Jane."

The room was silent. Caden could hear the rain falling outside; some of it hit the window with a clink. Soon it would turn to ice and snow. Caden didn't want to speak of Chadwin's death—not to Rath Dunn, not to anyone. "I know who took her," Caden said. "I want to know where she is, exactly where to find her. Tell me that, and it's a deal."

Rath Dunn raised his brows. Slowly, his sneer turned to his predatory, relaxed smile. With a dramatic flourish, he raised his hand. "I'll draw you a map," he said. He leaned in toward Caden as if they were sharing secrets. "Now, talk, prince."

Caden spoke the words as evenly as he could. "He was stabbed in the back, in the north corridor of the Winter Castle."

"Stabbed with what?"

Caden felt the words catch. "A rigging dagger."

Rath Dunn seemed to contemplate that; he seemed to enjoy it. "Such blades are jagged," he mused. "The mortal wound must have hurt. It must've taken time to do its duty. Was that so?"

Caden hugged his arms to his chest. Yes, the wound would have hurt. Yes, Chadwin was stabbed in the night and not found until morning. Maybe, had he been found earlier—

Rath Dunn slammed down his hands on Caden's desk. "Who killed him?"

Caden jerked and glared up at him. It sounded like that was what Rath Dunn really wanted to know, and it was information Caden didn't have. "I don't know."

"You don't? Interesting," Rath Dunn said, and his eyes lit up. "Were your other brothers in the castle that night?"

Caden kept his voice steady. He didn't like this conversation or what Rath Dunn implied. His brothers were honorable men. Elite Paladins. One day, Caden would follow in their noble footsteps. None would have hurt Chadwin. None. "Valon, Maden, and Jasan were there. As was I." He raised his chin. "Now, tell me where the lunch witches keep Jane Chan."

Rath Dunn laughed out loud. "Witches?" he said. "Is that what you call them?" He shook his head as if amused by Caden's ignorance. "Now, now, prince, don't insult them. They're ancient youth stealers, skilled in the darkest ritual magic. I'd guess Ms. Jackson's nearly a millennium old. When they drain the girl, the old ones will regain their youth. It's elegant when you think about it."

Still, the information felt incomplete. "Why Jane Chan? Why not another student?" Caden demanded. Even as he spoke, he still felt shaky from talk of Chadwin.

"Does it matter?" said Rath Dunn. "You didn't bargain for that information."

Caden took two breaths and looked down at Jane's desk. There was the tree that Jane had carved. Suddenly, he noticed something he hadn't before. In the corner, scratched into the desk, were letters that Caden recognized—but not from this world. From his own. Next to the tree was a word written in Elvish.

It was the Elvish word for mom.

Caden felt Rath Dunn looming over him. Rath Dunn swept his hand across the desk and rubbed his thumb over the Elvish word. "I hadn't noticed that before. That girl was always writing in Elvish."

"What?"

"Surely you've figured it out by now."

Caden thought. The magic trap. The enchanted necklace. The vial in Rath Dunn's desk labeled "Tear of Elf."

The Elvish word written on Jane's desk, next to the great Walking Oak.

"Jane's mother was one of the banished?" said Caden. "She was an elf?"

Rath Dunn sneered like it was insulting to group Jane's mother with him and the other villains. "No, I don't know how she got here. But, yes, her mother was indeed an elf. Jane Chan has more life force than most. Who better to devour than a half elf?"

"Her magic already drained her life force. She's enchanted metal. She has self-drained," Caden said, realizing that she must have done it on purpose. Had she suspected she was in danger?

"Yes," Rath Dunn said. "She's quite clever, Jane. Still, even as she is, half elf and enchanter, she has more than enough to revitalize them, more than any fully human child." He peered down at Caden. "Though I have to say, she's disposable to me. The *lunch witches* can do what they like with her. I'm not impressed with her talent. I'm impressed with power and skill, not novelty. Whoever destroyed my door is much more interesting."

"So you say," Caden said.

"So I do," Rath Dunn said with a mocking lilt in his tone.

The image of the vial in Rath Dunn's drawer flashed again in Caden's mind. He felt anger boil inside him. "You are involved with her disappearance. You have her tears in your desk. I gave you the information I have. Now tell me where she is!"

Rath Dunn raised a brow. He looked to the broken door then to his desk and back to Caden. "I never said I wasn't involved," he said slowly and coldly. "I said I didn't take her and I didn't have her. But I did need her tears. I've got what I needed." He sneered. "She did cry quite a lot."

It was fortunate Tito was not in the room to hear that. Though it would have been foolish, Caden felt certain Tito would have attacked. Caden tried to concentrate on the moment. He needed to know where Jane was.

"In the future," Rath Dunn said, and his voice was a growl, "stay out of my things."

Caden was disturbed by his chilled smile. "Where is she?" he said.

Rath Dunn walked to the white board. "You see, son of Axel, I keep my deals. Remember that." He drew a detailed map using green dry erase markers for trees, blue for water, and black for roads and buildings. Near the edge of a blue line he added a giant black X. "Just beyond the city limits, near the River Arts District, that's where the girl is kept."

Caden peered at the board and tried to commit the map to memory. With quick pen strokes, he also sketched the information into his notebook. When he glanced back up, Rath Dunn had added two red stick figures near the X.

"What are those?" Caden said.

"The beasts that guard her."

The ice dragons. "Such creatures can't be controlled."

"They can't," Rath Dunn agreed. "But they can be caged, directed, put into the right places at the right times. They can be kept hungry."

Caden added two stick figures to his sketch.

Rath Dunn looked at his notebook like he was evaluating his work. "Good enough," he said. He stalked over to Caden, and Caden knew his next words would hurt. "Your people," he said, "they sing songs of your brothers?"

Caden prepared for the pounce. "They are heroes."

Rath Dunn stood and cleared his throat like he was going to recite poetry. "King Axel and his seven sons, strong and brave, protect the Winterlands, through all her days." He laughed a weird, impish laugh and leaned back toward Caden. "You've heard that."

Of course Caden had heard it. He, above everyone, knew his brothers' hearts, his brothers' bravery. While they lived, Razzon would flourish. They would protect the kingdom. Even if Caden wasn't included in the song. "All in the Greater Realm know of my family's honor."

"That song will cease, I'd bet. With Chadwin dead." Rath Dunn sounded cruel when he said it. "Murdered at the castle, stabbed in the back. That sounds like a betrayal most foul."

"If there are traitors in the kingdom, my father and brothers will defeat them. They will catch Chadwin's killer." Caden glared up at him. "They defeated you."

Rath Dunn's face lit up like a sun. He laughed, this time almost giddy. His emotions were so quick to change, so strange and sudden, Caden was beginning to feel dizzy in his presence. Or maybe the dizziness was a result of such close proximity and such long exposure to the blood dagger.

"You don't see," Rath Dunn said.

Caden fidgeted, and he felt his anger spike. "See what?"

Whatever emotion flashed on his face, it wasn't anger. "If I were looking for the traitor," he said, and his words felt like blows. "I'd look at those who know the castle well. Those who were already in it. Who had spent their lives there. Growing up competing for their father's affection." He smiled. "Tell me, Caden, which—Valon, Maden, or Jasan—do you think most likely stabbed Chadwin in the back?"

"None would do that," Caden said, but his voice sounded weak.

Rath Dunn pulled his blood dagger from his red dress coat. He let it glint near Caden's neck, the metal now dark and stained. "You think not?" he said. "Maybe soon I'll get to speak to one of them." He moved so Caden could feel his breath tickle his ear and spoke in low, gleeful tones. "We'll talk more if you survive this rescue attempt. And I hope you do. I have time yet to kill you. I'd like to enjoy it."

From the corner, Derek was watching. His gaze was locked on the dagger, his notebook sitting forgotten on his desk, his hand gripping a cell phone.

For the first time since detention began, Rath Dunn's attention slid to Derek. "No cell phones allowed," he said. Then, with a burst of unexpected speed, he stabbed the blood dagger through the X Caden had drawn in his notebook, through the notebook itself, and into the desk. A second later, Rath Dunn was in front of Derek, Derek's cell phone in his hands.

Rath Dunn looked at it and shook his head. "Nine one one?" he said. He slammed the phone on Derek's desk, much to Derek's obvious distress, and only inches from Derek's notebook. "Next time you fear me, I'd advise you to run." Before Derek could say or do anything, Rath Dunn came back and retrieved his dagger. He glanced out the window. "Enjoy the snow, boys." He turned on his heel and walked out. "Detention's over."

The quiet that followed was loud but didn't last long. With a crude curse, Derek picked up his notebook and shoved it into his pack. He zipped up his jacket like it was his greatest enemy. The cell phone looked broken, and he picked it up gingerly. When he turned to look at Caden, he seemed furious. "Stay away from me, Goodwill," Derek said.

Caden had no problem with that. He disliked Derek, but then he hesitated. He could dislike someone and still not want him or his mother devoured by Ms. Primrose. And wasn't 911 the emergency number Rosa had mentioned? It seemed Derek was trying to help him.

"Wait," Caden said.

Derek's eyes were full of distrust. "What?"

Caden stood and gathered his things. His time was

limited. There was only so much he could spare for Derek. "Tell your mother to stop harassing Ms. Primrose. If she doesn't, I fear she will kill you both."

Derek just looked confused. "She's an old lady."

Caden pointed to the doorway by which Rath Dunn had exited. "Rath Dunn—Mr. Rathis—is dangerous and evil. You've seen it. Even he fears her."

Derek appeared unsure. "Look, it doesn't matter. I got detention because you threw spaghetti on me. My mother won't stop until she gets justice."

Caden wasn't sure what to do with that. He ignored his building headache and tried to concentrate. He needed to get to that X on the map, but honor dictated he at least try to save this unfriend, too. "Fine," he said, an idea form-ing. "Then tell your mother that I apologized and admitted fault."

"Here's the problem, you haven't actually—"

"I apologize and admit fault."

"All right," Derek said, and smirked, "and since you're all looney tunes and worried about someone killing my mother, I'll accept." He glanced toward the door like he feared Rath Dunn would come back, and Caden could tell beneath his bravado he was shaken. It seemed to make him more obnoxious, for he added, "But you and Tito nonbonito best stay away from me," he said, and hurried away.

Caden's hands shook, more from the earlier memories of Chadwin and the accusations about his brothers than anything else. He took a deep breath. Right now, he had to get home and get to that X. There would be time to figure out how to keep Derek from being devoured later. There would also be time to discover what Rath Dunn was plotting with his strange drawer of ingredients, and the information he needed from Caden. At night, when all was quiet, he could continue to mourn for Chadwin. But this day, at this moment, he had a half-elf enchantress to save.

WHITEOUT

aden's pocket, the one containing his phone, began to shake. Truly, he preferred the loud music to the buzzing. Any person who'd ever felt the debilitating sting of a Razzon crater wasp would feel the same. He answered it.

"Did he tell you where she is?" It was Tito.

"He drew me a map."

Moonrise was no more than two hours away. They would have to move fast. Caden heard Tito exhale a shaky breath; heard Brynne's musical voice in the background; and heard the comforting, unmistakable, and majestic neigh of Sir Horace.

"Meet us behind the cafeteria," Tito said. "We've got your horse and we're almost there."

Caden, though, glanced down the long hall to the twin front doors. "Rosa waits out front."

"Yeah, about that." Tito paused. There was a sharp edge to his voice. "Brynne tried to magic her. Rosa is pi—"

There was the sound of scuffling. "She's fine." Now it was Brynne speaking. "Her will is strong. He's angry because he was forced to sneak out of his room with your rope."

Tito's voice returned. "Look," he said. "I told Rosa about Jane. Any help we can get, right? Anyway, she said she'd send the police to check it out but . . ."

"They are neither prepared nor know where to look."

"Yeah." Tito paused. "And, um, sorry, bro, but I think Rosa's putting you in counseling next week. She's making me go, too—it's not that bad."

From what Tito had told Caden of counseling, it was something he neither wanted nor needed. "Why?"

"She thinks you're a *destabilizing influence*."

"My influence is nothing but honorable and good."

From farther away, he heard Brynne again speak. "We'd be there sooner if the beast would let us ride him." There was a snapping sound. "Ow. It tried to bite me."

She must have used all her tricks to get Sir Horace to follow them. "Put Sir Horace on the phone," Caden said.

"*What?*" Tito said.

"Do as I say, Sir Tito."

The next thing Caden heard was the mighty snort of his horse. He explained quickly to Sir Horace that he was not to bite Brynne or Tito. "You've followed them thus far. They're friends."

"You done?" That was Tito, not Sir Horace.

"Yes."

"Good," Tito said. "When we find Jane, we'll text Officer Levine and Rosa the location. It won't matter if they believe us or not. They'll come to get us either way."

"A wise plan," Caden said. Any moment, Rosa would come to find him. "You understand, however, Rosa will be furious."

Caden didn't care much about her wrath but Tito did. He heard Tito exhale. "Not if we find Jane."

Caden took the back exit. He adjusted his coat and held his damaged notebook to his chest. Outside, the air chilled. The snow plunged from the sky in stinging sheets. It was difficult to distinguish the snow-covered trees from the white sky, white ground, and white-covered building tops.

As he stepped behind the cafeteria, he felt his steps lighten. There, nosing in the Dumpster and crunching on apple cores, was Sir Horace. His mane was brighter than the falling snow. The hair on his bare back was a shade darker and looked recently groomed. Tito and Brynne were huddled nearby, taking what shelter they could by the building's wall. Tito was layered in dark clothing. The sparring broom was strapped to his back with a belt. His backpack was swung over his shoulder and stuffed so full that the zippers pulled.

Brynne was still dressed in her fuzzy white sweater and gray coat. She also wore sleek black gloves and a black knit cap. She'd brought only herself, but she was her best weapon.

While Sir Horace nuzzled Caden's ear, Caden shared his information. "She's near the river." He showed them his crude notepaper map. He pointed out the stick figure ice dragons while the gaping hole from the blood dagger collected snowflakes.

Tito opened his pack. Inside it, Caden saw matches, twine, first aid supplies, a spare blanket, and a flashlight. From the bottom, Tito pulled out a detailed map. "This one's official."

They held Tito's official map and Caden's bleeding, gaping sketch of a map side by side against the building's wall. It was easy to match landmarks, fit together bends in the river. Caden reached into his other pocket and pulled out his compass. Within minutes, they plotted a route to Jane.

Normally, Caden would have swung his leg up and pulled onto Sir Horace's back. Tito, however, looked nervous, and Sir Horace might buck Brynne off if she tried to mount. Caden patted Sir Horace twice and commanded him to kneel. "He can carry us all," Caden said.

"Well, yeah, he's the size of an elephant."

In obvious contempt, Sir Horace snorted. His billowing breath was like smoke. He looked like he breathed fire.

Tito glanced at Caden. "Right, no offense."

"It is to Sir Horace you owe the apology," Caden said.

Tito looked down and folded the maps so he would

have easy access to them on the ride. "You do need therapy," he mumbled.

The snow was beginning to fall thicker and faster. Caden felt icy flakes stick to his eyelashes; he felt his hands numbing. "We must hurry." He motioned for them to get on Sir Horace's back. "Hold tightly," he said, and gave Sir Horace a swift kick.

Caden sat in front where he could direct Sir Horace. Tito, due to his lack of riding experience and his navigational duties, sat in the middle. Brynne rode in the back to protect them.

Sir Horace sprinted toward the River District. He tore down the mountain like he was a flake in the blizzard—a Galvanian snow stallion riding the winds. They had until moonrise. With Sir Horace's power, they'd make it.

They sped to the river, followed it, slowing twice to cross icy overpasses, and once to trot down a slick sidewalk. When his hooves hit unpaved earth again, Sir Horace ran flat out.

"Just a little farther!" Tito said as they passed the city limits. He pointed toward the river bend. "There! That's where she is. She's got to be there."

Visibility was poor, but Caden made out a square metal structure in the distance. He directed Sir Horace toward it, still following what he thought was the river, but when the structure was no more than ten bounds away, Sir Horace planted his hooves into the snow and stopped.

Caden held on, his numb hands tangled in Sir Horace's mane. He felt Tito crush into him, and Brynne crush into them both. Sir Horace put his head down, his nose out, and his ears back. He looked from left to right and pawed at the snow.

"The dragons," Brynne said from behind him.

Caden glanced in each direction, but the snow blinded him. He wished to fight dragons, but not in conditions as these, and not with his underprepared friends at his back. Best they sprint for the structure. He gave Sir Horace the charge signal, but Sir Horace inched backward and loosed a mighty whinny.

From the left, Caden heard an ice dragon's wail. From the right came an answering one. The metal structure was close but was fading in and out of view in the snowstorm.

Only Sir Horace sensed the first attack. He went from a snow sculpture to a blur of speed, charging forward as the dragons attacked from each flank. Sir Horace moved so fast, turned so quickly, that the dragons crashed into each other.

Caden strained to keep astride. Brynne and Tito flew off in opposite directions. Once Sir Horace stopped, Caden could feel him breathing short fast breaths; he could feel the tightness in his steed's back.

Caden eased off and his boots sank into the snow. He needed to find the others, but he saw neither of them. Beside him, Sir Horace sniffed to the right, and Caden peered in that direction. Within the white wall of snow, something large moved. If not for the motion, it would have been invisible.

Tito stumbled from the snow. His broom was in hand. He stopped at Caden's side. "What's that?"

Then Caden realized two things. One, he'd brought no weapon, not even that poorly weighted sparring mop. Two, Brynne's silence might truly mean she was smarter than him and Tito. From the impenetrable white, the moving form shifted toward them. From the mountain road, car lights passed over the form and an ice dragon's blue eyes blazed.

"It's an ice dragon." Caden readied to dodge. "And it sees us."

Tito grappled in his pack and pulled out the matches. With trembling hands, he lit a match. It went out. He tried again. "Fire melts ice. They don't like it, right?"

Tito was quite smart. "No, they don't," Caden said, keeping very still. "Light the broom quickly."

The ice dragon moved closer, or at least its eyes did. The rest of it was a white haze, but Caden knew that its body stalked forward with its gaze. Tito was shielding his match with the broom bristles. It lit. Tito thrust it into the heart of the broom head and pointed the bristly end at the dragon.

"So how do we slay these things?"

Dragons were slain with swords forged by the great steelworkers and smiths of Razzon. A sword such as the one Officer Levine was currently keeping safe for him. As all they had was a smoking broom, that seemed an important discussion better suited for another time. If the broom started blazing, perhaps they'd have a chance. The dragon closed its eyes and disappeared into the snow. Then out of the white, the dragon charged.

27

THE GIRL IN THE SAND

It stampeded between them like thunder made whole. Caden scrambled left. He felt a rush of wind, felt his hair blow with the force. The dragon skidded, turned, and raised its snout. Caden stepped back, slowly, carefully.

No longer could he see Tito, but Caden heard him curse and he saw him wave his broom. It smoldered now, a spot of red embers waving in the storm. Even aflame, though, it would not penetrate dragon hide.

Whether the dragon saw the broom or smelled the smoke, Caden didn't know, but it angled toward it and prowled low, its frozen breath turning the hard snow to sudden ice. Its eyes and snout were the only weak points a broom—even one on fire—might pierce. "You must aim for its eyes!" Caden yelled.

The ice dragon cocked its head in Caden's direction.

Again headlights from the road passed across the hill. The dragon blinked its ice blue eyes and turned back. It seemed Tito was its prey of choice.

From behind Caden, Brynne emerged and touched his arm. He hadn't noticed her approach, but that was typical. She held her hat in her hand. Her cheek was bruised and her coat torn. Her hair was white with frost. She watched the right with what he imagined was the same careful and frightened gaze he cast to the left and to the ice dragon stalking Tito.

"Twin dragons," she whispered. "One a by-product of the magic that trapped Jane Chan, one a by-product of the magic that still holds her. Dark spells cast by dark souls." She nodded to the dragon in Caden's sight, the dragon that prowled toward the waving broom. "As this one hunts Tito, the other hunts us."

He shifted so he and Brynne were back to back. Their dragon-fighting weapons were few and the whitewashed world seemed to be dimming. Behind the darkening sky and the thick clouds, the new moon would rise, invisible and unstoppable. Jane Chan's time was short.

"We must get inside," Caden said.

The dragon to the right, the one Caden couldn't see, roared. The dragon in his vision, the dragon to the left, answered with a yowl that felt as if it sliced the sky.

The ice dragons might not think, feel, or talk like the Elderdragon Ms. Primrose, but they were not without instinct. On the mountainside, ankle-deep in building snow, Caden had no doubts they hunted him and his friends.

"I can't see them!" Brynne hissed.

The leftward ice dragon blended into the blizzard, moving closer and closer to the red glow in the snow, going in and out of view. Sight was of little use in this battle. For a second, Caden closed his eyes.

His hands were numb, as were his feet and his face. The wind howled, a high screeching that matched the pelting snow, and the ground rumbled with a pounding of feet. The rightward dragon attacked.

Caden spun and pushed Brynne from its path. "Move!" he said. The ground was slick, and he slipped on a patch of hard snow. The dragon did not wait for him to regain his balance. It rammed him. He sailed backward into a snowdrift, his breath knocked from him.

"Caden!" Brynne called.

Mouth gaping, teeth sharp with ice, the dragon bounded after him. Caden had no chance to move; he was too far sunken into the snow. He pulled his numb fingers into a tight fist. He would die fighting.

But ice dragons weren't the only creatures that blended with snow and reveled in the blizzard. The ground thundered with hoofbeats. A mighty snort rang on the winds.

Sir Horace rammed the ice dragon in midair. While it was true Sir Horace was smaller than an ice dragon, he was, as Tito said, big as an elephant—a snow-dwelling, brilliant, brave, dragon-hunting elephant. If an ice dragon could look surprised, the one trying to eat Caden and getting rammed by the eighth finest Galvanian snow stallion in the Greater Realm did. It tumbled out of sight, into the white, and loosed a terrible roar.

Sir Horace stood over Caden, teeth bared, and stomped at the snow. The darkness was falling fast. Caden couldn't see Tito, Brynne, or the dragons, but he saw a red glow dancing in the distance—Tito's broom. Then, a few bounds from it, a second fire ignited. Brynne's face was illuminated. She held her hat by one edge. The rest of it was alight.

Caden struggled to his feet. There were larger, more sinister blurs moving in the twilight. The ice dragons were going toward the small fires. He yelled to Tito and Brynne to tell them where he was, to distract the dragons. "I'm here!"

"Get to Jane!" That was Tito, his voice emanating from the direction of the dancing, fiery broom.

Caden hesitated, his hand against Sir Horace's warm coat. He was closest to the shed. With Sir Horace as his mount, and the others engaging the dragons, he could break for the structure. But could he leave his friends?

In the snow, the two spots of fire dodged and dived. One went out, only to light once more.

Caden's father always said not to hesitate in times like these. During battle, trust one's training, trust one's men.

Caden could do that. He would rescue Jane Chan and while he did, he'd trust Brynne and Tito to stay alive. He swung up onto Sir Horace's back with one smooth movement. In seconds, they were at the shed.

Caden ignored the roars and curses behind as they trotted around it. He ran his hand against the metal. It felt like ice, like a tomb of dark and cold.

He found the metal door frozen shut and locked tight. He neither dismounted nor hesitated. He gave Sir Horace the command to go through it. Sir Horace kicked the door with the same force he'd rammed the dragon. The door fell into the building. Yellow light rushed out. Sir Horace and Caden galloped in.

The inside was one large room, the floor covered with sand. Signs like those for the Ashevillian shops were stacked against the wall. Paints and brushes sat in the corner. Above, lanterns and animal carcasses hung from exposed metal beams. Heaters lit and warmed the room. Caden felt the cold snow blowing in from behind them, felt his face go prickly as feeling returned to it.

Then he saw them. In the exact middle of the room stood Ms. Aggie, bundled up in a shawl and hat. Mr. Andre was bent over with a cane and staring at them. Ms. Jackson was nowhere to be seen, but she was already young and beautiful. She'd no need to drain a half elf.

Mr. Andre brandished his cane. "Get out!" he wheezed.

Sir Horace reared up and kicked at the ground. Snow

and sand blew up. The lunch people lurched back and watched Sir Horace like he was a snow demon.

As Caden and Sir Horace trotted into the room, he saw her. He saw Jane Chan. She was covered in sand like a sculpture. Her fine hair and delicate face were completely encased. Her eyes were closed. The only break in the sand and sign she lived were the tears that ran down her cheeks.

The hot, dry room, the sand covering Jane Chan and the floor, the poor gutted animals hanging from above—all made sudden sense. This cursed structure was a second place where the ritual magic had been cast. The dead animals were the poor beasts snagged by the trap and now sacrificed. This sand was kindred to the sand he and Tito had deactivated on the mountain. The paint and signs a remnant of the structure's Ashevillian purpose.

Caden felt his anger heat to boil. He cantered toward Ms. Aggie and Mr. Andre. "This is dark magic," he said.

They stared at Caden and Sir Horace with twin expressions of horror and surprise, and hovered near Jane Chan like she was a trunk of elvish gold.

"Move away from her," Caden said with all the authority of his title and all the power of his anger.

They shrank back, but before they'd moved an entire pace, the sand began to glow. It was not, however, the soft golden glow as when deactivated. Jane Chan, the floor, and the sand glowed a sickly red.

The same sickly red color as the magic that had

stranded Caden in Asheville.

Ms. Aggie and Mr. Andre hobbled toward Jane and reached for her. "You're too late," Ms. Aggie said.

The new moon had risen.

Caden jumped down from Sir Horace. His boots kicked up glowing red sand and snow. Ms. Aggie and Mr. Andre were still old, Jane Chan still a sand statue, so he wasn't too late. Besides, he knew something of this magic. He'd counteracted it at the trap. "Chase them away from her," he told Sir Horace.

Sir Horace put his head down and moved toward them. Ms. Aggie tried to shoo him away like some sort of insect. Sir Horace bared his teeth and nipped. Mr. Andre swung his cane in attack, but Sir Horace bit it in half.

Caden ran to the doorway, dropped down, and filled his arms with snow. The room was warm and the snow would melt fast inside it. He dashed across the room and tossed it on sand-covered Jane Chan. She would be saved this night. She wouldn't die like Chadwin. He ran out and repeated the process. He had to save her.

On his third run for snow, he heard a terrible, inhuman screech from the dark mountainside. A huge flash of fire exploded in the storm, lit the sky, and went out. Caden felt his stomach flip, his jaw tighten. His friends still battled in the snow, and now the mountain was a wall of night. He had to hurry.

By the fourth armful, the snow on Jane was melting, the

sand beginning to fall away. She would not die alone and with tears on her cheeks like Chadwin. The glow from the sand began to change. From bloodred it turned to shining gold. The sand flaked off her body like petals on a wind. Her pale skin felt warm and she was breathing. Her dark hair fanned out around her shoulders. But she didn't wake.

Satisfied she was at least alive, Caden dragged her to the relative safety of the far corner.

Sir Horace had Ms. Aggie and Mr. Andre cowering in the back. "She'll get you," Mr. Andre said, but Caden did not fear little old lunch people.

"Keep them there," Caden told Sir Horace. Sir Horace put his ears back, bared his teeth, and neighed. Caden turned and ran out to the mountain, into the snow and darkness, into the battle.

Two steps out the door, though, he stopped. Tito stood uphill with his broom. Brynne's hat was draped on the charred bristles and it burned like a sun. One of the ice-dragons came into sight. It attacked with open mouth and ferocious speed.

Caden yelled to Tito and ran to help him, but the snow was thick. His boots sank deep with each step. His intended dash was slow and difficult. "It attacks!" he said.

If Tito heard him, he showed no sign. He stood motionless. Caden scrambled up the slope, but the dragon was closer to Tito and faster than Caden. Just as its muzzle made contact, Tito jammed the flaming broom right between its teeth.

Caden sank down almost knee-deep in the snow.

The dragon swallowed the fire. It lit up from inside, and blew up like a fireball. The wail was earsplitting, the flash blinding. Then all went dark and quiet. He didn't see Tito anywhere.

Caden feared for Tito's life. He sprinted uphill as best he could and called out in alarm. "Sir Tito! Sir Tito!"

The mountain was black and slick. Caden could hear coughing. He tracked Tito's voice and found him moments later, lying in the snow. "Are you well, friend?" he said, and patted Tito's arms. Tito still had two, so that was something.

"Yeah," Tito said.

He seemed dazed, but he recovered quickly and pushed Caden's helpful royal hands away. "Get off me."

As Caden's panic for his friend dimmed, something occurred to him. While he'd been threatening the elderly, Sir Tito, the Elite Paladin in training of Asheville, had slain a dragon.

Caden heard Tito rummaging in his backpack. A second later, the bright light of Tito's flashlight shone in Caden's face.

"Extinguish the light," Caden said. "The other dragon—"

"Your girl set her coat on fire and took out the other one with her bare hands. She's crazy, bro."

It was horrible. It was unfair. It couldn't be. Caden grabbed Tito's flashlight and shone it on him as he struggled to his feet. "Each of you has slain a dragon?"

Brynne staggered down the hill. "That's right, prince. We are mighty, Sir Tito and I." When he shone the light on her, her skin and lips looked blue, and as expected her coat was gone. Her fuzzy white sweater was the color of muck. She looked far too cold, sounded far too weak.

Caden gave the light back to Tito, took off his coat, and gave it to Brynne. Without it, the magnitude of the cold became apparent to him. Both Brynne and Tito had been in the snow far too long. He shielded Brynne from the stinging snow as best he could and helped her down the hill. "Jane Chan appears well, but she has not awoken," he said. "It's warm in the structure; we should get inside it."

Tito was already running toward the shed. "You left her alone in there?"

Caden bristled. "Sir Horace is with her," he said. As he watched Tito sprint, he felt a warmth in his belly despite the snow. They'd done it. Jane hadn't died like his brother. They'd saved her. Caden was almost speechless. Almost. "She's alive," he said, and in spite of everything, it seemed hard to believe. He turned to Brynne and felt his lips crack from the cold as he smiled. "She's alive," he said, "and we saved her."

28
THE LUNCH WITCHES

C aden and Brynne trudged into the metal structure. The storm's winds rushed through the doorway. Overhead, the lanterns flickered and the dead animals swayed.

Tito knelt beside Jane. His hands shook as he checked her; he seemed shocked they'd found her alive, shocked at the dead animals above and the evil lunch lady and lunch man huddled in the opposite corner. Jane's eyes remained closed.

Beside Caden, Brynne shivered. He tugged his coat snugly around her and helped her ease down and sit near Tito.

"I don't require your aid," she said.

"You're frozen, sorceress."

"As are you, prince."

True, Caden's face tingled and his hands were cold, but he doubted he was the same bluish color as her. "I had my coat."

Brynne reached in his coat pocket and pulled out his pink phone. Some of the sparkly stones were missing. The screen was cracked and it fell off as she held it out. "The ice dragon hit you hard, though." As she gazed at his phone, she looked sad. "Mine is lost to the snow."

"Mine's in my pack," Tito said. He opened his backpack and took out the first aid kit, and the blanket, then wrapped the latter around Jane's shoulders. "I'll call for help."

For someone who'd spent dusk battling an ice dragon with a broom, he looked amazingly unscathed. His hair endured in the same slick ponytail. His dark clothes were neither torn nor tattered.

Tito seemed to sense Caden's scrutiny. "What?"

"You look well."

Tito fussed between Jane and his backpack but stopped to spare them a glance. "Well, you two look like crap." He looked again and frowned. "Cold crap. You okay?"

"We're not as good as you," Caden said.

"Whatever that's supposed to mean," Tito said. "Here." He pulled his outermost sweatshirt off and tossed it to Caden. "Since you're so delicate and all."

Caden was an eighth-born prince, trained by the Elite Guard and his seven noble brothers, trained even by his father, the king. He was the opposite of delicate. Without his coat, however, he was cold. He pulled the sweatshirt on over his sweater. It was warmer than nothing.

Tito pointed at him. "Just don't tell anyone at school I gave you my shirt."

"Why would I do that?"

"You do all sorts of weird things."

Brynne laughed at that. She looked around, but her gaze seemed to set on Tito for a long moment. Caden peered, too. Tito was leaning over his bag, hunting for his phone; the half elf's necklace of protection glittered near his neck. Brynne nodded to it.

Tito slew the dragon with his bravery, wit, and fortitude. None could deny that. He had been brave and smart. His natural skill was unquestionable.

His quality of character, however, didn't explain his neat appearance. It was too cold outside, Tito was too new to battle, and the ice dragons too vile of opponents for him to escape without as much as a rip in his clothes. That was the work of something else, something powerful.

It seemed Rath Dunn was wrong. Tito's necklace was more than a mere trinket, Jane Chan's skills more than a novelty.

Tito found his phone and dialed 911. "The signal's breaking up."

From the back corner, Mr. Andre banged what was left of his cane against the wall. Without their youth and Ms. Jackson, without their magic traps, Mr. Andre and Ms.

Aggie seemed weak and pitiful.

"Let us talk about this; no need to call the police," Mr. Andre called out. "We should work together—we have much to offer." Cautiously, he peered around Sir Horace, hands out as he darted his gaze worriedly from Sir Horace to Tito and back again. He inched toward them. As he got close to Sir Horace, Sir Horace forced him back to the corner.

Brynne snorted and turned away. She bundled up like a ball in Caden's coat. "They have nothing to offer." She leaned her head against the metal wall and rested her eyes.

Caden used his foot to nudge her. "Don't sleep," he said. "You're too cold."

"I'm fine." The strength of her glare showed returning health and renewed vigor. "Caden, eighth-born prince of Razzon," she said. "You forget. I'm not your subject."

Caden glanced to the back of the shed. Mr. Andre and Ms. Aggie remained cornered by Sir Horace. "I suppose you sound strong enough," he said.

"Strong," Tito said. "That girl's a dragon slayer."

Caden crossed his arms and squared his shoulders. "I'm well aware that everyone's a dragon slayer but me."

Tito looked from Caden to Jane Chan and back. "You saved Jane," he said as if it was worthy of greater acclaim.

"Dragons." Brynne snorted. Then she glanced up at Caden. "Tito and I have slain ice dragons, but you faced and charmed an Elderdragon." She snuggled under his coat and raised a brow. "That is a feat of renown. Much more impressive than destroying a bundle of mindless chaos like an ice dragon."

Caden wasn't sure if his father would agree with Brynne on that or not. He looked away. His gift of speech was one he needed to better understand, that was certain. And the forgotten languages tugged at his curiosity. Beside him, Tito held his phone toward the rafters and tried 911 again.

"There's no need to call, no need for that," Ms. Aggie called out. She and her brother remained at Sir Horace's mercy. "No harm done. The girl's fine."

Tito's face turned red, and he clenched his fists. He'd been bound to explode or weep at some point and it seemed anger had won out. "Stop talking!"

His shout echoed against the metal walls. As if his voice broke the last shards of the spell, Jane Chan's eyelids fluttered. She looked at Tito with a slight frown.

The fury drained from Tito's face, and he dropped to his knees beside her, his phone held loosely in his hand. "Jane? Hey, you okay?"

"Tito?" She blinked at him. "Where . . . ? I've had bad dreams." She glanced to the rafters, to the animal carcasses hanging down. "The deer were screaming."

The animals probably did scream, and if anyone could sense wildlife's cries, it would be an elf. "Elves are close to nature," Caden said.

Jane turned to Caden. Her eyes were warm and kind,

her skin pale. She was pretty in a regular way, like a daisy in the Springlands. She scrunched her face and looked back to Tito. "Did Rosa bring home another one?" she said.

"Sort of. Don't worry, he's, uh . . . ," Tito said. "He's cool, I guess."

"Actually, I'm cold," Caden said, and Jane laughed. She'd been a long time kept in sand and nightmares. Recovery would take time. "She seems confused."

"She's been missing well over a week," Tito said.

"What? I haven't . . ." Jane struggled to sit up. Tito tried to help her, but she froze when she was eye level with his shirt. She reached for the glinting chain around his neck. "You're wearing my necklace."

"Oh, yeah. We found it on the mountain," Tito said. He blushed and reached to take it off. "I was just—"

"No," Jane said. She settled back and closed her eyes. "No, you keep it. I want you to wear it."

"You do?" Tito said, but she was back asleep.

Brynne opened her eyes. With an arch of the brow, she turned toward the lunch witches. "What of them?"

Tito also looked to the back corner.

Sir Horace pranced and nipped. Ms. Aggie and Mr. Andre trembled under his guard. Sir Horace, however, deserved a chance to run with the blizzard, to prance in the snow.

Caden stood and brushed dirt from his jeans. "Tell me,

Sir Tito, have you rope among your supplies?"

Tito pulled a spool of strong thin twine from his pack and tossed it to Caden. "Have at it."

Mr. Andre's eyes were full of hatred, Ms. Aggie's full of fury. As Caden reached down to tie her hands, Ms. Aggie whispered to him.

"Dear little prince," she said, and her voice was like the dead, "let us go and we can help you."

Caden tightened the knot. "How so?"

"We know how you and the girl came to be here."

Caden snapped his gaze to hers. "Tell me."

She shushed him. "Now, now. Let us go, leave the ropes loose, and keep the horse away, and we'll tell you, we will."

He moved to tighten Mr. Andre's ropes. "You know nothing."

Mr. Andre wheezed as he spoke. "We know everything."

"Everything," echoed Ms. Aggie.

They claimed to have answers. All he had to do was get them to tell him. If he could charm Ms. Primrose into liking him, certainly he could make these lunch witches tell him what he wanted to know. Besides, they were desperate. "If you can tell me how Brynne and I were brought here, and I believe you, I'll consider letting you go."

"Let us go, then we'll talk," Ms. Aggie said.

This wasn't like Caden's chat with Rath Dunn. With Jane rescued and his friends safe at the opposite corner near the paints, he had the bargaining power. "No," he said. "Tell me first."

They turned and whispered to each other. Ms. Aggie spoke. "One year ago, our sister was ailing. She needed another's life force to sustain her—and a powerful one at that. Rath Dunn knew of an elf trapped in this land and delivered the elf to her. She took her life force, was cured, and what's more, she regained her youth. Our sister owed Rath Dunn a debt."

Caden felt a sick turn to his stomach. "The elf your sister drained," he said. "That was Jane's mother. That's why she lived with Rosa."

Mr. Andre and Ms. Aggie cackled. Mr. Andre said, "As repayment, Rath Dunn asked us to aid him in collecting a list of strange items. He required tears of an elf, and so we lured the elf's daughter past the city limits during the night. The promise of seeing her mother made her reckless, and she went willingly into the woods," he said. "And in the woods, we set a trap."

Ms. Aggie leaned forward. "If we collected her tears for his use, he said we could do with her as we pleased. And on that same night, our sister, a master of ritual magic, retrieved for him two more items he was unable to procure on his own. Now, release us."

"No." The other vials had all been empty. "Tell me what they were?" Caden asked.

Ms. Aggie scowled but continued. "He asked her to

bring a great sorcerer and the seventh son of his enemy King Axel to this land. As a favor, he let us keep the young elf, so that we might regain some of our youth, too. The spell takes days to steep. It keeps those trapped alive and fresh and unconcious until it can be finished on the new moon."

"You've ruined it," Mr. Andre said, but Caden's thoughts were stuck on his sister's words.

A great sorcerer. A son of King Axel.

He looked between them. "Ms. Jackson cast the spell that brought us here?" Caden said. "But I'm not my father's seventh-born son."

"The spell doesn't make mistakes," Ms. Aggie said.

"Nor does our sister," Mr. Andre said.

Caden considered. The lunch witches allied with Rath Dunn. He'd befriended practioneers of ritual magic. In his desk, he'd had elf tears and vials for other things. He'd taken Caden's blood and seemed disappointed. The spell might not make mistakes, but Rath Dunn had.

Caden was eighth-born, and Jasan was seventh-born. But then Chadwin had been killed. Of the sons of Axel left, Caden was now number seven. "He asked for the seventh son, not the seventh-*born* son, just assuming the spell would bring Jasan," he said out loud. "He didn't know he needed to specify."

"Yes, yes," said Ms. Aggie.

Rath Dunn wanted Jasan, not Caden. Caden was a

mistake. Brynne wasn't, though. What she lacked in control, she made up for in power. She set the woods on fire and made a door explode through a phone. And one vial in Rath Dunn's drawer was for "magical locks." That was likely why he was interested in meeting Brynne. He wanted something from her for that vial. Knowing him, it would put her life in peril.

Ms. Aggie smiled in poor imitation of a kind old woman. "Now, let us go."

"Yes, let us go," echoed Mr. Andre. "No harm was done."

Caden glanced to his friends, to Tito and Jane. He looked at Brynne dozing and beaten up near the wall. Up in the rafters, the animals hung down lifeless and stiff. Jane's mother had met a fate similar to the poor animals; she hadn't been saved like Jane.

The witches were wrong. Great harm had been done.

"I need to know more." Caden crossed his arms and felt his stitches pull. "Rath Dunn is gathering ingredients," he said. "For what?"

They looked at each other.

"We don't know," Mr. Andre said.

"But," Ms. Aggie said, "our sister knows. Let us go and she'll tell you, she will."

Caden was certain she'd tell him nothing. He bent toward the ancient lunch people, inspected the ropes to make sure they were tight, then stood and straightened

Tito's smelly sweatshirt. "As promised, I've considered letting you go," he said. "And decided against it."

Their eyes widened in surprise and darkened with fury. Mr. Andre cursed. Ms. Aggie spat at him and said, "You wouldn't want to anger our sister."

Ms. Jackson was the least of Caden's concerns. He had other enemies at the school—Rath Dunn and quite possibly the creepy secretary. Ms. Primrose switched from enemy to friend with the winds. If he were to have more enemies, let there be more. Besides, he had figured out how to save Jane on his own. He didn't need the witches to tell him what Rath Dunn was planning. He, Tito, and Brynne could figure it out. "I'll take my chances," he said.

Later, after the heaters had stopped heating, and the lanterns flickered with low fuel, the emergency people arrived. Officer Levine was the first in the doorway. When he saw Jane, he turned up his mouth in a soft smile. He nodded back to a fur- and-leather-bundled Jenkins. "Tell Rosa we've found them. All of them."

Outside, the blizzard had finally stopped. It remained cold, but the wind no longer howled; the snow no longer stung. Behind the ambulance, Caden saw Sir Horace watching the flickering red and blue lights and signaled him to return to the horse jail. He deserved all the apples he could eat.

After that there were lots of blankets and hot drinks, prodding medics, and questions with difficult answers.

Jane claimed not to remember much from her days missing, but she named her captors with confidence. The police handcuffed a disgruntled and fearful Ms. Aggie and Mr. Andre. As they were loaded into the police car, Caden heard Ms. Aggie hiss, "She won't be happy . . ."

"I thought my mom was in the woods," Jane said as the four of them, Officer Levine, Rosa, and an on-duty social worker huddled in the warm and overly bright emergency room. "At school lunch they'd told me she was alive and living in the woods." She sat next to Tito on an orange-cushioned bench and leaned closer to him as she spoke. "I should've told someone. I should've told Tito at least. I knew she wasn't there. I mean, I know she's gone, but I had to see." Tears pooled in her eyes. "But it was them." She shivered, but Caden couldn't tell if it was from chill or memory. "They stole my tears. They were going to kill me like they killed those animals."

Brynne sat in a nearby chair, feigning sleep. It was a transparent ploy to avoid answering questions, but it seemed to be working for her. Caden, however, had no desire to be quiet. He added the information Jane left out; he told them of the magic sand trap and the lunch people's youth-stealing motive.

Officer Levine, Rosa, and the on-duty social worker stopped and stared at him. Caden squared his shoulders. "You should know the truth," he said.

Tito looked away; Brynne faked a snore.

Rosa put her arm around Caden's shoulder. "He's been through a lot. He's confused," she said. She cleared her throat. "He's starting counseling next Thursday."

Caden most certainly was not confused. He was quite the opposite. If not for him, Jane would have been devoured, hung from the rafters, and left empty like one of those unfortunate woodland creatures. He was about to argue his point, but Officer Levine's signals to stay quiet and Rosa's strong shoulder squeeze gave him pause. For once, he kept quiet.

Jane jumped in. "They did believe that," she said. "They were evil and they were wrong."

"How are you feeling, Jane?" the social worker said.

"Lost," Jane Chan said. "But found, too."

The questions continued, and sulkily Caden let Jane and Tito answer them. Eventually Officer Levine, Rosa, and the social worker started talking to one another and not them. Jane caught Caden's gaze then and mouthed, "Thank you."

29

SCHOOL GOES ON

etween the snow and the scandal, school was closed for several days. It finally reopened on the following Tuesday. Caden took time to measure and trim his hair. It had grown half a length too long since he'd left the castle. He dressed in a red plaid shirt with a collar and a pair of his too-long jeans. As always, he wore his coat.

He looked in the mirror and took a deep breath. Today Brynne started school. Rath Dunn would recognize her as a sorceress, and he wanted Brynne for something. He still had an empty vial in his desk drawer labeled "Magical Locks." She'd meet Ms. Primrose. Today was a day for great care.

Brynne came to the attic to talk to him and pretended not to care. "So, I want to meet her. And Rath Dunn can't do anything at school, no matter what he's planning."

She wore gray jeans and a purple top. Her hair was perfect. Her replacement black coat looked expensive. He held his tongue so as not to scold her for using magic to enhance her appearance. It was better to concentrate on the more pressing matter—Brynne, Rath Dunn, and the Elderdragon Ms. Primrose.

"I don't think you should go," he said.

"I'm going," she said.

"It's dangerous. Rath Dunn brought you here for a reason."

"As he did you." Her eyes flashed. "And yet you go. Tito goes. In a few days, Jane will also return to school. I'll go, too."

"You're being foolish."

"You're being annoying. Rosa won't let me stay home much longer anyway."

Between them, they were clever enough to find education options that excluded Brynne going to Ms. Primrose's school. Besides, if Caden understood this strange land, there were other schools in Asheville.

"Ms. Primrose likes to eat people," he said. "Not locals, she thinks that's impolite, but other people—people like you and people like me. You don't need to learn from her. You are a good enough spellcaster as you are."

Brynne seemed to take in a deep breath. Her expression became serious, became frail. She looked down and fiddled with the buttons on her new coat. "No, I'm not. I have fits when I do too much. I cast spells that burn down mountains."

"You slay dragons and help save kidnapped girls."

"I cursed you for life by accident." She looked up. "I'm not stupid, Caden. I know what a curse like mine could mean for you. You have enemies who could use it against you. Rath Dunn could find out." She twisted her hands together. "If any creature could teach me to break an unbreakable curse, it would be an Elderdragon. It would be her."

"She's a dragon."

"You like her."

Caden shouldn't like Ms. Primrose. Maybe he did, maybe he didn't. It was true, though, if any being knew how to break his curse, it would be an Elderdragon. So that was why Brynne had decided to go to school. "I see," he said.

"You need your curse fixed, and I need to control my magic. Tito thinks I should go, and you said she rewards people sometimes," Brynne said. She waved him off. "Have some faith I won't get eaten."

"You ask me for a lot of faith."

"Do you not have the gift of speech? If she gets angry, you can charm her and keep us from being lunch," she said, and smiled. Her eyes took on a mischievous glint. "That's what I'm going to call you from now on. Dragon Charmer."

"I'd prefer you not." Caden felt certain his brothers

would mock that title. He shook his head. "She might eat you when I'm not in the room."

Her pretty eyes narrowed. "You trust Tito and you met him two weeks ago."

"Tito's my brother."

"Your foster brother."

"I've concluded there's no true distinction. Besides, he's a local."

Quickly, her amusement at his nickname was being replaced by annoyance. That, at least, was familiar. "In this world am I not your foster sister?"

"It's not the same," he said, and grinned, for he'd figured out a way to catch her off her guard.

She put her hands on her hips and looked ready to hit him. "You've known me since we were four," she said. "If you should be close to anyone, it's me."

"Maybe," he said. "But understand, sorceress, I know your parents, and I know my family."

"And?" she said, clearly suspicious.

He grabbed his school things, made sure his science and math homework were complete. The school had a no-excuses policy for work. Caden finished it for fear if he didn't, he'd be dinner. He gave Brynne his most charming grin. "And I'd never consider you a sister."

That stopped Brynne.

In the truck, Caden asked Rosa for news of Ms. Aggie and Mr. Andre. "They're gone. You're safe now," she said, but she couldn't tell Caden where they were or what had happened after the police took them away. Neither had he seen any news reports about them on the television.

Sir Horace, though, it seemed was a celebrity. The morning news had shown blurry footage of him romancing the mare Cotton as well as a cell phone video of him prancing through the downtown sidewalks late at night and jumping one of their construction barriers. They'd named him the Ashevillian Stallion, which was nowhere near correct.

When they arrived at the school, Caden walked into the twin doors with Brynne at his right and Tito at his left. Ms. Primrose waited in the long hall. She wore a bloodred rose-embroidered dress with silver piping. She didn't look hungry at all.

Her satisfied expression made Caden queasy. Part of him wanted to keep Tito, Brynne, Jane, and even Derek as far from her as possible. Part of Caden, though, the foolish irrational part, liked the Elderdragon, people eater and all. Without thinking, he bowed when he saw her.

Ms. Primrose seemed to fight smiling, but the smile won out. It seemed they were alike in this way. Their fondness was mutual, cautious, and reluctant.

It seemed, however unlikely, that Brynne was right. He'd charmed the dragon.

Beside him, Brynne was wide-eyed. She sparkled in the hall like polished silver. The other students stared at her. She, though, looked only at Ms. Primrose. "I've wanted to meet you for a while," she said. "I'm Caden's friend Brynne."

Ms. Primrose looked at Caden. "The one you mentioned?"

"The very same," Caden said.

Brynne took a deep breath and held out her hand. Five mismatched, glitter-covered buttons sparkled from her palm. "I've brought you a gift, Ms. Primrose."

Ms. Primrose's face lit up like they were rare jewels. With little ohs and ahs she inspected each, and put them one by one in her dress pocket. Bribery, it seemed, was as good a strategy as charm for gaining favor with an Elderdragon. He'd have to remember that.

"Brynne's going to fit in fine here," Tito whispered. "If Ms. Primrose eats one of us, I'd put my bets on you."

"You're not funny," Caden whispered back.

"Dude, I'm not trying to be," Tito said.

Ms. Primrose paused and gave them a governess's glare. "Your input isn't needed, Tito," she said.

"Sorry," Tito said, and shrugged. "I didn't really mean for you to hear that."

Ms. Primrose continued to glare.

"I'll stop talking now," Tito said.

"That would be wise," Ms. Primrose said. She turned back and patted her pocket with the buttons. "Thank you, Brynne dear, what a delightful gem you are." She paused and cast Caden a weary look. "You do read English, right? Or Spanish, at least? I have the test readily available in both."

"I can read English," Brynne said.

"Oh my," Ms. Primrose said. "That's just splendid then. You'll have to take a placement test, but we'll get you started right after it." She smiled at Brynne. "Are you hungry? Do you need to eat before we start?"

"No," Brynne said quickly. "I'm not hungry at all."

"Oh good, very good." Ms. Primrose glanced at Caden, and he had the brief sense of power and heft emanating from her. And though he'd been certain her shadow in the bathroom had been blue, the one on the wall behind her now looked silver. "I had two big meals earlier," she said as cool as ice, and those shadowy silver tones turned blue before his eyes. "I practically stuffed myself." She laughed and motioned Brynne to follow her down the long hall.

Brynne hurried after her, stopping briefly to give Caden a horrified look. When Brynne turned back to Ms. Primrose, Caden heard her say, "I'm glad you're not hungry."

"Yes, dear," Ms. Primrose said as they disappeared down the hall and her silver hair shone. "You should be."

He watched them go. He'd grown certain she was the vicious Blue dragon. Now, however, silver hues seemed to follow her. He began to wonder if the myths were incomplete. Could the Silver and Blue dragons be two sides of the same being? He wasn't sure.

What he did know was that dragons had been slain and charmed, evil defeated, and innocents saved. Yet, the school went on as it had before. Caden learned words from the computer as usual. In science, Mrs. Belle gave him a sticker for doing well on his homework assignment. It was yellow with a smiling lifeless face, so Caden stuck it on Tito's back.

Lunch, though, was different. Caden and Tito waited near the door and watched Ms. Jackson. She stood behind the counter dressed in midnight black. She'd tied two red bands around her left arm. She wore the color of mourning; she'd tied bands of promised revenge.

Once the line of students thinned, Caden and Tito walked up to her and Caden held out his tray. She spooned fruit cobbler on it with a tight smile. "My little sister and brother have disappeared," she said.

"It was my understanding they were arrested," Caden said.

With sudden fury, she slammed down the spoon. "They were dragon's brunch. Tell me, young ones," she said looking from Caden to Tito with her voice sharp like a sword, "do you know why I, the oldest and smartest of the three, came to be so exquisite?"

"We know," Caden said. "You drained Jane's mother."

She smiled, but her eyes were mere slits. "That's right." She picked up her spoon and put cobbler on Tito's tray. The red bands on her arm stood out starkly. "But it means little to me without my siblings. You will pay for what you've done. As will Jane pay for surviving."

Tito seemed to have had enough. He turned away. "Don't feed the troll, Caden," he said.

Trolls were horrible, snot-ridden things, with foul stench and bad intent. At first, Caden moved into a defensive stance, but he neither saw nor smelled any trolls. Tito shook his head and walked out to their lunch table like his conscience was clear and his heart light. Tito was good at that. He knew how to walk away from instigators and insults.

Caden did not. "Now that I look closely," he said. "You do remind me of a troll."

She looked ready to jump the counter and throttle him. He stood his ground. Suddenly, the sound of slow clapping and booming laughter came from behind the partition. The next moment, Rath Dunn walked out. In one arm, he carried roasted pork, in the other buttered rolls. His beard was covered with a red hairnet. "Don't let the boy bother you," he said, and took Ms. Jackson's hand in his. "He's far too young to appreciate your considerable talents."

"I'm old enough to know a troll when I smell one."

Rath Dunn all-out guffawed at that. He seemed in a good humor, and Caden's arm didn't sting so he didn't have his dagger.

Ms. Jackson pulled her hand from Rath Dunn's and gave Caden a scouring glare. "I'll go check the beans."

Once she left, Caden said, "Does she know you helped me?"

"Helped? I thought you'd be eaten." Rath Dunn hummed as he piled meat on Caden's plate. "Tell me, prince, do you know of the Battle of the Bombadon?"

Bombadon was the great fight between the tree elves and the southern gnome people. "All of the Greater Realm does."

"Did you know I advised the gnomish queen and I sent supplies to the elvish dukes?" Caden doubted anyone in the Greater Realm knew that. With silvery tongs, Rath Dunn arranged the rolls into a tight pyramid. "You see," he said, "if the gnomes won, I'd gain the favor of their queen. If the elves won, I'd have the elvish dukes in my debt."

"No one won that battle."

"Indeed!" He held the tongs to the air like a scepter. "The gnomes and the elves decimated each other. Five moons after, my armies lay waste to what remained of each."

That part Caden did know. "So what have you gained here?"

"A chance to cook between math classes," Rath Dunn said, "and introduce you children to culinary genius."

Caden looked at the food on his plate. It wasn't square or triangular, but he still couldn't eat it. Never again could he eat the cafeteria food. Ms. Jackson and Rath Dunn seemed equally likely to poison. Certainly, they could do it and make it look natural. "You get permission to leave the city limits."

Rath Dunn's smile could have pierced armor. "We do buy from local farms. Only the very best for the school and all."

"Ms. Primrose is not so foolish as to trust you, even if she grants you permission to go get vegetables now and again. She'll never let you go."

Rath Dunn nodded, apparently in total agreement. "Yes, true indeed." Then he leaned forward and whispered. "But it's not foolishness that will bring her down, it's hubris. She's too arrogant to see any of us as a threat."

"I suppose you know something about that."

Rath Dunn straightened his beard net. He glanced at the butter packets and began to stack what was left into a cube. "Now, now, Caden, don't get snippy with me."

"What are you plotting? Why do you need elf's tears and blood from a seventh son?"

"And a sorceress," he said, and looked out into the students. Brynne sat beside Tito at a middle table. "I see you brought me one. How thoughtful." He laughed and seemed pensive. "She's young."

Caden didn't like the idea of Brynne trapped in Rath Dunn's class. He didn't like the fact that he seemed surprised by her age. "You thought she'd be older."

"Indeed, I did. Interesting magic destroyed my door." He hummed happily and stirred the pork. "Such a girl could be useful."

"Not to you."

"We'll find that out another day."

Caden had nothing left to say after that. He abandoned his tray on the counter and grabbed an apple for Sir Horace. As he walked away, Rath Dunn called after him. "As I believe one of your brothers may prove quite useful."

Caden stopped. Rath Dunn had wanted his seventh-born brother Jasan but gotten Caden by mistake. For all Jasan's prickly demeanor, he was honorable, and Rath Dunn wanted him for his blood. "My brothers are beyond your reach."

"We'll see," Rath Dunn said. He stroked his beard net with his fingers. "It's a shame, really," he said, "brothers killing brothers."

Rath Dunn made terrible accusations, but he'd been wrong about Jane Chan's skill and he was wrong about Caden's brothers, too. They were all loyal to Razzon, each other, and their father. With a deep breath, Caden put one foot in front of the other and headed to the table.

He worried for Brynne, Jane, and Tito. He feared for his father and his brothers in Razzon. Most of all, he feared the small part of him that wondered if Rath Dunn was right. Could one of his brothers be a traitor of the worst kind? Could one of them have killed Chadwin? It fit the facts of Chadwin's death far too well for Caden's comfort. Chadwin had been stabbed in the back, either taken by surprise by ambush or broken trust. Caden's throat tightened and his hands shook.

The night Caden left the Winter Castle replayed in his memory. Why had his father sent him away? They both knew it wasn't only so he could complete his quest. Had the king been trying to protect Caden from someone in the castle? From one of his brothers? If so, these were even darker times for his kingdom than he had feared.

He stopped and listened to the laughter and chatter in the cafeteria. He wouldn't let his enemy's words trump his faith in his family, not when they were a realm away and unable to defend themselves. He pulled his mind from his difficult thoughts and went to the lunch table. At this moment, at this time, he needed to sit with his friends.

Brynne had no tray but had swiped the roll from Tito's plate. Tito was eating the questionable food with full fork and much zest.

When Caden sat, Tito frowned at him. "Where's your food?"

"It's smarter not to eat."

Brynne smiled brightly and offered him half her stolen roll. "I was placed in the gifted class," she said. "Ms. Primrose and I were quick friends."

"She's not hungry today." Caden didn't take the roll. "And Rath Dunn finds you interesting."

Her smile dimmed, but only a little. She held up half a buttered roll like a goblet. "We have saved Sir Tito's lady and we have slain terrible beasts. Let us celebrate."

Tito answered her toast by raising a fork full of pork.

"Heck yeah," he said.

Caden's father always said, "Remember what's important, celebrate what victories you can." Caden had slain no ice dragon and he was at a school of villains, but Jane was safe. Tito was happy. Brynne yet lived. Sir Horace was pampered at his prison. And Caden had a gift that he was beginning to think would prove useful.

These were good things; these were things worth celebrating. He grabbed the apple from his pocket and raised it to the sky. On this day his friends laughed and his father would be proud. On this day they toasted with apple, bread, and pork on a fork. This day was a good day. There would be other days for dark thoughts and hard battles and there would be other dragons for him to slay.

ACKNOWLEDGMENTS

My sincerest thanks to Jocelyn Davies, my editor, who gave me so many great ideas with so many great exclamation points, and who helped me write a better book; and to my agent, David Dunton, who supported me and kept me sane throughout the year. And thanks to everyone at HarperCollins who helped turn my story into a real, not-imagined, paper-and-ink novel.

Also, I'd like to say thank you to my family for being there for me: my mom, Pat; my brother, Orren; my sister, Sarah; my brother-in-law, Stephen; and my nephew, Edward, and niece, Marie; as well as thanks to all those beachy Balls who read it for me, especially Sandy, Terri, Donald, and Jenn.

Lastly, I'd like to acknowledge my office mates Adrienne and Amy, who read and gave me feedback, and Janie, Erin,

Angel, and Lisa, who were always supportive; thanks also to my writing buddies Kat and Chelsea for brainstorming with me, and my friends Lorrie, Krista, Laura, Charlie, and Sam.